MW01147470

Set on cont
college professor
mystery surrounc   , drugs, kidnappings,
and police frame-ups cloud the landscape, but against all odds,
the good doctor solves the crimes with help from unexpected
quarters.

In the tradition of the recently deceased novelists William
Tappley and Philip Craig, the protagonist, Dr. David Knight,
works to solve the mystery with wit and acumen. Possessing an
esprit rivaling that of the late Robert Parker's renowned sleuth,
Spenser, Dr. Knight is also somewhat of a *wisenheimer* who
struggles against all authority figures from the college's
department head to the clinics' administrators to the State Police.

He knew Jimmy Farnsworth from the mental health clinic,
but now learns of his death. Knight, interrupted in the middle of
his lecture by the State Police, finds himself at the epicenter of a
murder investigation. Torn between disclosing all he knows to
the police and honoring the confidentiality that extends to the
grave for his deceased patient, he sets out on his own quest to
find the truth.

The violence that consumed Jimmy spirals outward and out
of control touching all aspects of Knight's life: college, clinical
practice, and home. His relationship with the police sours as he
learns they are angling for an expedient solution, which would
incarcerate for life an innocent man whose only crime is mental
illness.

Caught between the devil and the deep blue sea, Knight
seeks a possible solution in the waters off Chatham in order to
save his life and that of at least two others. This mystery/thriller
is set on Cape Cod, and the action encompasses the entire cape
from the canal bridges to the Atlantic. A diverse cast of
characters adds depth, intrigue, and even romance to the
frightening circumstances surrounding murder.

Writing in the first person singular, Browne has produced a
work of factual fiction based on his real-life knowledge of and
experience in academia and clinical settings.

Six Days In May

Six Days In May

Robertson Browne

ISBN-13: 978-1481299909

ISBN-10: 1481299905

First Printing

For Hilarie, Lindsey, and John

ACKNOWLEDGMENTS

To my wife, Debbie, whose faith in me and belief in my writing have made this book possible.

To Jay and Bobbe whose unflagging support, encouragement, and help have made this book a reality.

To Bobbe again for her willingness to review, edit, and critique revision after revision until this book achieved some semblance of order, consistency, and continuity.

PROLOGUE

Danny was cold; his cloth coat couldn't keep out the knife-like breeze coming off the cold Atlantic.

Danny was afraid; it was dark, and he'd been standing on this street corner for over two hours.

Danny was lost; he'd been dropped off here, in a place he'd never been before and told to wait until someone asked him for the package he'd been given. He had tucked the package wrapped in plastic under his coat.

Danny paced not only to get warm, but also because he was so frightened. The darkness did that to him.

Danny had grown up in one of the state's training schools for the mentally retarded. He was retarded and epileptic; he'd learned not to cry out as he thrashed in the grip of a seizure unless he wanted a beating from the night staff.

Danny, released to a group home as an adult when the courts demanded the institutions closed, was friendless, alone, and tormented by his own demons; he paced and paced in the night.

Danny headed toward the headlights of a car pulling up next to him in the hopes that it would be his ride back to the group home and maybe something warm. No such luck, two men dressed in heavy winter coats quickly got out and approached him.

Danny with the innocence of a child waved hello and asked if they wanted his package. Without warning, the first man hit him in the ribs with a piece of pipe. The second clubbed him on the side of the head, and he tumbled to the ground. Hands frisked him taking the package; and then the kicking began—head, kidneys, legs, and arms—steel tipped workmen's boots bloodied him.

Danny didn't cry out; he didn't know how to cry out any longer; he curled into a fetal position, and took the beating never asking why. Finally, one of them grabbed him by the hair and screamed into his broken face, "Who are you? Where are you from? You don't ever peddle shit on our streets, or you and your buddies will get a lot worse than this, get it?"

Not getting an answer and not wanting to wait around, the two got back into their car with Danny's package tossed into the trunk and left with tires squealing.

Danny tried to breathe and then vomited blood.

DAY 1: TUESDAY, MAY 6TH

-1-

"Let's see if we can't understand what Freud called 'infantile sexuality,'" I raised my voice purposefully for the last two words in an attempt, usually futile, to get a rise out of my sophomore level charges arrayed in a tier of rows in front of me.

"What do you think the term 'sex' in German means, and how was it used in Freud's theory?" I tried in a further attempt to jar a few of the eighty odd students in the lecture hall from their semi-comatose state. Jesus H. Christ, if our society didn't need these slackers to earn a semblance of a living to fund social security and my retirement checks, I'd quit. Then again, I might not have a choice come the end of the semester as my opinions were all too well known.

I easily nattered on about how the limitations of the English language somehow made "having sex" an adult activity when in fact in German the term means taking pleasure from the activity of one's body, yada, yada, yada. At times like this, I wonder if teaching is really worth the effort. Somewhere in my unconscious, a debate began to rage again about the value of my teaching career. On one side, I love the students—when they're awake, not text messaging, or asking the never-ending question, "Will this be on the test?" On the other side, I invoke the Lord's name in vain and scream silently, "Education is too precious to be wasted on the young!" But the paycheck comes regularly, the fringe benefits are great, the summer break is ten weeks long, ah if only they could spell, write, or even read!

While on vocal cruise control, I almost missed the rear door to the auditorium opening. Usually it's a student sneaking out for an early lunch or a smoke, but as the sun streamed in through the doorway, I was dragged out of my retirement reverie when two figures entered, closed the doors and stood at the rear of the classroom. They weren't students, even though they'd been backlit, I'd noticed that they wore uniforms—specifically, peaked, brimmed caps of some sort and jodhpurs—clearly a couple of Staties! Jodhpurs, when was the last time they rode a motorcycle much less a horse?

Gaining control of my own droning voice, I looked up and called out "How can I help you fellers?"

The shorter of two asked in an obviously female pitched voice, "Mr. Knight?"

Damn, I think they do that on purpose, no, not the female cop mistaken for a guy, but failing to use either "Dr" or "Professor" as part of the salutation. Hey I earned the title, but let me forget to call one of them "officer," they're insulted. Gee, life continues to be unfair; I know how Barbara Boxer must have felt when she asked the Admiral to call her Senator not "ma'am."

"Yes, I am Professor Knight," I acknowledged. "How can I help you?" I asked in the sinking hope that they wanted one of my students for the heinous crime of double-parking and not me.

"We need you to come with us," the male intoned with a no nonsense voice.

"Ok, just give me a minute to wrap this up," I replied and turned my attention back to the students, who by the way were all now sitting up in rapt attention. Maybe I should use a couple of rent-a-cops when I had to lecture on Pavlov's conditioning theory.

In the most sincere, yet serious, voice I could muster, I adlibbed, "Let's prepare an exercise for the next class; I want a short essay linking Freud's stages of child development to the stages of personality development giving real examples, not those found in the text! If you use Internet sources, be sure to cite them according to APA style. All right, I'll see you on Thursday morning ready to discuss Erik Erikson's psychosocial modification of Freud's psychosexual theory. Remember we have only three weeks left before finals."

As the students streamed past the two troopers who manned the door, I suppressed a grin at the thought of what would happen if they'd brought a drug-sniffing dog with them! Back to reality, I stuffed my laptop and notes into my book bag and joined the stroll to the back of auditorium. As I came abreast the two Staties, I stopped and asked with a sigh, "What's Manny want with me now?"

No answer, just a glower from the older one with the name badge "Victor Lopes." He was heavy set but powerfully built, although his Sam Brown belt strained more than a bit to hold in the beer belly. Not exactly, a pretty face was Victor. He looked hard. The younger, female trooper said, "We're here to ask you for help with our inquiries as the British would say." Her badge read, "Rachel Robbins," and seemingly, it was the only thing feminine about her. If it came to a wrestling match, I think I'd have a better chance against ol' Vic!

Hmmm, "Help with our inquiries" that was a sprightly response, and she almost smiled as she delivered the line. Maybe PBS's Mystery Theater has attracted a wider audience than I thought. "Ok, so Manny will tell me, but first I've got to check out with the head of my department lest he think I'm off fishing or sailing again."

Manny, by the way, is a Lieutenant in the Massachusetts State Police stationed at the barracks in Bourne by the bridge. He and I have a relationship: I want to avoid him at all costs; and he wants to interrogate me. Usually we split the difference and have a beer at one of the Cape's brewpubs. Most of the time when we're together he tries to pump me for information about the doings of my clients in the drug clinic or whether someone can con him about being psychotic. When I'm out with Manny, grabbing my wallet isn't about losing money, it's about feeling for my license which could be revoked if any part of the conversation was taken out of the realm of the hypothetical. Somehow, I got the feeling as we walked across campus that I wasn't going for a beer with Manny.

We entered the northern building where the faculty offices were on the upper floors. I could've taken the elevator, but the stairs gave me a chance to distance myself from my two shadows in Sam Browne belts. Down the corridor past the Xerox machines and secretaries' desks we went. At least they were a step behind me so I didn't exactly feel as if I was being frog marched along. Just as I entered the bay with the department head's office, I turned and motioned them to wait as the last thing I wanted was for the twit who makes my job miserable to take an interest in why the cops wanted me.

"Hey Fred," I called out in my most jovial, collegial manner. "Something big's come up, and I've got to cancel my twelve-thirty."

"Well, I don't know," Fred replied as he fixed me with a quizzical stare as if I had just sprouted a second head.

"No seriously, I've got to run right now, and either you cover for me in my abnormal class or cancel it."

"It's only twenty minutes to eleven; don't tell me you let your child class out early again."

The "again" pissed me off; Fred Dorfman was the essence of an academic turd. He had no life other than the college. I think he really hated having time off in the summer, but if he were good, talented, concerned about students, all that could be forgiven; but no, he was a turd, only interested in some arcane research topic that nobody knew much less cared about. When I asked why he had been elected department head, one of the better instructors pointed out that Fred got release time and taught fewer courses because of that. Just a way of helping our students, he told me! Great and now, I was groveling in front of Fred just for the opportunity to be hauled off by the state troopers hovering outside the door.

"Fred, please cover the class, have someone cover the class, or cancel it; I'll be back on Thursday no sweat, all right?"

"Dave, I really think we need to discuss your leaving like this. It appears you are not committed to your work at the college."

Yeah, Fred also had a hair across his arse because he knew that I also worked as a psychologist—gee, you think—in the local drug treatment clinic, and the mental health clinic. I believed that Fred who abhorred all things non-academic was simply jealous and wanted to bust my stones whenever possible.

I didn't have time to discuss this nonsense with him so I motioned with my left hand out into the hallway for the tough looking trooper to join the discussion. Fred blanched, gulped, and squirmed at the sight of the Statie standing there in his full uniform.

"Here, he's the reason I left class before the bell, argue with him willya?"

I don't think the trooper got more than the loom of his bulk into the doorway when Fred's already pasty complexion washed-out further. I'm sure Fred has never ever spoken to a member of law enforcement unless it's the campus cops to complain about students usurping his faculty parking privileges. This was a first, Fred was speechless; he just waved Victor and me away as if we were carrying the plague.

"Thanks Fred," I called over my shoulder. "I'll see you Thursday, and I'm buying if you're in the Sunset Room after four." The Sunset Room was the campus lounge serving beer and wine for older students as well as the faculty and administrators. Fred, on the other hand, considered any socialization with students or fraternization with faculty to be unprofessional. He was strictly an uptight, inadequate, and schizoid-disordered academic who measured his self worth in terms of space, be it office space or parking space.

Anyways, I was off the hook with the college, but clearly dangling on another as I trailed in the wake of the cops as they led me to their waiting cruiser.

.

-2-

Let's guess where the troopers parked their cruiser—not an unmarked job mind you, but the full Monty, with enough aerials to contact ET—yup, right at the entrance to campus. It was smack-dab where I'd be seen by as many students, faculty, and administrators as possible being ushered into the back seat and driven off. Talk about a perp walk. Just wait until I confronted Manny about his sense of humor for dragging me off like this. I know I hadn't done anything wrong, but knowing Manny, he probably wanted me softened up to tell him about who was scoring what and scamming whom in the drug clinic. I slouched down into the corner of the back seat as Victor at the wheel tried to make the cruiser airborne over the speed bumps. He wheeled left out of the college, caught the light, and left again up the onramp. Guess we weren't stopping at Dunkin' Donuts.

As Victor merged onto Rt 6, the four lane mid-Cape highway, he blew past a semi struggling up the hill outside of Exit 5 and pounded down the highway toward the Sagamore Bridge in the outside lane at a little over ninety miles an hour. As everything in front of us scrambled out of the way, I felt as if I were at the parting of the Red Sea behind Moses. Victor didn't flinch as he came up on the bumper of a Toyota trying to find an opening in the right lane to duck out of our way. I rolled my eyes, leaned back in the seat and decided to contemplate my existence as Victor ate up the seventeen miles from the college to the state troopers' barracks in record time.

I am, as my grandmother used to say, a *wisenheimer*, or smart aleck. My father usually said I had a "smart mouth," just before bloodying it with the back of his hand—knuckles—I always got the knuckles, never the fingers, or the fleshy part! Just before I was bounced from my last teaching job, the Dean told me that I had "hubris," a fifty-cent word for being arrogant or having that smart mouth. Ok, Ok, so I like a little acerbic repartee, and I've got more than an ordinary dose of chutzpah, and I've got a smart mouth, but I've never been in trouble, well, never real trouble. The problem is that I'm a loner, no, that's not right, I just don't get along with other people, but I'd like to. Unlike that twit, Dorfman, who just doesn't care about anyone else, I do! I want to be liked, but unfortunately, I am subconsciously afraid that I won't be liked, that I will be criticized and left out. To compensate, hey, this is what I get for spending six years earning my doctorate in psych and having a license to practice for almost twenty years, I fire the first shots. If you're going to dump on me, it'll be on my terms! Great strategy as I've blown through half a dozen psych jobs and two teaching gigs not to mention a marriage along the way plus more than a few friends. My dog loves me probably because he doesn't understand the insults from my smart mouth.

To top it off, I hate authority. There is an irony here somewhere I thought as the big Ford Crown Vic with Victor at the helm exited the mid-Cape at the Bridge by the Christmas Tree Shop (at least they don't tart it up with a "ppe" to try to make people forget that most everything sold is ticky-tack from China?). No I really rail against authority and authority figures (can we say dear ol' dad?), and here I am being escorted by two uniformed troopers who haven't even read me my rights.

I get along great with my students, it's just the Deans and Department Heads I can't stand; I work wonders with the mentally ill and drug addled in the clinics, I just rail against the clinical directors and program administrators because all them think that doing is less important than orchestrating. I think I'm one of these oddballs who isn't charismatic enough to be a leader, but isn't dumb enough to be a follower. Ergo, I crack wise! Why wouldn't I?

My boyhood hero was that nineteenth century English naval captain, Thomas Cochrane, whose audacity knew no bounds! The French dubbed him *Le Loup des Mers* or "the sea wolf." He was a great solo captain, but couldn't work with the fleet. Although I had studied and admired him, I conveniently forgot that he got himself tossed out of the Royal Navy after getting flogged for being an outspoken critic—a smart mouth— or maybe some unconscious part of me had already processed that tidbit!

We hit the Bourne Rotary where the state police barracks are just to the right of the bridge. Doing almost eighty in the rotary, I felt as if I was in one of the dodge-em cars from the amusement park, but nothing here was funny. Victor hit the gas as an opening appeared and gunned the Crown Vic at the exit for Falmouth on Rt 28. Well, I thought, so much for this being a prank by Manny to get me to buy lunch at the pub next to the cop house and pump me for information that ethically I couldn't disclose, but did so anyway with winks and nods!

"Er, um, hey, what gives?" I asked leaning forward to the cage like metal partition, which re-affirmed my status in the back. Neither trooper acknowledged my query much less turned in my direction. I noticed that both were stoically chewing on gum or maybe it was just their cuds, but I kept this smart mouth observation to myself.

"All right, all right, fun's over," I piped up in my most argumentative voice. "Listen up, you haven't told me what this is all about, but now I know it's not about the Lieutenant playing games. So let me know what you're doing and where you're taking me. This is kidnapping!"

I could see Victor in the rear view mirror as he bit down hard on his gum and stared straight ahead, but

Rachel half turned in my direction and said in an equally argumentative voice, "Shut up!"

Never knowing when to quit while I was ahead, I plowed on, "Come on, you've shanghaied me, you're holding me incommunicado, against my will, my rights." Then I delivered my best one-liner for the day, "It's not fair."

Rachel sucked in a full breath and blew back at me, "Hey, Knight, stuff a sock in it willya? You think we like not knowing jack about what we're doing? We were on 6A in Yarmouthport working that gas main detail when the call came in to fetch you forthwith. We don't know who you are, what you have or haven't done, who you know, and we don't care. We're out of the Yarmouth barracks not Bourne so stop whining about this Manny who we know from nobody."

We flew around the Otis Air Base rotary and barreled down the stretch of highway to Falmouth, I shut up and leaned back with the realization that the two troopers in upfront were as clueless as I was. Be cool, I chided myself; let them do their jobs; it was only a few more minutes before we ran out of road, as there's still no bridge to Martha's Vineyard.

The light banter, however, had pissed off Victor at the wheel. I could see the cords in his neck muscles stick out; he clenched his jaw and drove even faster. As we careened off the highway onto Palmer Avenue, he had a clear shot until we got to the lights next to the hospital when he hit the siren—is it still a siren if it only makes those ugly "oogah" and "baarch" noises? Right through the light, down Palmer Ave toward the center of town, aha, I thought, we're headed for the District Court over on Jones Road. Instead, Victor bore right in the direction of Woods Hole and the ferry terminal to the Vineyard; I sat up and leaned against the wire screen partition fixated as we hurtled past trees, pulled over cars, and blind driveways at an unthinkable speed. Rachel said something into the dash-mounted microphone, but I couldn't make out what she said, and the response was lost in static. At the last possible second, Victor, playing chicken with some semi just off the ferry, hung a left taking us away from Woods Hole and toward Nobska Point where the lighthouse is. Seconds later, we all saw the gaggle of town cop cars, state cruisers, town ambulance, and county meat wagon plus assorted unmarked vehicles. Guess we were there.

To his credit, Victor threaded the gauntlet of parked vehicles, right up to the crime scene yellow tape festooned around the seaward side of the lighthouse as if designed by Christo. By the time Victor had shut down the Crown Vic, Rachel already had gotten out and opened my door. Before I could say thanks, she slammed it shut and leaned back against the roofline of the big Ford leaving me to wander toward the yellow line alone. Her body posture, as well as Victor's failure to even exit the car, left no doubt that they had been hijacked just like me and just as much in the dark. I thought about turning and thanking both of them, but after our exchanges on the way here, I knew that even my most sincere effort would be rebuffed as sarcasm.

Walking up the rock riprap that protected the lighthouse and road from erosion, I could see a tall, whip thin, figure waving at me. With a considerable amount of fear and concern, I lifted up the yellow tape and crossed into what clearly, to anyone who has watched CSI, was a crime scene.

"Dr. Knight?" A lanky, black man dressed in a suit and an unbuttoned, stylish Chesterfield overcoat hailed me. An out-of-date fedora, a pair of bright yellow boots, and a badge clipped to his lapel completed the image. "I need you to come this way now!"

Oh well in for a penny, in for a pound—whatever that meant—standing on a cliff overlooking Vineyard Sound in early May, however, meant that I was more than just a bit chilly. The wind off the water was in the forties, and I was dressed only in my academic uniform: cotton Hagar's, blue oxford, and lightweight blazer. It was cold; I started to climb gingerly down the piled up rocks toward whoever it was who had called my name; and I knew I really, really, didn't want to be here.

"Dr. Knight?" again, he asked, but this time I was close enough for him to see my head bob up and down in affirmation.

"Look, I'm Lieutenant CJ Smith of the State Police, and you've got to get down here now before the tide changes."

"Ok, ok, I'm coming, but these leather soled loafers don't give me much traction on the riprap."

"Hey, wait a minute," and then he called loudly to a uniformed trooper standing guard at the yellow ribbon barricade, "Donnelly, change shoes with this fellow, he's got to get down on the rocks below the tide mark."

Great, I thought, another trooper who'd remember my face for life and hold it against me as he clambered down the rocks with a sour look on his face.

"Thanks, I really mean it," I said as sincerely as I could muster as I leaned against him to pull off my loafers. He accepted them without a word before bending over to untie his uniform shoes with a thick rippled sole. We made the exchange in silence, and he skidded in my loafers back up to the barricade while I made my way more surely down to where Smith was standing.

He held out his hand as if he wanted to shake hands with me, but when I reached forward, he grabbed me by the elbow and forcibly pulled me down lower on the rock wall. We worked our way over and down the steep granite face of the hundred foot high sea wall. Just ahead I could see a pair of yellow polypro ropes rigged up side by side to allow us to descend directly to the water's edge where a gaggle of people seemingly were milling about.

I was cold and getting colder as we got closer to the water's edge I could feel the water's bite start to suck at the marrow of my bones; I began to shiver.

Before penetrating to the inner circle of the fifteen or so men standing around just below the high water mark, I turned to Smith and asked, "Lieutenant, what's going on, why have you dragged me out of class and now down here, something not nice has happened hasn't it?"

I knew that when the circle of men parted, I would be looking at a dead body. Whose body I didn't know, couldn't even imagine, but I knew it couldn't be anyone I really knew or cared about. The only person I had left in life with true emotional ties was my daughter, and she was safely living in LA. So what's with this charade?

"Just take a look and tell us who he is so we can move him out of here before the tide turns," CJ's voice was firm and decidedly unsympathetic.

"Coming through," he announced. "Come on people, give us some room here."

I didn't know any of the men who were standing in a rough half circle; I looked in vain for Manny who'd at least be a familiar if not friendly face. After scanning the spectators, my eyes lowered to the body wedged into the rocks at their feet. It was a man, a dead man, splayed out on the wrack line. One leg was pinned through a crevice in the rock wall. My impression was of someone who had fallen and gotten hurt. He was looking up, but not at me, as the seagulls had been the first to find the body and scavenged his eyes for breakfast. It didn't matter, I knew him, and the realization that he was dead rose like bile in my throat.

"That's Jimmy Farnsworth," I said as I gulped back my own breakfast looking quickly away.

"So you do know him?" said Smith as he pulled me even closer. "Here look more closely."

Jimmy had been lying with his face up toward the top of the cliff when Smith squatted over and tilted the head downwards using the end of his pen to avoid touching the body. There were a couple of ugly lacerations in the back of his scalp, but no blood as the tide probably had washed it away.

"His leg is broken pretty badly, and you can see it's really wedged between the rocks. What we won't know until we get him over to the ME's office is whether or not someone smashed his head in and killed him first. It could have been an accident, and he drowned after being stuck down here. It doesn't really matter because we need to know how he got down here and why. Was he running from someone? Was he pushed down the riprap? Was this an accident or murder?" Smith continued. "We're treating this as a murder until the evidence proves otherwise. Because it occurred at the bottom of the lighthouse here, it's on federal property and that makes it a Homeland Security issue. We're trying to take the lead here, but we've got to move quickly and rule out any terrorist type of activity before the feds barge in and decide to take over."

I shrugged; I had never seen a murdered man before; I had no idea how to respond and still didn't know why I had been pulled down here to ID Jimmy.

"Okay, so I can ID him, but why did you have to yank me out of class and make me come down here to do that? Why couldn't I just have ID'd him at the county morgue?" I asked irritably.

"Two reasons," Smith answered holding up two fingers. "Number one; if he's a local guy we can claim some jurisdiction and get him out of here; otherwise it becomes a federal case, and they get to cart him off. Number two; there was no wallet or anything on his person to help identify him."

"And you just happened to decide to fetch me?" I shook my head disbelieving.

Smith held up his hand to silence me and continued. "Here, we found this, and it's the reason we wanted you here to see. Whattaya make of this?"

Smith motioned to a white coated technician of some sort to come over. Wearing white latex gloves, the technician was holding a clear plastic evidence bag. Using tweezers, he pulled out a card with writing on it, like a professional card or appointment card. He held it up for me to see but not touch.

Jesus, I began to sweat despite the brisk wind off the cold water. The card had been crumbled up and water damaged, but my name was clearly printed on the card. This was my card from the mental health clinic and read:

David L. Knight, Ph.D.
Psychologist
Eastern Cape Mental Health Center
State Rd, Eastham, MA
1-518-256-3501

"Yeah Jimmy was one of my guys at the clinic," I said. "How'd this happen? Why'd this happen?"

"That's what we need to figure out; we called the clinic for you first thing, and they told us that you were teaching at the college today, so we sent the uniforms to pick you up. Now let's get back up to the road and then you can start telling me everything you know about Jimmy, and what he's been telling you." Smith fixed me with a steely stare as he spoke, and then looking past me to the tech, he said to finish up and get the body to the county morgue in Pocasset, just a few miles up the road.

We grunted and sweated, at least this time from exertion, up to the top of the cliff face and across the road to the small parking lot next to the lighthouse. I looked down the road to where I'd left Victor and Rachel, but their cruiser was gone, so much for a quick lift back to the college. In front of me was Trooper Donnelly wearing a Victor-like scowl as he stared at his shoes I was wearing. Without so much as a word, he slipped off one of my loafers while I untied his broughams to make the exchange. My statement of thanks went unanswered.

To my left I saw a black ambulance with "Barnstable County Medical Examiner" in gold lettering parked nearby when overhead I heard the approach of a helicopter flying low. Just clearing the top of the lighthouse, a large helicopter with Coast Guard markings settled down to a hover. The noise was unbearable, but the scene was hypnotic as it unfolded. The copter was a search and rescue Dolphin used primarily along the coast in a variety of lifesaving tasks. The Dolphin unraveled a basket at the end of a cable toward the men at the water's edge. Not too gently, they wrestled Jimmy's leg out of the rock crevice, and in only a few minutes, the Coasties reeled in the basket bearing the body and lowered it again as the chopper repositioned itself above the medical examiner's van. Taking only a few minutes the transfer was completed, and the Dolphin wheeled away. A sobering thought was how all of this had been orchestrated around my arrival and identification of Jimmy's body. Something told me that the next round of questioning was going to make me long for Victor's stoic, silent stare.

"Let's start at the beginning," Smith jarred me from my brief reverie. "How do you know Farnsworth, and what was there about him that caused this?"

"Can't we get out of this breeze?" I asked. "If you're trying to break down any resistance I might have, you've succeeded. Look I'm cold, shocked, and honestly frightened by what I've just seen. I'm not looking for lunch, but at least some coffee out of the wind."

"Want to do this in the Bourne barracks?"

"I'd prefer a "Dunkin Donut," but I don't care, let's just get out of here."

For the second time in one day, I was hustled into the back of a cop car, although this one was unmarked, and I hunkered down in the back as Smith's driver retraced the road that brought me here.

-4-

Even though Manny had grilled about my heroin and cocaine rehab clients who might also be dealing drugs on the side dozens of times over the last few years, I'd never actually been inside the state trooper barracks. It was a two story brick building set at the end of a circular drive with a million dollar view of both the Bourne Bridge and the Cape Cod Canal. I'm sure the view would be distracting to anyone working much less being interrogated there, so that's why we entered a room with no windows. I had hoped to see Manny as we passed the front desk and weaved our way through the bullpen of desks and cubicles, but no such luck. I was clearly on my own with just a Styrofoam cup of wretched coffee and artificial creamer.

Smith sat in the middle of the table with his back to the door. This left me no choice but to sit opposite him and face the pictures of Jimmy. Spread out on the table before me were Polaroids of Jimmy taken only hours earlier. The shot of the compound fracture of his leg was gruesome enough, but the pictures of his eyeless face were horrible. I looked more closely, however, at the ones showing the lacerations on the back of his head. Sure there at least two jagged wounds, but there also was a six-inch long depression with faint scratches visible. A quick knock at the door and a uniformed trooper passed a folder to Smith. He scanned its contents before pushing toward me a FAX blowup of a driver's license—Jimmy's. I opted to initiate the discussion just because I am used to doing that in my clinical work as well as when teaching. Besides, I was trying to regain my composure and steady my nerves. This wasn't funny at all, and I had no wise cracks to make!

"I don't know what you want me to say about Jimmy, he always seemed to be one of life's lost souls," I offered. "What's that along the right side of his head? It doesn't look like something you'd get from falling on the rocks. Did you see it?"

Smith didn't even bother to look; he said knowingly, "The ME commented on that when he did his prelim exam of the body 'in situ.' It doesn't fit and makes me think murder not accident; what can you say about it?"

"Who'd want to hurt Jimmy and why?" I whined.

"That's what we want to know," Smith grunted. "How long did you know him and in what capacity? Look I didn't say anything when you were IDing the body, but your card was stuffed in Farnsworth's mouth. Either he was trying to swallow it to protect you, or someone stuffed it into his mouth before or after killing him to get your attention."

I gulped and said, "Jimmy was a client at the Eastham Clinic, that's where I knew him from. That's all; I don't understand any of this."

"There was something written on the reverse side, but it got pretty much washed off? Any ideas? And why did he have your card, or did someone else have it for him to choke on?"

The coffee roiled in my gut, my voice subdued. "On the backside I probably would have written a time and date for his next appointment. Jimmy wasn't the most reliable of my guys, so I normally would make a big deal of giving him a new card before he left after every visit. Do you have a blowup of the back side for me to see?"

Smith rummaged through the folder he was holding and with an exasperated sigh slammed it down on the desk. He stormed out of the room.

Before I could decide whether to stay or leave, he was back with an eight by ten enlargements of both sides of my card. The front was the same printed stuff as I'd read on the original, but the back was blurry and smudged as if the writing had been in pencil and not pen. I only used a pen, as pencils are *verboten* in the clinics because our notes are legal entities. I'd spotted an inconsistency.

"To me," I said carefully, "this looks like 'Friday 2-4.'"

"Does that mean Farnsworth had an appointment with you on a Friday afternoon, or did you have one with him last Friday?" Smith demanded.

"I don't really remember the last time I saw Jimmy," I answered which was true, but I did know damn well it wasn't last Friday afternoon as I have open office hours at the drug clinic then.

"Ok, we're going to need his records, your session notes, and anything else connecting you to him," Smith persisted.

"I'm not sure what I can tell you and what materials you can have access to."

"What's that supposed to mean, we can get subpoenas, warrants, and whatever we need. You can't hide behind 'privilege,' 'cuz he's dead."

For the first time, I looked at CJ Smith; I mean I really looked at him. Although seated, I could tell that he was tall, very tall, at least six and a half feet, and rail thin. His head was shaven; his baldpate glistened in the reflected glare of the fluorescent ceiling lights. His cheekbones were prominent, his jaw line etched, and his nose aquiline. As an Afro-American, I would have to guess that his family hailed from Ethiopia or somewhere in sub-Sahara Africa. What surprised me was that his eyes were a deep shade of green and intense as he glowered at me. Even more surprising than his eyes were his hands. Given his height and build, I anticipated the long almost delicate fingers, but I was surprised to see that they were manicured—buffed and polished. Looking more closely, I noticed that Smith's suit didn't seem to be something "off the rack" from Sears or even what passes for a boutique haberdashery on the Cape, Pilgrim's. No, it was smooth and expensive.

CJ Smith wasn't a regular state police detective assigned to Troop D, which covered southeastern Mass; no way, he was right out of Troop H, probably assigned to Boston's Beacon Hill barracks. I know all of this because Manny usually spent part of our lunch times pontificating about how great it was to be part of Troop D. He crowed that he didn't have to spend half his salary buying Armani suits. There hadn't been time to bring in Smith from Boston as a heavy hitter. My guess was that he'd fouled up somehow in Boston and came to the Cape under duress to repair his record. If this were true, then I figured that I was in for a rough ride. Smith had to be eager to get back to Boston in good graces.

"Look let's get off on the right foot, I want to know what happened to Jimmy and why as well as getting whoever did this, but there are ethical issues and federal laws to consider," I came back at him. Right now, all I really wanted to do was to get to the Eastham clinic and grab all Jimmy's files. If I poured over them maybe with Smith or alone, I could figure out who'd have done this to him. I just didn't know where I stood especially with all the new HIPPA regulations, which governed all sorts of disclosure stuff.

"Hey, Doc, he's dead, and he may have been killed. His killers could be out there. Not only that, but they know who you are. Didn't you see that Farnsworth had nothing on him except your business card stuffed in his mouth?"

"Yeah but," I started to respond.

Smith interrupted raising his voice, "Yeah but nothing, what if someone thought he was a rat, and you're the guy he'd squealed to. That means you have the info they want. Either that or someone has found a convincing way to get your attention. So I want you to tell me all of the details, and I'll figure out which are relevant or confidential."

"Jesus, you mean if Jimmy were killed, then the same guys who killed him may want to have a conversation with me?" I asked.

"No, asshole, they probably are looking to kill you too—remember 'dead men tell no tales'—at best they'd make you talk and then kill you, so talk to me first!"

"You can't be serious about this being a message for me," I protested. "Killing Jimmy and dumping his body off the rocks at Woods Hole to get my attention is off the mark; it's at the wrong end of the Cape even."

"Yeah right," taunted Smith. "The body was found right after low tide by a jogger, and within a couple of hours we have you on the spot—do you think they've gotten your attention yet, asshole?"

"Well asshole or not, let me make a call to my mentor to see where I stand legally, then I'll do everything I can to help you and me." I leaned back in the chair to fish out my cell phone.

With a look of disgust, Smith got up to leave me to my call. I tried to signal by pointing at my coffee cup that I wanted a refill, but he pointedly ignored me.

Without hesitation, I flipped the phone open and punched in the number of my "rabbi" in all things ethical and diagnostic, Dr. Mary Kilpatrick, one of the sharpest minds and even sharper wits I've ever met. Luckily she was between patients so I could explain what had happened and asked her what limits were imposed upon me by HIPPA regulations and APA ethical standards. In less than five minutes, I had all the information I needed, thanked her, and hung up. Why did I think that Smith was listening in when within seconds, the door opened and he returned?

"Yeah so?" he asked as he sat down with a refilled Styrofoam cup of coffee in front of him, and none for me—talk about cruel and unusual punishment! I was getting my mojo back.

Using the suggestion given me by my mentor, I looked Smith straight in the eye and said as sincerely as possible, "I can only discuss Jimmy in generalities and the hypothetical, anything said specifically including access to any of his case files and my notes would violate federal law."

"Gimme a break, who's going to complain— Jimmy?" Smith sneered at me with derision.

"What happens when the defense attorney asks whether you violated federal law to gather information leading to the arrest of his clients, and the answer is yes? Your case would go out the window just as fast as my license as a psychologist."

"I'll worry about cleaning up that detail if and when we ever get to trial on this one." Smith leaned in toward me.

"Why don't you call the DA's office to find out what's legal, maybe there's an exemption under the Patriot Act and Homeland Security. After all, Jimmy was murdered on Coast Guard property up there by the Nobska light so by rights it would be a federal case." I tried to deflect his rising anger and have him call the DA to see if he couldn't wrangle for an exception to the privacy laws.

Without comment, Smith got up again and stormed out of the interview room for a full fifteen minutes. When he returned, he appeared calmer but not happier.

"Right, so far what you've said checks out at the AG's level, so we'll play it your way for now," he said. "Start with what you can tell me about Jimmy, how you know him, and anything that might be relevant, but keep it general," he said the last words with distain.

"I've been working at the Eastham clinic for the last four-five years, since I came to the Cape, and Jimmy has been around for all of that time. His diagnosis is paranoid schizophrenia. He receives medication regularly and counseling to help him continue functionally. Typically, a paranoid schizophrenic has pervasive themes of persecution and believes that all sorts of forces are arrayed against him. These delusions are far-fetched, like being chased by little green men from Mars; they are unbelievable to everyone except to the paranoid schizophrenic himself. Along with the drug therapy, the psychologist or social workers would attempt to help the patient find and maintain reality."

"Too vague," Smith snapped, "who's the shrink?"

"The clinic uses Dr. Jose DeVelez and a couple of nurse practitioners," I was able to answer with confidence.

"Good maybe we can squeeze him," Smith said writing Jose's name in his notebook.

"Hey Smith, Dr. DeVelez saw Jimmy at most twice a year over a five year period, or whatever was the absolute minimum set by law. The most the nurses could tell would be in which cheek they'd stuck him. Jimmy was on the far side so he couldn't be trusted to take his meds using pills. They had to shoot him up with a long acting antipsychotic. Most of my work was just getting him to show up for his shots otherwise the clinic would have had to go to court to get an order and a Rogers monitor." My mind was spinning, I had to get away from Smith and think about what had happened, and whether I was in danger too.

"That's nice and all that; I don't want to know squat about Rogers monitors, so don't waste your breath and stop beating around the bush. You want to give a psych lecture, and you're not being helpful, y'know," he came back. "Why don't we get down to specifics about Jimmy, what he told you, and when he told you it that might have led to his death?"

"I haven't an answer, this is off kilter, people like Jimmy find threats and fears in all kinds of things, most of them are just crazy,—like sometimes he was afraid of license plate numbers."

"What numbers, was someone following him?" Smith pressed on.

"He was paranoid; he believed someone or something was always following him for the years I knew him. As far as numbers are concerned, guys like Jimmy think that there are codes and secret meanings in the numbers, it's like they talk to him; but what's worse is he talks back!" I was getting exasperated as I really had nothing to tell Smith and didn't know how to convince him of that fact.

"Tell me more about Jimmy's condition?" Smith was nothing if not persistent.

"Look he wasn't involved in drugs; I didn't see him in the drug clinic, he was mentally ill, he couldn't hold a job, he went to the day treatment program, he drove around in a beat up Chevy station wagon, he had a dirty mouth, and that's all I know." I sighed and continued, "Jimmy had no friends as his type doesn't trust, and the biggest part of my job was to convince him that his meds were not poisoning him. The day treatment program threw him out regularly for being verbally abusive toward the staff; but this was because he believed they were all talking against him. I saw him for one-on-one therapy and believe he had made some progress after he'd joined my weekly men's group. Poor Jimmy, he wouldn't have hurt anyone unless threatened, and he felt threatened every day."

Smith pounced on that last remark, "So you say he threatened to hurt people—who, when?"

"No, it wasn't like that, he just felt he should carry a knife or learn karate or something to make sure that he wasn't attacked. Part of my job is to help lessen the perceived threat in people like Jimmy. Really, his only defense was to run away.

"Hey, what about his car?" I asked feeling as if this wasn't part of any federally protected info. "Jimmy trusted his car, he wouldn't have left it or abandoned it, it was the only safe relationship he had. You'll find his license and registration in the car taped under the steering wheel column. I know because I convinced him to tape them there because he didn't want anything to identify him. For the same reason he never carried a wallet, just some cash in his pocket. Have you found the car yet?"

"Did you say he had a relationship with his car? Come on Knight give me a break and tell me something I need to know?"

I took a deep breath, I was getting tired, this was too intense, and I wasn't used to being on the hot seat as I reserved that for my students. "Patients like Jimmy sometimes see themselves as mechanical and 'bond' with machinery like their cars. It's almost autistic-like in the caring they have for their possessions but so little concern for their fellow humans."

"Stop the psych lecture, Knight, I need to have somewhere to start," Smith was getting testy.

"Find the car! He'd have had to be dragged out of it. He never left the lower Cape unless in his own car. How'd he get to Falmouth? Trace his steps!" I was agitated and stood up. I only wanted to leave.

"All right, all right, I'll take you back to the college, but then I want you to meet me at the police station in Eastham to share anything you might know about where Jimmy went and with whom. I need to have that information to help the locals do some grunt work."

"Why don't we meet at the clinic itself? You can hear from my bosses directly what I can and cannot say to you. If they give you his files, I'll decipher my handwriting, but that's not going to happen." I leaned my chair back against the wall; I had just turned off the interview.

Even Smith knew that we'd wound down, he got up and didn't say a word as I followed him out of the room and into a corridor where he grabbed a set of keys off a rack. Without looking back, he kept going out of the building with me wallowing in his wake. We got to the parking lot, and Smith opened the door of a nifty BMW 355 coupe, his own car, no driver, or Crown Vic now. He looked across the roof and said with resignation, "Just get in, Knight, let's go, I've got a crime to solve and not much time to do it."

-5-

It wasn't even two-thirty when Smith dropped me off at the college. All of this started only four hours earlier but I felt that days had gone by or years had come off my life. After dutifully promising to meet him at the mental health clinic in Eastham in less than an hour, I decided to avoid contact with Fred, the departmental fink, and thought about a late lunch at the Land Ho in Orleans. No, that wouldn't work; I'd have a burger and couple of Harpoons on draught and end up blowing off Smith leaving him to the pair of nasties who masquerade as my clinical supervisors. Better to raise my cholesterol at Burger King by the highway and get there in one piece with only French fries on my breath.

Tooling down the highway toward the clinic, I was on the cell phone giving Jen, the clinic director, and her partner, MaryBeth, the clinical supervisor, a heads up about Jimmy's death and Lieutenant Smith's demands. Those two were quite the pair. MaryBeth was an earth mother, talk about smother-love, with an overwhelming desire to make the world a better place for all of us. Let's see, MaryBeth meant well, but she was so intrusive into my clinical work that she usually mucked up any progress I made with her misguided enthusiasm and unsolicited suggestions. In addition, her feelings were easily hurt when rebuffed by either staff or clients. MaryBeth was the type of person who held staff meeting and brought homemade cookies and brownies. Yes, we were all her children.

On the other hand Jen, oh she prefers to be called Jennifer if one must use her given name, was a skinny, uptight, emasculating bitch, and those were her good qualities. Talk about a neurotic whose life revolved around submitting invoices to the state and hounding staff about filing paperwork as she lived in mortal terror of an audit. Of the two, I could see MaryBeth all atwitter about meeting the cop and his demands while Jen would just be pissed at not being able to bill Medicaid for the meeting.

I hit the rotary at Orleans at the eastern end of Cape Cod and turned north toward the town of Eastham. With about a quarter million full time residents, the Cape is like a midsized city. Only difference is that it has fifteen towns each with numerous villages and ports stretching some thirty-five miles eastward into the Atlantic and another thirty miles north into Cape Cod Bay. It's known for its beaches and the beautiful people who try to keep everyone else off what they consider their beaches. They've come from New York and Connecticut totally convinced the Cape needs to be saved from itself and reconstructed into whatever they had in New York or Connecticut. Ugh, shades of the *Stepford Wives* only made worse by the destruction of every cottage and camp rebuilt into McMansions or starter castles. Somewhere under all of this ostentatious wealth, good restaurants, and a neat national seashore resides poverty and mental illness. The poverty is corrosive and manifests itself in a street drug subculture as well as minimal treatment facilities for those whose ability to function in this world has been severely compromised.

I work with these two groups of displaced and disheartened people. Besides teaching at the local college, where my tenure always appears tenuous, I ply my trade as a psychologist for the Eastern Cape Mental Health Clinic and work with the men and women who have been severely hurt by some strange confluence of brain dysfunction and environmental insult. I have almost twenty on my list, and they mostly live in a couple of state-sponsored residences or town subsidized housing. Some live in one room apartments; some live in unheated summer cottages, and one poor soul lives in an old school bus. They all want to be normal, to be happy, to quell the noises in their heads, and to stop the chemicals from eating through their livers, kidneys, and most of all through their brains. Jimmy was just one more member of my ragtag group!

In contrast, well it's not really a contrast it's just another point on the continuum of human misery, are the drug addicts. I spend part of each week at the local drug treatment center run by a for-profit group called Ramparts. It sells methadone, a substitute heroin subsidized by the government. Addicts are simply switched from one drug to another. Looking at the literature shows that quite possibly the only lasting benefit to a methadone clinic is a drop in the crime rate. Methadone addiction seems to be more resistant to detox than heroin, but it's legal and for the junkie it's cheaper as you and I foot the bill via taxes! In order to hook 'em on methadone, the laws require that counseling must be provided—that's me, counselor Dr. Dave! Talk about a losing proposition, as the name of the game is to beat the system, not be cured. Most of my troopers are lifers, and as usual, I get the anti-social psychopaths, the truly fried schizos, the junkies who snort coke and wash it away with beer, or some combination of all three.

All I can say is that heroin must be a hell of a drug, as it wipes out all pain— physical, psychic, and moral. This is why Manny as a Lieutenant in the State Police bugs me for information as often as possible—addicts steal, scheme, and scam! The same ethical standards, however, bind me in my work with those vilified as the dregs of society as I would be with hoity-toity private paying patients—as if I ever saw any of those.

Manny has said more than once how he'd like me to wear a wire to record some of the details of the crimes committed by my guys whether in the past, the present or preparing for tomorrow. Yeah right, I don't like knowing that the Cape is under siege from the scourge of drugs and drug users as I live here too, but ratting out these druggies would keep them away from any help physically or mentally they might ever receive. Oh yes and don't forget about the only demonstrated benefit of methadone—lower crime rate. Manny and I play word games about "hypothetical" situations as I try to deal with my sense of civic responsibility balanced against my addicts' need to trust me. Jimmy was not part of this sorry bunch; as far as I knew he'd never used any drugs with the exception of nicotine and alcohol, but that defines a lot of us.

-6-

Pulling into the parking lot of the mental health clinic, I noticed that Smith had beaten me here so stopping for a burger hadn't been such a hot idea even if I did eat it in the car on the way down. Good thing I'd gotten both Jen and MaryBeth on the phone before the Statie sauntered through the reception area and into their offices. As predicted, Jen was all business about having a cop let his eyes do the walking through clinical records while MaryBeth, I swear, was ready to break down into tears learning of Jimmy's death. I think she wanted to organize a service or celebration of his life, maybe on Nauset beach at sunrise, and then give us all herbal tea with tofu muffins—yuck!

Jen must have set some tone with Smith as he was sitting, somewhat uncomfortably, in the waiting room surrounded by our usual flotsam and jetsam of society. I had to hand it to Jen; she has a pair of brass cojones when someone challenges her authority in her own lair. Smith literally jumped out of his seat seeing me walk in and asserted himself saying, "Hey Knight, you were right behind me when we left the college—what did you do get lost on Route 6?"

"No, just drove slowly thinking over what I saw down at the lighthouse and trying to make sense out it all." I did my best to placate an angry state trooper that I really didn't want to add to the list of all those regularly pissed off at me.

Jen must have been lurking just inside the receptionist's cubbyhole because she forcefully opened the door to the clinical office area and announced herself with, "Lieutenant Smith, now that Dr. Knight has arrived, we can go to the conference room to discuss this matter further."

Kudos to Jen, she drawled out the "Dr." as if it were six syllables long—I liked that! Also using the conference room was a good ploy as her office was adjacent to the records room while the conference room was about as sterile a place as possible except for the interview room back at the Bourne barracks where Smith first grilled me.

"Please sit, Lieutenant or do you prefer to be addressed as Detective?" Jen waved him to a seat on her right leaving me to plop down wherever I could. She continued, "You need to start again as I don't know anything more than what you told me in the reception area. I have to tell you that standing there announcing that you were a state police detective and wanted to seize our records wasn't the most sensitive strategy in front of a room full of clients for whom confidentiality is our guarantee."

God, but Jen could be icy.

"Ms Pearlman," Smith responded using Jen's surname, "don't play me for a fool. I don't care if you call me Lieutenant, Detective, or just plain Mister. I also know Knight here has been on the phone with you since I dropped him off in the college parking lot. You know damn well, who I am and why I've come here. If you'd invited me into your office, I wouldn't have had to 'announce' who I was and why I was here, so after spending half the morning with one of your clients who's dead now and the other half with Knight here, let's cut the crap and start solving a potentially nasty murder."

It wasn't the words themselves, but the way CJ Smith said them. He got through to Jen; she caved.

"How can we help you with Mr. Farnsworth's death?" she asked nice as pie.

"Dr. Knight has said that the clinical records for him remain confidential, and the AG's office has said that might be true, so I won't waste our time trying to get them directly from you. What I want is to know something about Jimmy; his friends, his hangouts; and some leads so I can talk to others who aren't caught up in all of this paperwork bullshit," Smith replied forcefully. I noticed that the beads of sweat gathering around his temples—he was getting angry and impatient no matter how "slick" his attire was.

"Well Lieutenant, we will try to help you there and sooner than you think." Jen looked at me in a way I couldn't decipher. She continued, "Our clinical supervisor, MaryBeth Andrews, is quickly organizing a memorial service for Mr. Farnsworth. We feel that it's best for his friends, especially those connected with us, to have the opportunity to come together. I'll ask her to have Dr. Knight say a few words to encourage anyone who'd like to contact you directly. Obviously Jimmy had issues otherwise he wouldn't have been in our care, and that goes for many of his friends too. We want to be able to reassure everyone affected by his death that we are here in case we're needed professionally.

Nice, I thought, MaryBeth does her thing as resident earth mother, and Jen parlays it into billable hours! This might get me off the hook with Smith; he could get to interview some of those attending Farnsworth's service without having to grill me further.

"Thanks," he replied. "I'll leave some of my cards so I can interview those who attend. I have to try to get around what seems to be this foolishness about the sanctity of a dead man's records. It's a start, but before I leave, I want Dr. Knight to get Farnsworth's records and go over them with me. I won't look at them or attempt to read them, but I need to know if there are any clues to get us immediately on the trail of whoever did this."

"Well," Jen was trying to buy time, "I would have to ask our legal office for advice here as that seems just on the line."

Smith anticipating her dancing for time routine was ready for her. He said without hesitation, "Hey, if Farnsworth's death was not an accident; and it's looking less and less likely that it was, so beating a guy to death and wedging his leg into the rocks like an anchor is a pretty violent crime.

"Oh, there is one more thing about his death that I am sure Dr. Knight did not tell you," Smith added with a wry smile. "The reason I am so interested in the good doctor here and Jimmy's treatment at the clinic is that we found Dr. Knight's card from the clinic on the body. It was the only piece of identification, and it was stuffed halfway down his throat! Not only did it have Knight's name on the card but also the name and address of the clinic, so while there may be a link to the good doctor here, there also could be a link to the clinic itself. That card could be a warning for someone either to shut up or maybe to spill the beans, I don't know which, but I need to know who that someone is if he's not already sitting in this room with me."

Jen blanched at the thought of the clinic being involved in any way. She gulped and nodded to me conveying her irritation that I'd neglected to tell her the details. Her posture let me know that I was going to spend the rest of the afternoon if not evening deciphering old case notes whether or not they ever got to CJ Smith.

"Look I will do my best to separate what can be shared and what has to be kept confidential. I want to help but I don't want the Board to yank my license. I need to know that you're onboard with this and won't file a complaint against me at a later time," I offered to Jen.

Jen didn't even blink; she nodded her assent—damn, my luck for being a fee-for-service clinician—she didn't have to pay me anything unless she could bill it out, so I was going to be stuck culling the case notes as a freebie.

"Ok," I said to both of them, "let me get into Jimmy's file and start sorting out what might be allowable and see if I can find anything remotely related to what's happened to him. He might have said something I noted that was more than just his regular paranoid ramblings."

Smith knew when he'd gained an advantage and seemed to agree adding, "I'll leave you my FAX number at the barracks in case you find something. I'll have to live with your insistence on privacy issues for now, so if you want to black out portions of the notes, go ahead and redact them, just send me what might be important to moving this case forward. If I have to, I'll get a judge to issue a subpoena for the full file then you folks can fight it out in court. Right now I just want to get someone besides you, Knight, as a person of interest or better yet a suspect."

As if on cue, Jen got up and left the conference room along with Lieutenant Smith, escorting him away from the reception area and out into the parking lot. Her hard line obviously had melted after learning the details of Jimmy's death. For my part, I pulled the file from the records office and started reading the case notes going back a couple of months as a starting point. There wasn't much I didn't already know; and what I'd written mostly dealt with some of Jimmy's worst fantasies— wrong word—these were delusions of the darkest sort. Jimmy was a prisoner of his own thoughts, which often had no contact with reality. I had tried to inject reality into Jimmy's world, challenging him to understand the illogical nature of his ideations, which would lower his level of panic, hostility, and suspicion. In addition, I noticed that a lot of time I spent with him was spent defending the Prolixin injections he'd been receiving. Jimmy wanted oral medication, but his compliance record was so bad that giving him a biweekly shot with all its side effects was preferred; at least that was the clinical staff's opinion, certainly not Jimmy's.

Just as I had arrayed all of the notes on the conference room table, Jen returned accompanied by MaryBeth, the clinic's official supervisor of the therapy staff. MaryBeth and I got along even worse than I did with Jen; but in reality, I liked MaryBeth as she really tried to nurture us as staff members and supported us in every way she could. MaryBeth scheduled peer-review meetings with each clinician to go over case files and give advice on handling the client as well as evaluating the work overall.

The problem was that she was a social worker with a master's degree, and I am a psychologist with a doctorate; bottom line, she isn't my peer much less my superior! As the only licensed psychologist on staff, I wasn't about to listen to her social worker drivel about "being in the moment" or some other new age psychobabble. No doubt I could learn a lot from her, but I wasn't about to accept her as a peer, leave that to those with master's in psych to be on a par with her master's in social work. Yeah, I'm an academic snob, but I worked long and hard for my degrees, so there! Oh trust me, I do know how I come across to those with whom I have to work; there's not a lot of collegiality lost between me and the rest of the staff. At least I don't insist upon being called "Dr" as just plain Dave works nicely.

One of the biggest issues separating us has had to do with what constitutes therapy or even a therapeutic session. For MaryBeth and Jen sitting in an office holding a strictly timed fifty-minute session followed by a ten-minute write-up was the only appropriate format. Aaaargh, for me, I do what was necessary to help my patients—hmmm another bone of contention—psychologists have patients, after all I am licensed by the state as a "health care provider," and social workers have clients. Sometimes I would actually drive with Jimmy as he read license plates and hallucinated over the meaning of the numbers. I needed to confront him about his delusions, as they occurred, not his memory of them days or weeks later. The same was true for any number of unruly mentally disturbed patients that didn't fit the neat social worker's model meaning they often got sent down to me as a last resort before being dismissed from the clinic altogether. I often was the odd man out with the oddest of the odd patients. I remember the time both MaryBeth and Jen told me to discharge one of my patients because he had been arrested for possession of heroin in addition to being a manic-depressive, oh excuse me, but that now officially is called a bipolar disorder and is the disorder *du jour*. They didn't want "his type" in their waiting room! Add to that they really didn't want "my type" in their office space either!

Looking up, I acknowledged the duo's presence and asked, "Should I highlight what could be sent to the cops and have you take a look? If it passes muster, you can have one of the secretaries type them out and FAX them off."

"Nobody is going to be able to read your handwriting, sometimes not even you can make out your scribbling," MaryBeth said with a smear of sarcasm in her voice. "I think you should transcribe what you feel is allowable into a word document and let us review it, then you can send it to Lieutenant Smith after both Jen and I have approved it."

"You know that if you both review and sign off on what I can send Smith, and then both of you as well as the clinic itself will share responsibility for any problems if it gets out that we're feeding clinical information to the cops," I said with malice.

That took both of them aback. Neither wanted to give me a free hand regarding what could or should be sent; but neither wanted to put her license on the line or risk dragging the clinic into either a lawsuit or worse, a compliance review by Medicare/Medicaid auditors. Hah—as if I was going to sit at a computer half the night typing up snippets from old clinical notes for administrative review—set, point, and match, I thought!

"You have a point," conceded Jen, the more pragmatic of the pair. "Let's do it this way, you highlight what may be allowable and relevant going back to the beginning of the year and leave the case file on my desk for me to review in the morning. If everything is acceptable, I'll hand them back to you to send to Smith."

"No, that's not the procedure," interjected MaryBeth. "Dave needs to return the file to the records room, log them in, and lock both the cabinet and the door. He knows the routine; and I don't want any files, much less these, left on anyone's desk. Besides, do this once, and Dr. Knight will make a habit out of the exception."

Gee, she knows me so well! "All right, I'll return everything to the records room as soon as I've finished. Tomorrow I have to be here for the staff meeting at eleven, so you can tell me then what to send to Smith," I offered. "Oh Jen, please let me know what to do about the notes from group sessions—there's another half dozen guys who are still alive and need to be protected."

She paused for a moment, then replied, "Just make sure their names are blacked out or any reference that could be traced back to a particular client of the clinic's except for Jimmy."

"By the way," MaryBeth added emphatically, "don't miss tomorrow's staff meeting. I'm going to have to tell the rest of the clinic about Jimmy's death, and I'll need you to answer questions, as word will get out quickly about what happened to him. Of course, we're going to have to do something for him as a family. I want to have a celebration of life on Thursday, let's get this done as soon as possible, so make sure you are ready to say something about him and his life to all of us."

Jen nodded in agreement, and the two left me to toil in solitude. The conference room had a window overlooking the parking lot, and I watched as both of them packed it in for the day about half an hour later. As soon as their cars turned out of the lot, I shoved all of the case notes back into the file folder and dumped it in the records room, locking doors and hitting light switches on my way out. If I got into the clinic a couple of hours before the staff meeting tomorrow, I could get this finished, but right now I just had to get home.

-8-

I live at the end of a "non- accepted" street at the very edge of South Chatham. Chatham, for a dinky three by five mile town, is divided into the villages of Chatham, West Chatham, North Chatham, and South Chatham. There's no East Chatham as it would be out in the Atlantic. Throw in the Old Village and Chathamport, and you have some interesting divisions among the locals to say nothing about the visitors. North Chatham, Chathamport, and the Old Village are where the swells live. Some of the residences on Shore Road overlooking Chatham harbor would have made the Great Gatsby proud. Town residents don't live there, can't afford to; we live in the hollows at the end of roads, underneath power lines, or hard by the town dump—for the politically correct that's now the "transfer station." After all, we really shouldn't be seen by the annual influx of those from across the bridges. Nevertheless, we do live here and eke out a living as best as we can. At one point, the very rich and the very privileged wanted to ban lobster pots from our yards or even keeping our boats on the hard next to the house. They were concerned about the smell, the noise, the impact on property values. Well just as long as we kept to ourselves at the bottom of these unpaved or pot-holed roads away from their unobstructed views of the harbor (with the quaint fishing and lobster boats, but that irony is lost on them), then we can stow our gear and work on our boats.

My house is a converted fifty-year-old summer cottage with insulation stuffed in the rafters to keep the nor'easters at bay and a wood stove to help the propane floor furnace warm the inside. I live right next to the marsh separating Chatham from Harwich called the Red River. Why Red?—because the mud has a reddish hue from the bog iron in it. Probably way back when, they worked this marsh for its iron ore and smelted it into wrought iron for boat nails and fishhooks. Today it's home to foxes and coyotes, skunks and rabbits, and me. Yes, I have electricity, but no cell phone service or even cable. I'm not the only one down here to have an antenna on top of the roof.

After all of my affairs and mess-ups across the bridges, I live alone thank you very much. Well not quite, I have Toby, my fourteen-year-old Springer Spaniel. He's been with me through a lot, so even though he's mostly blind and deaf, he stays with me.

By the time I'd gotten home after starting to go over case notes looking for clues, some to share with CJ Smith and some to file away mentally for me, I was exhausted. What a day. The only good part was opening the door and having Toby wagging his stump of a tail just as eager to see me as if he were only a six-month-old pup. Talk about unconditional love and never any back talk! Ok so it was late, and he needed feeding which ratcheted up the activity just a tad.

First I grabbed a beer out of the refrig; two glugs, and it was history! Working on a second cold one, I mixed kibbles with some canned glop for Toby who downed it as quickly as I did the beers. Next, I lost the tie, jacket, and blue button down, putting on my fisherman's sweater and jeans to go out back and attack the woodpile in the yard. I don't know what it is, but doing something, almost anything, helps clear my head. Tonight it would be splitting a few logs from the last half cord to get me through the nasty cold of what passes for spring around here.

I didn't really feel too sorry or broken up by Jimmy's death. There was a professional separation between me and my patients; and Jimmy—he was a handful. He often didn't take his medication if prescribed orally, and then he'd hallucinate and get delusional about irrational stuff that made the little green men from Mars laughable. In his demented thought process was his belief that he got special messages from the TV to crack the code embedded in license plates. He was forever trying to get me and anyone else who'd listen—I listen, I am paid to listen—to understand that certain cars were out to get him because their license plates told him so.

As a psychologist, my goal with Jimmy and his ilk in both individual therapy and group was to get him to ignore the commands whether from the TV or license plates. He could be as crazy as a loon, but he just couldn't act on his craziness. On the other hand, the rest of the clinic wanted him shot up with a high-powered antipsychotic that left him in a semi-vegetative state. Jimmy's only friend was his old Chevy wagon, which he drove in a rage because someone's license plate was bugging him; or he weaved across the median in a thorizene-like stupor. Additionally Jimmy wasn't the nicest of people. His paranoid schizophrenic thoughts caused him to lash out at everyone. His family had turned him aside as had most of his friends, even the day treatment program designed to be like a club had banned him. This left me, and I was the last in the long line of therapists who been assigned Jimmy. Still why did he end up at the other end of the Cape with his head bashed in and my card in his mouth?

Two hours of splitting wood didn't bring me any closer to an answer, so I buried the axe blade in the chopping block and headed in for a shower and bed. Climbing the steps to the back stoop, I heard the telephone start its incessant ringing. After the day's events, I hesitated to pick it up letting the answering machine click on instead. I heard the mechanical voice say "Leave a message," and then Fred's voice from the college came across the ether.

"Dave, it's Fred, pick up please, I need to talk to you right now!"

There was such an air of apprehension, almost panic, in his voice that I picked up the receiver quickly and said, "Hey Fred, it's Dave, you sound pretty ragged man, what's up?"

"Where did you go with the cops this morning, and what have you done that involves the college?" he was at his most insistent and annoying self.

"That's a long story, Fred, I'll tell you about it Thursday before my class over coffee, but it's just too long and complicated to rehash over the phone right now. I can tell you that it has absolutely nothing to do with the college or any of its students," I tried to assuage him.

"Yeah you think, then tell me why I just got a call from security at school? Someone broke into your office and ransacked the place. Who'd do that—one of the psychos or dopers you're so fond of?"

"'Psychos' and 'dopers,' are we talking professionally here Fred?" I hadn't processed what was going on at the college, but Fred's behavior, for a fellow psychologist, was just too much to take, especially now. "Look Fred, it's probably some student in danger of flunking out looking to grab a copy of the next test or even the final. You know that I keep my professional practice away from my teaching. All my files from the clinics are locked up in the clinics—those are the regs, get it?"

"I don't believe that this has ever happened before and certainly not while I've been the chair," Fred was determined to assert himself. "You'd better get in tomorrow first thing and straighten this mess up. I need to know what's missing, and if I find that it has anything to do with your outside activities, I will go to the Dean about you."

"Chill Fred," I added. "Look I might have just left my door unlocked, and the mess probably isn't ransacking but just my normal mess; I did leave in a hurry this morning, y'know. If it makes you feel any better, I will come in early tomorrow to figure out what's gone on. Have there been any of those book buyers around, remember last year when one of them hit a couple of our offices stealing psych texts?"

"Well that might be true, but I want you here early enough to review the situation thoroughly and file a report with me and security."

"Fred, I'll see you first thing in the morning, but I have to move quickly as I've a staff meeting at the clinic at eleven, and I need to be there before that." I was going to regret agreeing with Fred because I would need the time to finish reviewing Jimmy's file, but whatever, I had to get Fred off the phone. Before he could object or say something academically pompous, I hung up on him.

I grabbed a couple of beers and headed for the shower—seems as if that's a metaphor for my life these days—multi-tasking!

DAY 2: WEDNESDAY, MAY 7TH

-9-

When the closest living things besides the snoring of Toby in the hallway outside my bedroom are the skunks that live under the front porch, the foxes across the road in the marsh, and the coyote that patrols the yard nightly looking for rabbits or a tasty kitty-cat, I don't feel the need to lock myself in. In fact, I don't have a key for either of my doors, and the only place I leave the ignition key for the car is in the ignition—where else? Of course, there's crime everywhere, but if you looked around Chatham, you'd see much nicer and easier homes to break into. Just last year over on Martha's Vineyard, there was a guy posing as a real estate agent who'd call the cops to tell them that he was showing a house that'd been closed up for the winter, then go in and clean it out! He must have hit half a dozen homes before the owner of one of them showed up right in the middle of winter and in the middle of a heist! It was chutzpah, but it worked. So I don't lock my doors and sleep soundly too, plus a few beers helps the process along.

Just before dawn, I woke up hungry for the dinner I hadn't eaten last night. Around four am is the false dawn as the sun won't break through for another two hours, but the sky lightened in the east enough to let me know that I'd survived to see another day. I splashed water on my face, pulled on my fleece vest and watch cap, and decided to walk the good mile and a half down to the breakfast joint where the fishermen would be congregating right about now. Toby barely stirred in the semi-darkness as I let myself out and headed up the pot holed, rutted road.

I couldn't put the pieces of what happened yesterday together as I followed the road up to the main street and walked along it until the "Java Hut" guarded by two rows of pickup trucks came into sight. I sat on a stool in the middle of a half dozen arguments about government intervention and their God given right to reduce the fish stocks to zero, or was it their right to take every lobster or whatever? I was alone in my thoughts going through the motions of downing a couple of mugs of steamy coffee and working my way through runny eggs, burnt bacon, and blackened toast. I didn't notice any of this as I wrestled on this new day with the thoughts that I couldn't drive out of me last night at the woodpile. Why, what did I have to do with this mess? Jesus, as if my life wasn't enough of a mess all by itself. I knew Fred was agitating to take away my job at the college, and this stuff with canceling class to go off with the state police along with the office mess was just the frosting on the cake. Talk about complications, I had to go back to the college to straighten out my office—why or who'd break into it? I must have left the door open with my papers and books strewn over the desk and onto the floor as usual. Next, I had to go to the clinic to go read all of the files a second time—actually really for the first time, but who's counting?

On top of it all, I knew that this would trigger a review of all of my files. MaryBeth would take the opportunity to make sure all my files were documented properly in case of an audit by either the state or feds. That was Jen's nightmare because if the feds found missing documents they could ask for all of their money back. Of course, it all fell upon me to straighten this mess out. In addition, I had to meet with all of my guys who'd been in group with Jimmy to give them the news and ask if any would like to meet with Smith to share.

Add to that was MaryBeth's insistence that a "celebration of life" be held for Jimmy on Thursday morning. Jesus some life, filled with mind-bending drugs masquerading as medicine. Aw shit, I muttered to myself, I'd forgotten to tell Fred last night about it and now I'd have to see Fred at the college to get him to cover my classes on Thursday morning. No way was this fair.

I got up, dropped a few bills on the counter, and stomped out into the gathering sunrise to slog home and face the new day breaking. Usually I feel better after breakfast with a good coffee high working, but this morning I just dragged back toward the lane leading down to my small cape. Dawn had broken, and the sun was starting to dry out the night air. I heard one of the male cardinals up in the tree with his mating song— sounded good and normal—I thought maybe the day wasn't going to be all-bad after all.

I turned down the lane to my place and heard the throaty growl of an engine revved up in low gear. Looking up I barely had time to jump into the brush alongside the road. A too large for the lane, black, badass Caddy screamed past me. It was rocking and rolling in the ruts and banging its oil pan as it bottomed out. I stayed hidden behind some scrub pines, no doubt standing waist deep in poison ivy. Once the Caddy fishtailed onto the tarred road, I started to run toward my house.

The front door was wide open as well as both doors on my old Ford. Toby was nowhere in sight. I bounced up the steps onto the porch calling for him as I entered. The front room was a mess with every book I owned tossed onto the floor; the sofa cushions strewn about; and even the scatter rugs kicked into a corner. No Toby. I called again as I entered the kitchen area. It was like the living room; every cabinet and drawer opened, and the contents dumped. Crossing the kitchen to the back entryway, I saw Toby lying there—eyes open and dead. That did it for me; I just sat down in all of the crap around me; hugged my dog and cried. I'm not a tough person, sometimes I have a smart mouth, but never have I tried to hurt anyone. Here was Toby, my only real friend through all that had gone on in my chaotic life, lying dead.

What was going on? Whatever it was, it wasn't fair. What else I could do? I tried to put stuff back where it belonged, but I didn't care. Nothing had been taken; I had nothing to take. My emotions started to run the gamut from fear to rage with a lot of sadness mixed in. Why Toby? He couldn't hurt anyone. It was just past eight when I bundled him in a comforter and put him in the back of the SUV to go to the vet. I needed to know how he died—did some sonofabitch kick him to death? I just needed to know, and besides, the local vet's office is less than half a mile up the road by the four corners.

I parked in the back of the office and knocked on the locked door. One of the vet assistants let me in, helping carry Toby into an examining room. She didn't say a word to me; she could no doubt read the grief on my face.

Within a few minutes, Dr. Stone, the vet, gently pried me away from Toby and looked me square in the eye saying, "Dave, I'm sorry for your loss, but in the couple of years I've known Toby, he'd gone down a lot. What happened, and what do you need me to do for you or him?"

I briefly explained the break-in, and how I found Toby lying on the floor by the back porch. "Doc, I need to know if Toby died because he'd been hurt or what?"

"I'm not going to perform a formal necropsy on this old guy," He replied. "Let me see if I can't see if there's any trauma."

Using his flashlight to peer into Toby's sightless eyes, examining his mouth and teeth, and feeling up and down his rib cage, Dr. Stone was as gentle examining the body, as he would have been with a new puppy. After just a few minutes, he looked me squarely in the eye and said, "No Dave, Toby wasn't kicked or hit or beaten to death; I think his heart just gave out. He probably died barking away in his protection of his master. Ol' Toby was a true trooper."

I started to tear up all over again—it was my fault. I should been home when his warning barks could have roused me. I thanked the Doc, signed the papers for Toby's cremation, and wrote out a check to cover the expenses as well as a donation to the fund that helps take care of pets when their owners can't pay.

I went back home feeling empty, angry, and cold. The house wasn't any better than when I left it an hour earlier, but I couldn't have cared less. The emptiness and cold was in me, not just the house. Something else was there too—anger—I wasn't afraid even with Jimmy's death, the break-in at the college, or the Caddy barreling up my road past me; I was pissed that for nothing poor Toby had died. I vowed to myself that I would get to the bottom of this mess no matter what was going on. I just didn't know the how or why right now, but I wasn't going to leave it to the authorities who dispassionately clear cases; with Toby, this had become personal!

I realized that it was after nine in the morning, and I wouldn't have time to drive down to the college, check out my office, talk to security and Fred, and get to the clinic in Eastham to sort through the notes before the staff meeting. No way, something had to give, but I wanted to see what might be in those case notes that might be a clue about what was going on. I called security at the college and told them that I probably had left the door to my office open. I'd be in soon to check it out. Next, I called Fred, remembering at the last moment that he had a nine am class on Wednesdays— whew—I could avoid the confrontation and just leave a message. I told Fred that something serious had happened to one of my clinic patients. I needed to be at the clinic today and tomorrow. Would he please cover my Thursday classes for me? I knew I would have to deal with some serious fallout when I returned to school, but *que sera*!

-10-

I left my home for the clinic driving the back roads through Harwich and Orleans until I hooked up with the mid-Cape at the rotary and took the right down to the Eastham clinic; I kept a wary eye out for a black Caddy, but saw nothing. Arriving a full hour early for the staff meeting, I grabbed Jimmy's file from the records room, noting that neither Jen nor MaryBeth had signed them out so far this morning—maybe I'd luck out and sort through them before having to sit for an hour through the pablum and sorry clichés called a staff meeting.

With a fresh cup of coffee in one hand and a yellow highlighter in the other, I sat down to review my notes for the last couple of months. Each clinical note summarized the contents of my time with Jimmy. Most of them documented his hysteria over imagined slights and threats. Part of what I had to do was to get Jimmy to appraise his stressors before acting on his impulses. He, like most of us, felt that picking a fight was wrong, but it was Ok to retaliate when provoked. The problem, however, was that nobody else would ever agree to what Jimmy considered extreme provocation. I saw nothing in the notes to warrant murdering Jimmy, much less trashing my office and home. I was having a harder time trying to find anything worthwhile in these notes to pass on to Smith, who no doubt would be on the phone by noon if he didn't get some viable info.

I gave up and carried my files drifting down the hall looking for a spare office to duck into until the staff meeting. I didn't rate my own office at the clinic, barely even squatter's rights—no respect—but I was only there two days a week. Ken's office was vacant, so I dumped the files on his desk and grabbed the phone to call Smith directly. When I got through to the Bourne barracks, I asked for Manny DeSilvia, the lieutenant with whom I had a relationship no matter how shaky instead of Smith.

"Manny, my friend, I need to talk to you soonest," I just launched into it with any preamble. "Can we meet for lunch today—I'll even buy?"

Manny's response was just a bit chilly, "Look Dave, I don't know if meeting with you privately is going to be a good career move; right now you're a cross between toxic and radioactive waste in the barracks. In case you haven't noticed, Smith's pretty much a Prima Donna. Boston has sent him to us in the boonies for an attitude adjustment. He still has friends in high places who are watching him and how he handles—meaning solves— this case, pretty closely."

"Yeah but, I've got to lay this stuff out for you before I get hung out to dry by Smith. Jesus, he's got me between a rock and a hard place and doesn't seem to want to play the wink and nod games that you're so good at."

That got a chuckle over the line from Manny who added, "Maybe I should bring him with me so he can see how it's done."

"Manny, I've been straight with Smith, but I think he doesn't believe me, and I don't want a stand-off; he's got to continue his investigation even if he can't get leads from me. Trust me, at this point, I know nothing, but a couple of things have happened that really piss me off."

I explained briefly about the college, the home, and the dog. Manny finally agreed to meet me, maybe with and maybe without Smith tagging alone, at the Hearth 'n Kettle just off the mid-Cape in Orleans about twelve-thirty. I felt relieved!

I had only a few minutes before the staff meeting, so I flipped open Jimmy's case file to re-review the notes. Each file has separate sections dealing with therapy notes, medication log, physical eval, history, and at the end a place for group therapy notes. I flipped open the section for group and started at the end to re-read. That was strange, I thought, because the last note entered was three weeks old. I run group every week, there should have been a clinical note for the last two weeks if Jimmy had been there, but there wasn't anything.

I checked my appointment book, which is the only way I know whether I'm supposed to be at either clinic or the college. I teach and hold office hours at the college on Tuesdays and Thursdays, have individual appointments in the mental health clinic on Mondays and Friday mornings, do groups at both clinics on Wednesdays, and hold open office hours at the drug clinic on Friday afternoons—busy schedule for sure.

I had put a checkmark next to my listings for group at both clinics the last two Wednesdays. Where were the notes for the mental health group for the last two weeks? Maybe I never wrote them—hey, God knows I've done that before. Wait one, I still had a copy of my billing sheets for the last couple of weeks tucked away in my appointment book. Sure enough, I had billed for group therapy the last two weeks, so I must have held them. Even more telling, I couldn't bill for services without including a copy of the note for the front office as proof. Then why weren't there any notes in Jimmy's file?

Being in Ken's office reminded me that one of his clients was also a member of my Wednesday's group. One particularly annoying—i.e., time consuming without remuneration—aspect of running a group was that I had to write up the clinical note, make copies, and stuff them into therapist's mailboxes for inclusion into everyone's clinical record. Most of the time I didn't even know who the therapists were. Normally I just used first names and left the copies with the receptionist along with my billing record so she could get them sorted correctly. Ken and I had talked about this one fellow; but what was Ken's client's last name? I knew his first was Frankie, but nobody every used last names; I couldn't remember—

began with a "C" I thought, maybe something French Canuck sounding.

I picked up Jimmy's file and hustled back to the file room, looking to avoid both Jen and MaryBeth knowing they'd be looking for me before the staff meeting to review my findings. I opened the file drawer for the Cs and rifled through them looking for a first name of Frank. Bingo, two thirds of the way through, I found "Cournoyer, Francis" and pulled his file. At the end of section for group notes, I found not only a copy of last week's note but also the one for the week before. Looking at the top part listing only the first names of attendees, I saw that Jimmy had been at the meeting two weeks ago but not at the last meeting. He had bailed on the last group meeting—it happens; but he was at the meeting two weeks ago, and that session note was missing. Prying open the metal clips, I removed both notes and returned the file to its place in the cabinet. I was puzzled. Sure, I wouldn't have put a note in Jimmy's file if he missed group, but I would have put a copy of the note in Jimmy's file when he was there. What that meant to me was that somebody had removed it!

I put both notes in my pocket; returned quietly to Ken's office and locked the door. I reread the notes for the last couple of months—individual and group—in chronological order to see if there was something going on either with Jimmy or one of the group members. As I read—or more accurately deciphered my scrawls—I realized that Jimmy not only was on the far side of reality most of the time, but he was frightened badly. My notes recorded a growing escalation of paranoid ideation along with greater decompensation in his personal life. He rambled more and bathed less as time had gone on. What had frightened him to that extent? I searched my notes for a clue. All I could find was Jimmy complaining about driving around too much. I figured that just gave him more time to stare at license plates and get threatening messages via telepathy. I went back to the missing group note from Frank's file—what could be so different about it? Why remove it from Jimmy's file? And by whom? And was I involved?

Looking closely at the note, I tried to piece together the names of the other members of the group that day. Besides Jimmy and Frank Cournoyer, there were another half dozen names, which was typical for attendance at my group. Altogether there might have been twelve to fifteen eligible to show up, while getting more than fifty percent to show up was a pretty good turnout. I tried to picture the room with the group sitting in around the conference room table (I did that just to whiz Jen off as her office was next door, and men's voices do carry) with me by the door (first rule of therapy with guys as loosely wrapped as these was never to get cornered). Jimmy was my only patient in the group, and he sat on my right hand side as if entitled. The rest of them didn't have any particular seating pattern that I could remember. What had happened? We started as we usually did—each taking a turn commenting on the week past—nothing strange there according to my notes. Again, Jimmy complained that he was driving too much; he was too stressed; and he was too scared by being followed by big black cars. Nothing different there—but wait, what about the big black caddy with tinted windows that barreled up my road at dawn this morning? Coincidence, sure, but I made a mental note anyways. What else?

At the very bottom of my note, two things stood out in this second reading. First, Jimmy had asked me why I never visited the day treatment program anymore. Jimmy and I first met at that program. I had wandered over to check up on how one of my new patients was getting along—or was he even there—when I found Jimmy barricaded in a back room. The staff had demanded that he hang out there and not mix with the rest of the program as he was actively hallucinating (gee so were half a dozen others) and threatening to fight with everyone around him. I went in to spend some time with him and see if I could calm him down. Funny they didn't mention that Jimmy always, I mean always, carried a knife or if more crazy, a baseball bat. To my knowledge, he'd never used either against a real person, but I have seen him swinging his bat and jabbing with his knife against imaginary foes that were out to get him. Well that day I was able to calm him down, got him to face what was scaring him, and got him back into the day program for some coffee and doughnuts. Jimmy knew that about six months ago Jen and MaryBeth had told me not to visit the day program. According to them doing therapy there was best left to the day treatment staff, leaving the clinical staff to be stuck behind their desks. In fact, the director of the day program was part of our clinical review team and held firm to the position that his program was a viable alternative to therapy. Mavericks like me just weren't welcome there. Jimmy knew that because twice in the last month or so he'd had an eruption in the day program resulting in being banned from the program as a time-out. According to him, he'd asked for me to come over to help him, but the program director was adamant. Jimmy was left to storm to the clinic in the hope that I was there. So why would he mention my not going to the day program anymore?

The second thing I noticed, and even more confusing, was my note about an exchange between Jimmy and one of the others—Kevin, a guy I knew only slightly if at all—about finding things that didn't belong to them and doing the right thing. This led to a general discussion about what the right thing was. I remembered the conversation—more of an argument than a discussion of ideas. My note said that I would help Jimmy with what was right next time we met for individual therapy. Hurriedly I flipped to the section with individual notes and saw that Jimmy had missed his last two individual therapy sessions with me; and I'd logged his absences—the last one was Monday, the day before he was found dead at Nobska Point. I went back to the group notes—the one for just a week ago. There was nothing at all about stealing or doing the right thing. In fact, I didn't log a single mention of Jimmy, as he wasn't there; and the conflict from the previous week had evaporated. More to the point, Kevin wasn't at group either. I had to find this Kevin character who'd started the argument over taking things that weren't yours.

First, priority was to get something for Jen to review, and time was short. Taking a yellow marker, I highlighted the most innocuous stuff I could; none of it was helpful in any way about who killed Jimmy or why; but at least I'd have something to give Jen for the staff meeting. I still didn't know what to do about the group note taken from Jimmy's file, so I kept that one under my hat. With only a few minutes to spare I left Ken's office, grabbed another cup of coffee from the staff's break room, and headed to the conference room for the meeting.

Jen and MaryBeth were already seated—each at either end of the rectangular table—like bookends with most of the staff seated in between. The table held the ubiquitous plate of homemade muffins flanked by piles of paper napkins. Heaven help the clinician though, who helped himself because we'd all learned the hard way that these goodies were just props. They were to be put out in the client waiting area as soon as the meeting was over—MaryBeth liked to contribute whatever she could to those more needy than ourselves.

I nodded to Jen and gave her Jimmy's file so she could checkout my highlights during the meeting and said, "Jen, this is the best I can do given what I understand are our restraints about confidentiality. There's nothing helpful; I made sure that nothing's shared about Jimmy's diagnosis or treatment. If Smith wants to read about the times I tried to get Jimmy to discuss something other than his paranoid ideations like what the Sox or Pats were doing, then that's fine by me; but it sure isn't going to help. I know this might just piss him off big time, so if you want to give him more about Jimmy let me know."

I was going to tell her about meeting Manny and maybe even Smith for lunch after the meeting, but thought I'd rather wing it alone. Could she have pulled the group note? Could MaryBeth have done it, but why?

Jen just nodded, but had her red pencil handy to check off what I could use. MaryBeth caught my eye motioning me to sit up at her end of the table; no doubt, she wanted me to say something about Jimmy to the others who might not have known him well. She started the staff meeting, beginning first with the regular stuff about notes, time cards, keeping track of appointments, and the thousand little details she went over each time we met. Then she got to Jimmy and his demise. Thankfully when she asked if anyone didn't know who Jimmy was, no hands went up—not surprisingly as most of the social workers in attendance had already had Jimmy on their client list and discharged him for a variety of offenses ranging from too many missed appointments (no money there) to feeling threatened in their office by his rage-like outbursts. The reason to get rid of him I liked best (or actually least) was this one fat, middle-aged, lesbian (hey she lived in P'town) social worker who'd accused Jimmy of sexual assault. For Christ's sake, when Jimmy didn't take his Haldol pills regularly, he got worse, and to help his mental state the shrink ordered Haldol shots for him. The side effect was that Jimmy felt like he was running in place—he couldn't stop moving; but the social worker, like all of

MaryBeth's good clinicians, demanded that he sit for his fifty-minute therapy session. The result was that Jimmy sat slouched in a chair pelvis thrusting to ease his discomfort. It's a good thing Jimmy didn't take one of those erectile dysfunction meds because if he had the erection lasting four hours, she'd have screamed rape. When Jimmy was all wound up with me, we just went for a walk; but then I'd have to put up with MaryBeth's wrath as in her world such behavior was unprofessional and certainly not therapeutic at all.

MaryBeth managed to annoy everyone at the meeting by announcing that all clinicians had the obligation to call their clients to tell them that a celebration of life for Jimmy would be held at Coast Guard Beach in the National Seashore tomorrow at ten in the morning. She cancelled all clinical appointments for the morning as well. The thought of losing money was an anathema to most of the crowd, so pandemonium broke out. A telling point by Ken—not an unreasonable guy even for a social worker—was that most of our clients didn't have wheels and getting down to the beach would be almost impossible. The compromise was to have the celebration in our parking lot with appointments cancelled only for the ten o'clock hour. MaryBeth ended the meeting by saying how I'd have something special to say about Jimmy tomorrow, and how I'd discuss his death in the men's group this afternoon. She said not a word about how or where Jimmy died, and no one around the table cared enough to ask. This wasn't exactly Dunne's "Ask not for whom the bell tolls" moment.

I grabbed Jimmy's file from Jen as I passed her. She said, "Dave, I checked off the parts you can give Smith, and I found some other stuff you could share with him without betraying confidence like how many times he'd been seen in the clinic, who treated him, stuff like that. I hope this satisfies the state police and keeps them from trying to get a search warrant to rummage through our files."

Although I only nodded in assent, I couldn't help but think that she and probably everyone else in the clinic really didn't give a damn about Jimmy's death. To be honest, I wouldn't have either if I weren't affected personally. Jimmy really was unlovable. I left the highlighted files and CJ Smith's FAX number with Deb, the receptionist asking her to get them off soonest. She rolled her eyes, but agreed to the task.

Oh well, I thought, time to boogie and get to the Hearth 'n Kettle to meet with Manny. My hope was that he wouldn't bring Smith along. I was in a quandary: someone killed Jimmy; someone stuffed my card down his throat; someone ransacked my office at the college; someone ransacked my house; and someone killed my dog. Now add that someone rummaged through my files and took the clinical note from Jimmy's file, a copy of which was now in my pocket. Time to find Manny!

-11-

I pulled into the lot of the Hearth 'n Kettle a few minutes before noon but noticed that Manny's unmarked, midnight blue, Crown Vic was already parked there. If anything screamed cop car, it was this one—a dinosaur among the Jeep and Prius population of the Lower Cape. To boot, there were the three or four squiggly aerials on the trunk and roof, just in case anyone mistook it for a family sedan. I made my way into the restaurant and found Manny seated alone, thank you God, in a booth toward the back. With his brylcreemed hair, dark suit, and perpetual sneer, you'd have thought he was a mobster not a state cop—hmmm maybe not a lot of difference there at times. I slid into the booth opposite him and sighed heavily; he looked up.

"Manny, thanks for driving down here on short notice, but I really need to talk to you," I began without any preamble niceties. "You heard anymore about what happened yesterday down in Woods Hole at the lighthouse?"

"Yeah, sit down and get something to eat, maybe their chowder, it's pretty good with some crackers to thicken it up. What do you think about the Sox this year? That kid going to be able to play the field Ok?" This was Manny-speak for "give it a rest" or maybe to chill so we look like two businessmen just having lunch together before we talked business. Manny always seemed to have a sixth sense about what was going on around him. He didn't want to attract attention to us, which meant to me, that something was up!

We both ordered, Manny had a burger with fries and coffee; I got a bowl of quahog chowder along with half a turkey club and coffee. Yup, we were just a couple of middle-aged capitalists sharing lunch, idle chitchat, and maybe over the coffee doing some business. For fifteen minutes, Manny talked in generalities about this, that, and absolutely nothing of interest to me. After the lunch plates were removed, and the second cup of coffee poured, he opened up, "The ME had just finished the autopsy when I left; prelim report at least from what I heard is it's murder; his skull was caved in with something like a baseball bat. Wooden splinters ID'd as ash, were found in his scalp; no way in hell that this was caused by a fall on the rocks. What the fuck have you gotten yourself into this time, Dave?"

"I don't know," I admitted, "I really don't have any idea why what happened and how come I'm in the mix."

"Yeah, but bopping a guy and tossing him off a cliff with your card stuffed halfway down his throat sounds like stuff out of the Godfather or mobbed up wiseguys. What's with this guy who got wasted?"

Gee, Manny was slick—he just had a way of getting me to open up—I had to be on guard for letting it all out. "Manny," I said, "The guy killed was Jimmy Farnsworth, one of my patients that I saw in therapy and in group, but I hadn't seen him for a couple of weeks."

"Listen boyo, Manny leaned forward almost conspiratorially, "I shouldn't say this, but the ME also found bruising that wasn't obvious at first. He said that someone definitely shoved your card down Farnsworth's throat. There's a clear left-handed thumb and finger marks on either side of the jaw meaning that someone held his mouth open and jammed the card down the throat with the right."

"Manny, that's gross. Would Jimmy have already been dead when that happened?" I asked.

"No, doesn't work that way, my friend. In order to get bruising, blood has to be flowing, heart has to be pumping, and the vic's got to be living. In addition, and don't let this spoil your lunch, but when the ME got his shirt off there were some unbelievable burn marks on his arms and chest. Looked like cigarette burns, and all of the fingers on his right hand were broken, so he was tortured too."

I shook my head in disbelief and denial. After a pause, I said, "Last time I met with him was in group—three weeks ago today—he didn't show for his last two individual sessions with me or his last group one either. That's not unusual, he was flakey—hey if he wasn't he wouldn't have been at the clinic in the first place."

"Sounds good, but you told me over the phone about your office at the college getting trashed and your home too. Look, I'm sorry to hear about your dog—you and he were a pair I know. There's too much going on involving you to be any sort of a coincidence. You've got a bulls-eye painted all over your back!

"I know, I know, this sucks, and I can't make sense out of what's going on. I've nothing at my house or college office to connect me to the clinic much less Jimmy Farnsworth. Try telling that to Smith, Christ but he's all over me like a cheap suit," I pleaded.

"I've talked a bit to CJ—cut him some slack if you can—he's been transferred down here from 1010 Com Ave and thinks it's some sort of punishment to be banished from the big city. Apparently, he got all jammed up with the Fart, Belch, and Itch crowd by blowing the cover of a CI whose identity he should have checked first. If he's pressing, it's because he wants to score a quick solution and get back to Boston. You of all people should be simpatico with the guy."

Manny and I were both "washashores," the derisive name given to those living on the Cape who came from over the bridges. We originally met in New Bedford when I was the psychologist in the drug clinic there, and Manny worked out of the North Dartmouth barracks. He was an undercover agent in the drug task force out of the DA's office when I blew his cover by accident. Long story made short, but Manny had to "get out of Dodge" and relocated to the Bourne barracks. I followed him to the Cape under a different set of circumstances as I got myself transferred out of the university only a year later. He figured I owed him big time for my gaff, so he struck up a relationship trying to make me give him something on the druggies with whom I worked. Ok, so I owed Manny one, but not this guy Smith.

"Well Smith sure seems to be an eager beaver, but you know the rules about disclosures, and he should too," I took a hard line. "I can't let him run roughshod over me, the clinic, and poor Jimmy even if it helps nail his killer.

"If he's from Boston, he should know the old pol's line," I continued. "'Never write if you can speak; never speak if you can nod; never nod if you can wink.' I can wink and nod with the best of them, but nothing can either be spoken or written—that's the game we've played for the last few years here on Cape, right?"

"Sure, but we haven't been playing for the same stakes; this is a murder investigation, and it's all hands on deck," he countered. "Look we could play it this way—you become an anonymous informer, and I'll protect you by listing you as an official CI. That way anything you give up will be washed through me before getting to Smith. I'm sure he'll be sensitive to the CI label this time around."

"No, it's not that I don't trust you, but I don't. Someone will tumble on our meetings or past affiliation in New Bedford, and I'll be hosed by my Board of Registration. Also, and I told Smith this, a smart defense attorney will get everything I've said or disclosed thrown out. Can you imagine the stink if the killer gets away scot free on appeal?"

"Play it your way, but what about your life? Someone trashed your house and your office, and for what? You say you don't know. Look Knight, haven't you heard of obstruction of justice? Ask ex-Speaker of the House

Finneran about lying —he lives down in Eastham. Being politically connected got him probation; you'd be looking at jail time. Holding stuff back just because you think a dead guy would complain isn't going to fly. Give it up, let us take it to the DA to see if he wants us to pursue any leads we get. Besides talking to us may be a better alternative than having whoever did Farnsworth do you."

"Manny, I want to help—this thing is out of control. I can't talk about Jimmy's condition, his therapy, his meds, and there isn't much else in the files. I don't want you guys breathing down my back because you think I know more than I do. Look, just between us, I've a note from my men's group that Jimmy was part of in my pocket; it's from last week. Take a look at this right now and tell me how this would help Smith's investigation." I unfolded the note for last week's group, which Jimmy had missed, and passed it over to him.

Manny made an annoying production of fishing out his glasses from his shirt pocket, putting them on, and smoothing out the note I had given him. After he scanned the paper, frowned, and squinted, he looked up and said, "Jesus, Knight they pay you to listen to this crap? I can't decipher half of what you wrote, and the other half is gibberish. Talk about psychobabble!"

I pulled the note back to my side of the table and pocketed it. "Hey I told you that these notes aren't designed to help. They don't have any purpose except to pass muster when the state or feds audit our records to see if we really performed the services for which they've paid. Most of the social workers use a formulaic approach—it's called SOAP and stands for four aspects of the therapy session. First there's the subjective, like he looks nuts; next it's the objective—yup he sounds nuts; followed by the assessment—still nuts; and finally the prognosis—he'll stay nuts if he doesn't get more therapy. Let's face it, these notes aren't intended to be an accurate recording of what was said; they're just crib notes to help us pick up the thread in the next session as well as showing MassHealth that we're doing something."

"Enough, I get the point," Manny admitted. "Getting the notes verbatim won't help us find the killer, but getting information about Jimmy, his friends and habits, might help us trace his movements up to the time he was killed. I talked to Smith before meeting you, who said he has butkis so far. He can't find the car or anyone who saw Farnsworth on Monday or even over the weekend. He seems to have vanished for up to forty-eight hours before showing up at the low tide mark."

"Here's the best I can give you right now," I said. "Tomorrow morning in the parking lot of the clinic at ten o'clock there'll be a service for Jimmy. I have to meet with the men's group this afternoon to make sure that they'll be there. All of us are supposed to call our people to get a good turnout. You guys could join us—in mufti of course—and see who knew Jimmy. I don't think we can stop you from talking to anyone except the clinical staff. Just don't let on that you learned from me about this—the clinical director will have my balls for breakfast."

"Sounds good, Dave," Manny nodded in agreement. "Why don't you stand with those from the men's group so we can single them out more easily?"

"I'm targeted as a speaker for this dog and pony show so I'll be onstage literally," I protested. "Why not just circulate and casually ask about how they felt about Jimmy or even his death? You'll find that most everyone really don't give a damn; our client list doesn't exactly include the Mother Theresas of the world. Besides having major mental disorders, most of this crowd—clinicians included—have some sort of personality disorder. Jesus, Manny, please don't make a scene there."

"We won't," he said. "I'll get some undercover cops from New Bedford to help out. I agree having Smith show up wouldn't work—he'd stand out something awful given that the lower Cape's ninety-seven percent whitebread—and besides he's already been seen at the clinic. Thanks for the tip, Knight. I'll make this square with Smith and unless something else turns up, you'll be off the hook. If I go to Smith and get him off your case, you'd better not be holding back on me."

"What you need to understand is that these people are different from the ones you know from the drug clinic. They don't connect with reality unless their meds have kicked in. Compared to the shenanigans played by the druggies, these guys are just babes in the woods. I gotta trust you, so it cuts both ways."

I picked up the tab left on the table by the waitress— there was a clear quid pro quo and buying lunch was part of it. Manny left without further comment; I dumped some bills on the table and headed off to my next stop—the drug clinic.

-12-

I jumped on the mid-Cape just behind Manny's cruiser and trailed in his wake as he hit speeds of seventy until he caught up with some biddy doing exactly the fifty mile per hour speed limit around Exit 10. No doubt, Manny was already on the phone to Smith rounding up extras for tomorrow's event. The cynic in me justified the disclosure by saying that at least there would be a better turnout for Jimmy that way. I tooled off the highway where Rt 6 double-barreled and worked my way down to the drug clinic.

Pulling into the near empty parking lot behind the non-descript brown sided, two story office building, I grabbed the first spot by the entrance and was buzzed inside by the receptionist. Security tends to be tight, and during the morning, there's a security guard to help direct traffic and keep the druggies from doing the hang all day around the clinic. Think about it, if you wanted to score dope or sell something to an addict, what better meeting ground than a drug clinic. The clinic kept the cops away so the addicts didn't freak out as most of them had outstanding warrants for defaulting on court dates. For the clinic, this had been a major PR coup. But nature abhors a vacuum, so without the cops, two things happened—first the clinic parking lot started to look a lot like a tail gate party before a Pats game. The clinic opened at six in the morning to dispense methadone and by mid-morning, the lot was full of cars, addicts, and even their families. It was a safe place to gather. Secondly, the absence of cops brought out those who wanted to score dope or sell it. We'd had a couple of bad incidents with dealers looking to find junkies who owed them money and then hung out in the parking lot looking to nail the deadbeats. Once they even chased one right into the waiting room—I got him into an office, but they confronted the clinic director and beat him up instead—hence the improved security at the door and in the parking lot!

My group at the drug clinic varied from week to week because I got the addicts who had blown off the breathalyzer in the morning during dosing. Methadone is a central nervous system depressant as is alcohol. Mixing the two can be a deadly recipe—in fact, most deaths in the clinic occurred because the addict drank and drugged. We couldn't stop them from drinking after they'd gotten their methadone-laced juice in the morning, but the clinic refused to dose anyone who'd been drinking when they showed up in the morning for their legal fix. Besides random tests, anyone who the nurses thought might be under the influence was breathalyzed. Booze in the morning meant withholding the methadone dose. Now here's the problem—Ramparts, the clinic, is a region-wide, for-profit corporation, they are paid for distributing methadone—no dope, no income! Withholding someone's dose because he'd been out boozing limited the corporation's liability in case of death, but it sure didn't feed the bottom line. I was the solution—if you'd been drinking, the morning dose was held, but you were allowed to stay at the clinic or come back after lunch and if clean, dosed then. The response cost, as we say in the trade, was that you had to attend the alcohol awareness group for a month of Wednesday afternoons. If the number of offenders got too large I added a Monday or Friday group, but right now I was down to half a dozen on Wednesday afternoons and whatever newcomers had been condemned to my care over the last week.

I smiled at the receptionist, Angie, and picked up my folder with the list of names for group plus all the paperwork need to facilitate the billing and processing of the paperwork. What a difference between the two clinics; the for-profit drug clinic was fast and efficient compared to the laid-back attitude of the non-profit mental health program. I had the entire list of drug clinic clients with those consigned to my group ticked off. I had all of the paperwork necessary for processing and filing the group note as well as submitting my invoice. Time was money, and the clinic didn't run a tab on the addicts—strictly cash, unless they were insurance eligible. Another scam was to get our addicts enrolled in a disability program like Medicaid or SSDI. It used to be that having a drug or alcohol addiction was enough, but now the state required a mental health diagnosis as well. Heck, you have to be crazy to shoot dope, so it's a slam-dunk—depression, bi-polar, attention deficit, you name it we can document it. Most often, we called it "adjustment disorder," getting us six months of treatment without a problem. This allowed the addict to get his methadone and receive therapy—a double bonus because Ramparts made a profit on both ends. Me, I just did my job trying to keep the problem under control, but it always seemed as if I was shoveling sand against the tide. Heroin and cocaine are just too tempting and too available for too many. I really thought that all we did was act as a pit stop whenever the habit became too large or too expensive. Take a break, detox, reduce the need, then bam back on the street. Talk about a vicious cycle that usually ended in death by overdose. There is always the hope, however, that someone would kick the habit and leave the clinic for the straight and narrow. Hmm, now who had the needle in his arm, I wondered?

On the way to the meeting room, I grabbed a diet coke from the break room and quickly scanned my list of offenders. No surprises here. A couple of newbies referred over the past week; for two others, today's session was their last; and all the rest were working their way through the month long purgatory. Entering the room, there were all of my guys and two women seated around the table. Angie had let them in once I showed to facilitate matters. I called the role, ticked off names, started to take notes, and began the process anew.

Like AA group meetings, we began by sharing our names and acknowledging what got us here. It happens every time and without fail that one of the tyros bitches and moans that he'd been setup, that the nurses had it in for him, that the breathalyzer was wrong, and that he'd really not been drinking that much. What's neat is when the old timers who've admitted to their drinking get on his case. Less work for me, I can just referee. In my mind I was back in the mental health clinic trying to place this Kevin guy when I started to look over the names of the client list in the drug clinic—there were half a dozen Kevin's, and I couldn't place any of them either. I was brought back to the present when I realized that one of new group members was talking about Jimmy and his death.

"Wait a minute, wait now," I jumped in to the exchange. "Back up and tell me about Jimmy and what you know."

The big guy, I think he had said his name was Alex, looked at me and said, "Yeah this fruitcake, Jimmy whatever, got himself offed a couple of days back—I mean they found him yesterday morning—and I hear that he was whacked."

"No, no that's not true. I mean he did die sometime Monday night, but it might have been an accident. The real question is how he'd get to Falmouth where he was found. Any thoughts about how he'd get there or with whom?" I tried to wheedle more information from him.

One of the women, probably in her late twenties but aged to at least forty from a decade of chasing dope, spoke up, "I seen this guy hanging out behind the clinic all the time the last week or two. I asked who he was 'cuz he was weird, and Kevin said his name was Jimmy, and he was a wack-job from that Eastham place."

Alex started to say something, but I held up my hand and said rapid fire, "Whoa, wait, backup, who's Kevin? Is he on the clinic? What's his last name?"

She said, "I think it's Kevin Turcotte—I know I called him Turbot once, like the fish y'know? Funny he told me he fished before he got hooked himself."

I quickly checked the client list for the clinic, and there was a Kevin Turcotte listed.

"What was this guy Jimmy doing? Why did you think he was weird? When did you see him last?" I blurted out. My intensity woke up the other half of the sleepy group, and everybody stared at me as I leaned forward. "Look I need to know about you seeing this guy, not simply because he's dead, but because I knew him from the other clinic."

Elaine, the one who said she'd seen him, continued, "Like I said I seen him behind the clinic; you know how the parking lot backs up on the bike trail, and it's like uphill; well he was walking up and down real weird, just looking and looking into the lot."

"What do you mean by 'real weird,' Elaine?" I asked.

"He walked funny, y'know like his pants were on fire, all herky-jerky like."

That was Jimmy all right, without a doubt. "Did anyone else see him, or did you see him talking to anyone?" I pressed.

True to form, half of the group said sure they had seen him too, but none was able to add any further details. I'd shown some interest, and these psychopathic personalities all wanted to jump on the bandwagon— maybe there'd be something in it for them—my team!

I had another forty minutes before I could let the group out, and each minute dragged worse than the one before it. With ten minutes left, I had already written the complete session note and was ready to get it and the forms to Angie for processing. Come on, I thought, lets wrap this up now. Finally, I let them go close enough to the real break time so anyone who was looking or timing would be satisfied. Usually I was the last out of the room, but this time I was first.

"Hey Angie," I said breezily handing over the billing form for the session. "You look busy; let me make the copies for you."

Angie, whose idea of being busy was chewing on gum, nodded and waved me toward the copy machine. After getting the copies made, I headed for the records room as if I were going to find each person's file. No, I just wanted to look at Turcotte's file.

Pulling it, I flipped open to the first section done at intake into the clinic. Here was supposed to be all of the relevant information about new clients to the clinic; the file was empty. When Angie sets up a file for intake, all of the sections are there with blank forms—one for intake, another for diagnosis, treatment plan, physical, whatever— so we'd know what to do and when it was due each time we were assigned a new case. This file was trash, all of its material missing; it was just an empty shell. After putting his file back in place, I unceremoniously stuffed all of the copies of the group note into an envelope, wrote Angie across the top, added a smiley face and "thanks, Dave" at the bottom, and dropped it into the interoffice mail box.

Waving good-bye to Angie, I left the clinic and walked to the end of the parking lot where Jimmy had been seen last week. The clinic parking lot backs up to the old railroad bed now converted into a bike trail. The trail winding around the back of the parking lot is elevated about six feet and gives an unobstructed view of the clinic setting. I climbed over the low split rail fence and up to the trail. As it was early spring, not a whole lot of people were bike riding, roller-blading or walking with the wind whipping off the Atlantic just two miles east of here; talk about cutting right to the bone! I started at the far end of the trail where a view of the clinic began and carefully walked along with my eyes glued to the ground. Just about two-thirds of the way around, I found what I was looking for—cigarette butts and gum wrappers—Jimmy's MO all right! He smoked incessantly; well more like he chewed on the filters while chewing gum at the same time, probably to ease the discomfort of the stiffness in his jaw. Just another in the list of side effects of the meds he took. No doubt about it, Jimmy had been here and more than once too. But why? He had no reason to hang out behind the drug clinic. I never heard him ever speak about it or any of its clients.

Looking at my watch, I realized that I'd barely enough time to get back to Eastham for my men's group and spread the word of Jimmy's death. I needed to line up the crew for tomorrow's celebration at ten that for many of my guys would be early in the morning. With more questions than answers I headed back down the mid-Cape to Eastham where I needed to see whether Kevin Turcotte had been treated there, and if he was, in fact, the same Kevin who had been to my group two weeks ago.

-13-

The only saving grace to working three jobs with all of the driving I have to do is that I write off the travel expenses. Probably a tax fiddle, I know, but otherwise I'd go broke having to pay the extra cost at the pump for the privilege of driving the length and breadth of Cape Cod daily. Right now, the traffic was bearable, but in less than a month, it'd be wall-to-wall with out-of-state cars. I was able to make good time down to the Orleans rotary and then up to the clinic just inside the Eastham line. I entered the clinic on time, waved a greeting to the receptionist, signaled for my guys seated in the waiting room to follow me, and headed for the conference room.

As usual, I circulated a sheet of paper asking each one to write down his first name only. Because we were a little more lax than the profit-driven drug clinic, the receptionist who doubled as the billing clerk would insert the right last names when I sent in my billing sheets. As the sheet wound around the table, I started by telling the group that Jimmy had died and asked if anyone had heard about it.

To me it seemed as if his death was weeks ago, but in actuality someone murdered him less than forty-eight hours earlier. I wasn't surprised that nobody in the group had heard of his death. I didn't get nor did I expect to have gotten an outpouring of emotion, as Jimmy wasn't anyone's favorite.

"Hey come on guys," I said. "Who knew Jimmy; I mean if not well then some way?"

Max, one of the old timers in the clinic whose claim to fame was that he'd survived over one hundred acid trips in the sixties and seventies, said, "I lived with Jimmy in a halfway house for a couple of years maybe ten years ago, he was a strange dude."

"Ok, but how about recently?" I tried to head off war stories about Jimmy from the distance past. "Did anyone run into him in the last two weeks?"

Max wasn't one to give up once he got a thought—he could be locked on for weeks at a time—so he started again, "At the halfway house, Jim posted signs on the walls to tell Lenny that he wasn't wanted there. Those two went at it all the time."

"Max," I said gently, "how long ago was that? Who's Lenny anyways, and when was the last time you saw them fighting?"

Max looked down at the table, started to count on his fingers, and then looked up smiling saying, "I saw Lenny since the last group meeting, he's still on the clinic, but he sees one of the women here and doesn't have to do group. All I know is that Lenny and Jim really had some go-rounds back in the halfway house days and later in the day program."

Ah, that jogged my memory. When I first took a job at the clinic, I had to separate Jimmy from Lenny over some incident that had taken place years earlier. If memory served me correctly, Lenny lived totally in the past; I'm sure his therapy sessions revolved around his belief that his mother liked his brother better. Besides, I did know Lenny a little bit, and in my humble, but professional opinion, he was a gentle giant. Thinking of him and Jimmy together made me think of Lenny and George from Steinbeck's *Of Mice and Men*—I smirked if not smiled. I make a mental note, however, to check his file on the QT before leaving for the day.

"Great Max, that helps a bit, I'll have to talk to Lenny and see if he ran into Jim around the clinic any time in the last couple of weeks. Good work! Now who else can help me out?"

No response, but one person wouldn't make eye contact with me as I panned the room. I glanced down at the signup sheet and saw that his name was Ted.

"Hey Ted, what do you think could have happened to Jimmy; how well did you know him?" I tried to elicit a response.

"I don't know, Doc, but I ain't seen Jim since group a couple of weeks ago when he got into it at the end with Kevin," was his response. There was some head nodding around the table in confirmation.

"Did you see Jimmy outside the clinic with Kevin; did they continue to argue when they left that day?" Again, I tried to get the dialogue going.

Max spoke up softly, "I tried to get Jim to give me a ride back to the day program, but he wouldn't even talk to me. He just hauled ass out of here"

"Was Kevin around?" I pressed on.

"Yeah, I saw him leave; he was yammering at Jimmy all right," this from a third guy, Craig, who'd been a member of the group for over a year now.

"What was going between them? Was it more about someone stealing stuff like they'd been arguing about in here?" I asked remembering the contents of that next-to-last session note.

Craig, who had been a college student until he started talking to the light bulbs after the onset of schizophrenia, was a reasonably reliable reporter and said, "Kevin was following Jimmy to his car trying to get him to stop and talk, but Jimmy seem scared-like and just drove off."

I didn't want to press too hard, most of my group function at a low level and stressors such as trying to get answers to questions just overwhelms them; I had to back off. I said instead, "Tomorrow morning there'll be a service for Jimmy here in the parking lot for all of us in the clinic. It's at ten and will last about an hour. I don't think coffee or doughnuts will be around, but I could be wrong. What I'd really like is for all of us to stand together as members of the group Jimmy probably trusted most. I might have to say something and some of you might want to tell a story about Jimmy and how you wanted to remember him."

I could see already that Max and Ted along with a couple of others were squirming in discomfort. Standing in front of even a small group while you were fighting off the voices in your head was a recipe for disaster. I said, "Ok, ok, nobody is going to have to speak; tell you what, lets each take turns right now saying something nice about Jimmy, and I'll put our thoughts together and speak for all of us tomorrow. How'd that be? And just for helping out, I'll stop by Dunkin' Donuts to get a box of munchkins to share."

After some head nodding, I thought I had a consensus and started going around the table. I took the lead trying to think of something nice or kind that Jimmy had done for me or someone else. I admit it was hard, but I did remember the time that he had offered to give up his appointment with me because one of my patients had burst into the clinic in a full-blown panic attack. That seemed to break the ice, and the others chimed in with similar small but innocuous remembrances of Jimmy. At least I could work from these notes elaborating them or just downright lying if I had to.

"Hey," I added. "Did Jimmy ever mention anyone down in the Falmouth area? Did he ever talk about driving down there or to Wood's Hole?"

Max, who seemed to have known Jimmy best, said, "No, Jimmy never went up Cape farther than the Rt 28 Bridge over the Bass River. He hated Hyannis and was afraid of getting lost in all of the traffic especially around the mall and all. The only place I've seen Jimmy out of this area was down in P-town, but that was a couple of years ago. I know he liked to drive up and down Rt 6, but getting off the highway spooked him."

"How 'bout the drug clinic over in Dennis? Think he would have had any friends there?" I threw out the question.

"Bunch of coke whores; Jimmy was freaked by them," Max replied adamantly.

After a few more comments in the same vein, it became clear that Jimmy typically would not have visited the drug clinic under any circumstances. Standing on the bike trail behind the parking lot made even less sense. Trying another tack, I asked, "What about Kevin, who'd he hang with? I haven't seen him around the clinic hardly at all and not since group a couple of weeks ago."

I tried to make eye contact with Ted, Max, and Craig first as they'd been the most forthcoming about Jimmy but to no avail. Finally, Frankie started to say something, but his voice was low almost as if he were chanting.

"Kevin's not from around here; he's from New Bedford; he's bad; he's mean; he called me names; he pushed me."

"How long have you known Kevin?" I tried to keep Frankie talking.

"He's mean" was all I could get as a response.

I knew not to push the issue, as Frankie's hold on reality was tenuous enough to begin with. I'd just have to check Kevin's file once I figured out who was his therapist. Something didn't seem kosher as most of my guys had long histories with each other and knew each other almost from the day each had entered the system; talk about a closed group! I then told the group that we'd break early because I would credit them the time spent tomorrow at Jimmy's celebration of life. With that, I left them to wander off while I found Deb, our receptionist cum billing clerk, at her desk. She juggled answering the phone, scheduling appointments, collecting co-pays, and preparing the billing forms sent off Cape to the head office. In reality, she knew more about both the clients and clinicians than anyone in the clinic did.

As breezily as I could, I asked, "Hey Deb, I'm concerned about one of my guys in group; he's missed the last couple of sessions, and I'd like to discuss the absences with his therapist."

Deb looked up from the stack of billing forms on her desk, sighed, and said, "What's his name, Dave?"

"Kevin, I think, but I don't know the last names." I lied not wanting to tip my hand.

"Jeez we've at least half a dozen Kevin's in the active files. I'll have to go back to your billing form to find his case number, cross match that with his name, and then I can find his therapist. I can't do it now, but maybe by next Wednesday when your group meets again I can get to it; I'll leave a note in his therapist's box to call you."

"Naw, Deb that seems like a lot to ask just to chase down a missing guy what with all of the fuss about tomorrow, y'know. Hey, just give me the master client list for five minutes, and I can find his file in the records room. That way I can talk to his social worker tomorrow and maybe see Kevin too."

I could see that Deb wanted to help me out—I get along great with my fellow peons—but I was sure that she wanted to look over her shoulder to make sure neither Jen nor MaryBeth saw me get carte blanche in the records room.

"All right, here's my latest list of clients and their case numbers; get it back to me as soon as you figure out your guy's therapist," she relented.

"Gotcha and I owe you, you're the best!" I enthused.

With the list in hand, I checked over my shoulder to see if either Jen or MaryBeth was watching. Thankfully, they weren't about, so I barged into the records room, opened the file cabinet for the T's and pulled Turcott's file. It was blank. No intake form, no diagnosis, no treatment plan, no progress notes, no nothing. There wasn't even the stuff Deb automatically puts in like billing information and the assigned therapist. This was a repeat of his emptied chart at the drug clinic. Not good!

Next, I decided to check Lenny's file; I hadn't had much contact with him in at least a year or so and wanted to see if there was any mention of Jim in the file. This time I didn't know the last name, which made the task more difficult but just as unrewarding. I had to scan the master list to find all those with first name of Len, and then yank each file to see if it was the right one. File by file I eliminated all of the ones who were in group or had male therapists and simply ran out of files to match up against names. There was a name on the master list for a "Len Rudkowski," but there was no file for him at all. I even checked the sign-out sheet over by the door of the records room to see if his therapist or someone else had it out—no luck. Not good at all! I had to get answers, but I didn't dare get caught thumbing my way through files in the record room for which I had no reason. MaryBeth would skin me alive.

I handed back the client list to Deb and began, "I know you're jammed right now, but there was just an empty folder for this Kevin guy. My session note for group should have been there from two weeks ago, but it's all blank. Can you check the client number and see which therapist billed for services, please? Also, ditto for Lenny Rudkowski. His name's come up in group, and I'd like to discuss him with his clinician. Their files aren't there, so maybe they've been discharged or something, but even so, I'd like to know who saw them here"

"I can't cross therapists with clients here at the clinic. It became such a hassle when therapists would call in and demand that I call each of their clients to cancel appointments. I'm too busy running the waiting room, making appointments, handling the co-pays, and being the phone receptionist without having to pull all of a therapist's files for contact numbers. Finally last year Jen had that info sent off Cape to central office's billing department. Only by going through them can you cross-reference clients with therapists. But call them, they'll get back to you—someday," she responded with a smirk.

Damn, our clinic was part of a larger group of clinics banded together for all of the accounting functions. Money drives the ship, and our clinic lives uniquely on disbursements from the state and federal government. These payments can be months in arrears, so the clinic needs a bank. Right! Try getting a line of credit from a commercial bank using invoices to the government for services rendered as collateral, as I said—Right! The answer had been to sell out to a mother organization that collectively billed the state and feds for a dozen small clinics. Think of it like a bank offering bridge loans so that there was a constant cash flow. If MassHealth or the Department of Mental Health delayed or denied payment on a bunch of invoices for one clinic, there was enough cash flow through the central office to offset any shortfall. In addition, a head honcho coordinated all the clinics and had introduced a standard form for billing and record keeping. I hadn't met him, but he seemed to be a good guy in that he never hassled me. In fact, he only huddled with Jen as he made his weekly rounds, and of course, our checks were in the mail.

"Deb, I know what you mean—why don't I see if Kevin comes to Jimmy's celebration tomorrow. I'll talk to him then and find out who's his therapist, maybe there's a simple answer about why his folder is empty," I dissembled and headed for the door. With a final wave to Deb who was back answering the phone, I headed for the parking lot and a return drive to the drug clinic.

Sometimes I think I know every pothole along the single lane portion of Rt 6, but that didn't stop me from thumping into them as I sped back to the Dennis clinic. Pulling into the parking lot, I headed back up to the bike path where I'd found the gum and butts from Jimmy. I took a panoramic view of what he could have been looking at or for. Nothing in the parking lot, but as I turned away from the lot, I noticed a glint of reflected sun light from next to a house a hundred or so yards away. The houses east of the bike path formed a summer colony of fifties ranches along the shore of the Swan River. I looked down at the overgrown slope that led up to the bike path. There was a clear path of trampled weeds and broken scrub pine branches leading to the cul-de-sac at the end of the summer colony's main street. I hustled down the slope and wandered in the direction of the sun glint I'd seen. In a driveway about three houses back, just peeking out past the summer porch was Jimmy's car.

I'd have known his old Chevy wagon anywhere; it was at least twenty years old, rust pitted, and full of the debris that defined Jimmy's life. Although the doors were closed, I noticed they were unlocked. I didn't bother to open the doors; I could see Jimmy's license and registration still taped around the steering column undisturbed. I knew there wasn't going to be anything there for me, and I didn't need to add my fingerprints to whatever mess was inside for the police to find. I thought of calling Manny immediately or even Smith, but then I'd have to wait around for them to show up and answer questions for half of the night. Looking around I saw evidence that somebody had been raking leaves and pulling weeds recently. Probably homeowners down over the Patriots' Day long weekend, so I didn't think anyone was now living on the street at all. I figured I'd see Manny or his minions tomorrow and could give them the location of Jimmy's car then. I had put in a long day and now wanted to get away from all that had happened.

-14-

What a day, I said to myself as I climbed back into my SUV and headed off to Chatham. I rambled along the back roads, not to avoid the traffic on the mid-Cape, which wouldn't start for another couple of weeks, but I wanted some solitude to assess what had gone on since I got hauled out of class yesterday. It had been a pretty traumatic two days; I was exhausted and wound up at the same time. Nothing seemed to add up. Why kill Jimmy and dump his body down at Nobska Point? Who was this guy Turcotte who'd been at both the drug and mental health clinics? How come his folders were blank at both places? Why had someone yanked his files? He'd had a beef with Jimmy, so it had to be all connected. Add to that the missing folder about Lenny. Too much of a coincidence that two guys who'd had beefs with Jimmy would have their files pulled. Why had Jimmy been down at the drug clinic—not his patch at all? Both my house and office had been tossed, but by whom and why? Too many questions, I was tired, as I turned left onto the dirt lane leading down to my house.

Wait a minute, I thought. Driving down to the dead end at twilight might not be the smartest move, so I backed up and decided on Plan B. I turned onto the main road and headed toward town. First, I stopped at the local liquor store to get a decent bottle of wine—a J Lohr cab worked fine—then I hit the village market to grab a steak. It was just past closing time, but there were a couple of blue hairs still checking out. The butcher was cleaning up the meat counter, but seemed Ok about selling me a good-sized hunk of rib eye. Back in the car, I zigged and zagged over what must have been cart ways a century ago before pulling up in the driveway of a newish cape style house overlooking one of the kettle ponds in town. I hoped I'd found a sanctuary and safe haven with Chris.

I headed for the back steps and knocked on the door. The porch light went on, and the door opened wide. I waved my goodies as if in supplication.

"For Christ's sake, come on in, Dave," she welcomed. I didn't need a second invite as I crossed into the kitchen where her two overactive terriers greeted me. Did they want to see me, my steak, or did they smell Toby on my clothes? Probably the answer was yes to the latter two at least!

"Beware of Greeks bearing gifts," I said lightly as I knew I would be baring my troubles to her soon.

"Yeah, but you're Irish," she retorted.

Giving her a hug and kiss on the cheek, I handed over the supper goodies and started to unburden myself over a glass of decent wine. I'd known Chris ever since I had lugged my sorry ass all the way down Cape after getting the heave-ho out of the university a few years ago. I'd had tenure as a psych professor but got myself mixed up in an affair with a close relative of the chancellor. I was recently divorced and didn't think twice about dating—Ok, call it shacking up if you will—with someone from the administration, but I didn't know who her auntie was. When it all blew up in my face, I made a personal enemy out of every top floor executive in the university—yikes! Now there are only three ways to fire someone with tenure: insubordination, incompetence, and moral turpitude. The first two seem easy enough to figure out, but the last one can be sticky as it can define behaviors that aren't actually against the law. I'd say sleeping with a student would fall into this category, but the Chancellor interpreted it as sleeping with her niece, and she wanted to have me stripped of my tenure then fired. Problem is the tenure hearing has to be in public and the record available to all. To avoid litigation (I'd have sued) and to spare all involved the sordid details we struck a deal. The compromise was that I'd accept a transfer from the state university to the state college and a reduction in rank from full professor to the associate's level. I kept my tenure in the higher education system (Fred obviously didn't know the details, or he'd have stopped bugging me by now) and my professorial salary (more than Fred makes, I'd bet). How do I get myself into these jams?

Chris had been working for a local realtor down in Chatham village when I showed up one day with Toby in tow. She really hit it off with the old guy; probably couldn't have cared less about me, but she and Toby instantly bonded. After that, I got to know Chris; she helped me find the little place I call home and funding through the local bank too. I'd been pretty well stripped of my assets between paying off the ex-wife and the host of attorneys. I had a salary but no track record at the college as the transfer happened so quickly. Chris knew people, and in small town America that still counted for something.

Bottom line, I got my loan, closed on the house, moved in, and made a friend of Chris. We'd seen each other a couple of times for dinner or just walking the dogs on the beach. Now I was in her kitchen trying to tell my story while she fired up the Webber on her deck to grill the onions, potatoes, and steak.

As I brought Chris up to speed, I got to my point, "I really didn't feel safe going back to my place tonight. It's a mess, and then there's Toby's bed and food to get rid of. I just couldn't sleep at all. Here's the pitch—you know folks with rental properties that won't be used until June sometime—I'd like to move into one until this mess gets cleared up. Any thoughts?"

I had had my head down staring into my wine glass when I looked up to make eye contact. Chris was just sitting at her kitchen table with tears running down her cheeks. She knew how much Toby had meant to me and to her too.

"You can stay here," Chris suggested. "I've an extra bedroom or whatever."

"Thanks, I'd hoped to be able to, but what if someone was following me or saw my car here? I can't put you in danger," I answered.

"Easy, just go park your car in the Hill's driveway, just behind this house and walk back through the yards. They won't be here until June the earliest, and even if someone followed you they'd have to know the path through yards to get here."

"I don't know," I protested. "I didn't come to make trouble for you, but I really appreciate you putting up with me and putting me up."

"Most of rentals are still shut down for the winter. Getting electricity and water turned back on without the owners knowing would be a pain—stay here, I insist."

"Gee, Chris, thanks and I mean it—good thinking about my car—I don't think I was followed here, but if so it's too late, so I'm here for the duration," I relented.

Dinner with Chris reminded me how seldom I ever shared my thoughts and feelings with anyone else. Literally days if not weeks went by when I talked only to students, drug addicts, the mentally ill, and of course, Toby. These were the normal ones compared to my railing at administrators—hmmm my authority problem again. Chris was good at listening, letting me just let it all hang out without a critical comment or trying to solve the problem for me. We killed the J Lohr along with a second bottle, ate the steaks and veggies, and finally I relaxed enough to give the mess I call my life a rest. While I cleaned up the kitchen and fed scraps to her dogs, Chris made sure the spare bedroom had sheets and blankets in case I ended up there. I had been up since before dawn and needed a sound sleep even if alcohol induced. Chris, on the other hand, was a night owl and not an early riser at all. She laughed as I started to nod off on the couch trying to catch the ten o'clock news and suggested that I hit the hay. With more tenderness than I deserved she gave me a good night kiss and told me not to leave without waking her in the morning.

Robertson Browne

DAY 3: THURSDAY, MAY 8TH

-15-

I awoke refreshed having slept the sleep of the damned and no dreams either. I grabbed a shower, saying thank you silently to Chris for leaving out a toothbrush, razor, and comb for me. Down in the kitchen I fixed coffee and rummaged around for cereal or maybe an English muffin. With a mug of coffee in one hand and the muffins lathered with marmalade in the other I headed for Chris' computer to read the morning papers. After logging on, I glanced at the national papers like the NY Times, the regional rags like the Boston Herald, and our local entry, the Cape Cod Times. In that one, I looked for an article about Jimmy's death or the investigation, but found nothing; I checked the feature called "Police Blotter," but again no mention; finally, I looked under "Death Notices," again nada. Either nobody cared, wasn't news, or the cops had this pretty well bottled up. Looking at my watch, I figured I had time to get to my place, throw a few clothes in a duffel bag, make sure the doors were at least closed, and get to the clinic with the box of munchkins I had promised the guys for attending. I went upstairs, woke Chris up, gave her a kiss on the cheek, and said I would call her later and would be back for supper. She just smiled, thank God for one good friend!

I forgot that I wanted to stop at my box at the post office. There isn't any delivery down my dirt road, and I got tired of having my mail box on the main road run down by drunks, kids, and the snowplow at least three times a year. I got a box in the post office instead. Last time I checked it was back on Friday—jeez and today was Thursday already, oh wow time flies when you're having fun. I crossed the lobby and fitted my key into the lock, swung open the door and took out a handful of bills and useless advertising circulars. What else did I expect? Stuffed in with the assorted junk mail was a yellow card telling me that I had a package waiting to be picked up? With card in hand, I tried the door leading to the counter only to find it locked. I couldn't get in until after nine-thirty, but by then I needed to be on the road to the clinic, so it would have to wait. Now I had to remember to get back to the post office before four in the afternoon before the counter closed!

After springing for a couple of boxes of munchkins at the Dunkin' Donuts inside the local gas station, I turned up the dirt lane to the clinic's rear entrance, but turned around and parked on the street near the front driveway. I wanted to be able to make a quick getaway back to the college in case the lot was full of celebrants for Jimmy. Walking along swinging my boxes of donut holes, I passed two unmarked, but not unnoticeable, cruisers positioned on either side of the driveway leading into the parking lot. So much for being undercover, I thought.

Getting into the parking lot itself, I realized how nice the day had become. The sun was actually warm, and the high trees blocked the breeze, which was still cool off coming off the water this time of year. There was a fair number of people milling about, and it appeared that MaryBeth had set up a podium just outside the clinic's main door with a microphone hooked up to a pair of speakers in the windows of the reception room. Someone had set up a table to the left that looked as if it held a punch bowl of some sort and a couple of plates with crackers or knowing MaryBeth twigs, leaves, and granola. I saw a couple of the boys from the men's group looking around, no doubt for me, or more likely my doughnuts. I waved to them and lifted the boxes in the air. Like bees to honey, they made their way over to me.

"Hey Max, hi Craig," I called. "Any of the others here yet?"

"Yeah Doc," Max said, "most of us are here but hanging back up against the trees. The sun's pretty bright so we'd better stay out of it, I think."

I'd forgotten, and I would bet MaryBeth had too, that most of our clients were taking some sort of psychotropic med increasing their sensitivity to sunlight. Not only were their eyes supersensitive, but also their skin could more easily burn and even blister when exposed to sunlight. Cynic that I am, however, I bet that the real reason for standing in the shadows was to be able to smoke undetected and as far away from MaryBeth's hectoring lectures on the dangers of tobacco use. Whatever, I left Max and Craig to take the doughnuts to the gang while I checked in with the boss.

Entering the reception area, I counted all the clinicians from yesterday plus a few who'd skipped the staff meeting. Apparently, I was the last to arrive—typical. MaryBeth peeved with me said, "Glad you could make it Dave; we were waiting for you to begin."

Mumbling my usual mea culpa, we all marched out to the parking lot, where MaryBeth stepped to podium and gestured all those spread around the parking lot to come closer. Besides the dozen or so therapists, there were about forty-to-fifty clients moving slowly toward the front of the clinic. I noticed too the three or four others not part of the clinic bunch. Probably they were Manny's undercover cops. No matter how they tried to sidle up alongside one of our crowd and start a conversation, it never worked. Looking around I could see groups of clients huddled together and then the cops with a five-foot radius of open space around them. I never told Manny that it'd be easy, but in reality, the mentally ill have a strong sixth sense about who is like them and who isn't. These cops didn't make it at all.

MaryBeth led off the celebration praising everyone for being here and talking in generalities about the clinic as a family; how everyone here was part of that family;

and how the clinic was there to help and support everyone in the family. Sure, I thought, and how many times did MaryBeth try to get Jimmy booted? Listening, I realized that MaryBeth wasn't going to say anything about Jimmy because she didn't know anything about him other than his clinical record of being a paranoid schizophrenic. After a few minutes of platitudes, she called me to the podium to share my thoughts and feelings over Jimmy's death. Personally, I'd rather have talked about Toby, but that was something I would have to share with Chris.

I've never been good with microphones and have a leather set of lungs from lecturing to college students all these years, so I stood in front of the podium and made my voice heard across the gathered group. "Jimmy died during the darkness of Monday night, and this morning we have gathered in the bright sunshine to remember and share something of him and his life. Yesterday he was missed at our men's group, and his friends there each gave me something to share with you today."

With that, I pulled out of my pocket the notes I'd taken yesterday and embellished them as I read aloud. I added a couple of his peculiar behaviors that were the least offensive and most of us had experienced. I mentioned a bit about his life, being born on the Cape, attending local schools, having a variety of jobs, that sort of stuff—pretty thin stuff. Finally, I said, "You all knew Jimmy one way or another, you knew him for good or bad, but you knew him. I'd like each of us to find one thing in our memories of Jimmy that wasn't hurtful, hateful, or frightening. It doesn't have to be a good memory just not a bad one. Hold on to it; think about it; and make it how you will remember Jimmy forever whenever his name comes up. Also if anyone wants to talk about Jimmy's death, we're here to listen; and if anyone has any information about Jimmy that helps us understand what happened to him or why, please see me or Marybeth."

I paused long enough to let those who cared find a memory, then said, "I've talked too long, but I do want to share a quotation from Hemmingway that touches and describes all of us, 'The world breaks everyone and afterward many are strong in the broken places. But those that will not break it kills. It kills the very good and the very gentle and the very brave impartially. If you are none of these you can be sure it will kill you too but there will be no special hurry.'"

I just stood there looking over the faces of broken men and women. Their minds had been crippled by mental disorders, neurological malfunctions, and even the damage done by psychedelic drugs like LSD. Their bodies bore the ravages and scars of the side effects of the most virulent anti-psychotic; anti-manic; anti-everything drugs we could prescribe. Just as I turned away to give the podium back to MaryBeth, I noticed someone staring at me with undisguised hostility. It was Mike Pitts, the director of the day treatment program. Jimmy and the majority of patients I saw hung out there. Boy, if looks could kill, but why? It could be because I had spoken, and he was just pissed that MaryBeth didn't ask him. More likely, I guessed it was because of the animosity between Pitts and Jimmy over his refusal to let me into the program to advocate for him.

MaryBeth gushed her thanks to me for my comments and wrapped up the celebration of Jimmy's life with more pap. I'd already tuned her out and probably the majority of staff and clients had done so too. After a couple of minutes, she thanked us all for taking time to come and said good-bye. Whew, now I could head back to the college and teach my afternoon classes that I had bailed out on Tuesday. I wondered if Fred covered them for me then, and if had, did he plan to do it again today? Ah the heck with it, I'd better get back to school and face Fred's wrath along with the vacant faces of the horde of not so eager students.

Walking down the driveway back to my car, I realized that something terribly wrong was happening. At least half a dozen Staties in plainclothes were isolating and buttonholing clinic clients. Max, Craig, Ted, along with a couple of others were surrounded by the cops and were being herding off to one side. I saw one reach out and grab Max by the arm when Max tried to turn back to the clinic. Looking up I saw to my horror a paddy wagon backed up to the entrance of the driveway. Flanked by the two cruisers, it blocked the driveway totally. I turned around in time to see a couple of uniformed Staties emerge from brush on either side of the drive to keep the clinic clients from retreating to the safety of the clinic itself. This was insane; the cops were going to round up as many of our clients as possible to grill them about Jimmy; this was a pogrom. I was caught in the middle—Sweet Jesus, I was the only sane person on the street and that included the damned cops. I pulled out my cell phone and hit #6 to speed-dial the clinic. Deb answered, and I told her to get MaryBeth out into the parking lot toward the street. I told her that the cops were rounding up our clients—I didn't tell her how they knew to be here.

Max saw me standing there and called out, "Doc, Doc, help me, tell them to leave me alone."

I walked over to the cop and put a hand on his shoulder to get his attention and keep him from tightening his grip on Max's arm. The cop, dressed only in jeans and sweatshirt, turned and screamed at me to get back. I still didn't see a badge or any identification so I screamed back, "Hey leave him alone, he doesn't know you or want to go with you, who the fuck do you think you are?"

Nothing gets someone's attention than yelling obscenities. Pulling up his sweatshirt, he pointed to a badge clipped to his belt saying, "This is who I am, fuckface, now get out of here!"

I stepped back and looked around for either Manny or Smith, but couldn't see either. What I did see and hear was MaryBeth screaming at the top of her lungs coming at a dead run down the driveway. Bright red face, kinky grey hair, heaving bosom, and two hundred twenty-five pounds of tofu, she led the charge and was followed by half a dozen social workers. Coming up behind the uniformed troopers, she broached their line like a modern day version of Delacroix's "Liberty" at the barricades. Talk about a mother hen and her chicks. She was all over the Statie who was trying to usher Max toward the waiting Black Mariah. Looking around, I saw the pandemonium that had broken out. For the first time in my life, I felt a kinship with the social workers. They'd entered the fray doing all they could to keep the cops from scooping up our clients. A couple of them had their cell phones out taking pictures of the cops. If these were really undercover Staties, posting their mugs on the Internet would out them and end their undercover careers along with any investigations underway. The Staties didn't know whether to keep at our guys or go after the social workers and grab their cell phones. By now, the uniformed Staties were running up to help their colleagues when what I feared would happen happened.

Many of the meds our clients took lowered their threshold for an epileptic seizure. Depending on diet, exercise, and dosage, the risk varied. With the emotional stress of what was going on, a young woman, rail thin, probably anorexic, started to convulse. I rushed over to her as she flopped on the pavement and pulled off my sweater to put under her head and keep her from getting a concussion too. After a minute, which seemed like an eternity, the convulsion eased. I looked up away from the spreading stain on her jeans as she'd lost bladder control to see the uniformed Statie just standing there.

"Hey," I called, "give me a hand; let's see if we can get her to a sitting position."

He looked me squarely in the eye and said, "No, I can't do that. It might constitute a liability situation."

I laid the girl back onto my sweater and rose to confront him, "What do you mean by constituting a 'liability situation'? What about 'Protect and Serve,' or don't those words mean anything to you."

I was nose-to-nose and chin-to-chin with him; I was enraged; there was an innocent young woman caught up in this stupid riot instigated by even more stupid cops; and idiot boy here refused to help. I didn't get a chance to say anything more. Another jackbooted fascist roughly shoved me away with his baton in my back. As I wheeled around to confront my attacker, a dark suited Lt. Manuel DeSilvia stepped between us. He pushed me farther off and said to the two troopers, "Get down and help this woman; make sure she is Ok, and call the EMTs to get her to the hospital now."

He looked at me and said, "Don't take it out on them, take it out on me, this got out of control; I didn't want to do it this way! Smith found out what I was planning and took over—it's his murder case. Why don't you get that big one off my men before she gets smacked in the mouth—let's get this under control—I need your help!"

"I'm not helping you any further than stopping this clusterfuck, you asshole. How the hell could you be part of this?"

I didn't wait for an answer but turned away and headed toward the confrontation between MaryBeth and a couple of undercover thugs. Over all of this, I heard the whoop-whoop, oogah and baarch of modern day sirens. At the top of the driveway, I saw a couple of local cop cars pull in to block the Staties' paddy wagon. All of a sudden, the appearance of the local gendarme stopped the commotion.

Local cops protect their turf jealously. They don't like to be tread upon by the county sheriff's department, and they hate being left out of the loop by the state troopers. I'd bet that nobody cleared this operation with the chief. The ramifications were going to be far-reaching and long lasting, but they weren't going to help find Jimmy's murderer. Almost as soon as it started, it was over. The Staties got into their cars; the chief and DeSilvia were going at it hammer and tong; the paddy wagon was replaced by the EMT ambulance; and the girl I had helped got professional treatment. I made eye contact with MaryBeth who was getting everyone, client and therapist alike, to head back up the driveway and to the clinic. She rolled her eyes and pointed to the clinic; it was clear she wanted me to go back with her and the others.

I caught up with Max, Craig, and Ted standing together, actually more like huddled together, and asked if they were Ok. Each nodded in agreement, and I suggested that we all go back to the clinic. They started back up the driveway with me following when Smith touched me on the arm saying, "Why don't you come with me, Knight? There are more questions I need you to answer."

Yanking my arm away from him, I whirled around and hissed venomously, "Look at this mess; you expect me to help you because you're so incompetent you couldn't pour piss out of a boot with the instructions on the heel. I don't have anything to tell you."

"Hey wise guy, if you'd given me what I asked for in the first place, this wouldn't have been necessary," he said and again grabbed me just above the elbow.

"Don't bullshit me, Smith, if what you wanted was legal, you'd have had a subpoena and gone through all of the files already. It's not legal, so you think a terror campaign will work, well it won't. I'm done, and so are these undercover cops once the staff uploads their pictures to the Internet. Good move, Smith, busting the career paths of half a dozen cops," I taunted him.

"Don't make me put you in cuffs, for Christ's sake just get in the back of the car."

"Yeah, and while you're at it, you can have one of your goons beat me for resisting arrest, you're pathetic."

"Look, this didn't work out well, I admit, and I'll take the blame, but I've talked this over with DA Bayreuth personally, and he's got an assistant DA waiting for us at the county complex in Barnstable. Come with me and talk to him; if he says so, you'll be off the hook with us."

By this time, Smith had steered me over toward his unmarked cruiser where the rest of the uniformed Staties were gathered. I pulled away again saying, "There's nothing more to be said here, except you and Manny need to try to smooth things over with the clinic director. Right now I expect she's on the phone with every politician she can find; this ain't over yet by a long shot."

Raising his voice, Smith barked, "I haven't the time now, I've a murder on my hands, just get your ass in the car, Knight!"

Pushing away from the car, I was knocked off balance and forward by a sharp blow to the middle of my back. Twisting around I stared at the same thug who'd crosschecked me earlier. He was daring me to make a move and justify his taking another swing at me. Hey, I might be dumb, but I'm not stupid. Not wanting to end up in the hospital ER, I backed off, pulled open the cruiser door, and got in. Needless to say, the drive to the DA's office in Barnstable was made in stony silence.

-16-

We pulled into the County Complex off 6A and wheeled around to the DA's office next to the bank. Smith got out and made a cell phone call while leaving me to stew in the handle-less backseat. I think he enjoyed letting me sit there while he did whatever damage control he wanted knowing that I was a virtual prisoner. Games that people play, but hey, I'd had Psych 101—even better I taught it too!

After a suitable interval designed to irritate and intimidate me, Smith opened the backdoor and ushered me into the DA's office by a side door. We went right to a small conference room where, according to his nametag, ADA McGuire sat. Without ceremony or salutation, McGuire started with, "Tell me why we shouldn't arrest you for obstruction of justice, Mr. Knight?"

"Well nice to meet you too, Mr. McGuire, that is if your tag is accurate," I replied scornfully. "You can't charge me with obstructing justice, when it's not me that's keeping the files confidential; it's the clinic, and Smithie here knows that. I don't have the authority to graze through the file folders, and now that Mr. Farnsworth is deceased, technically he is no longer my patient so I don't have any authority to pull his file or even read what's in it. All I have responsibility for is the adding of a 'case discharge' form indicating that Mr. Farnsworth no longer needs or receives services from the clinic due to his death. His case is closed, and my hands are tied both legally and ethically."

"Our position," he responded, "is that this is an ongoing murder investigation and some leeway needs to be given. We would like the case files including all of the notes by those treating him; but failing that we want you to tell us what you can remember or recollect having reread all of the notes, I've been told, within the last 72 hours."

"If you had a legal leg to stand on, you'd already have had a search warrant or subpoena executed," I countered. "You don't because any judge will tell you what you want is illegal under federal rules. I'll grant you that nobody designed the HIPPA privacy act with a murder investigation in mind, but it's there nonetheless. I told Smith on Tuesday that having his case file or getting the information from me leading to an arrest would get the case thrown out. It's the fruit of the poisonous tree. At least that's what it's called on *Law and Order.*"

Smith jumped in, "Look we've been able to go nowhere with this. You are the only positive lead, and we're wasting time."

Turning in my chair to face him, I said, "What you did this morning was moronic and wrong. You were ready to beat up and haul away a bunch of people whose only crime was being mentally ill and attending a pseudo funeral service. How many of those people won't come back to the clinic; not because they've something to hide, but because they're scared of black paddy wagons, your boys and their batons?"

"Yeah, yeah, it didn't work out so well," he admitted. "But we had to try something. You saw that we tried just to talk to the nutcases, but they wouldn't go near us. This was a fall back plan."

"And that makes it right?" I was getting hot again. "If Manny hadn't stepped in, I'd have been beaten like a rug because I was trying to get help for a woman who'd had a seizure. Some plan!"

"Let's stop this bickering now," McGuire attempted to regain control. "Knight you're correct that the legality of a fishing expedition in confidential files is shaky. On the other hand, you are here now, and it's time to get off your high horse and start answering some questions. Can we be clear on that?"

"Sure, you ask the question, and if the answer doesn't compromise Jimmy's confidential file material, I will answer it," I conceded. "But, and there's always a but, you will no doubt ask me a question such as 'did Jim have any enemies?' to which the answer is yes—he pissed everyone off. You'd have to bust just about every convenience store owner on the lower Cape as most had banned him for his crazy behavior. But, this is your show, give it a shot."

"All right," McGuire cleared his throat, nodded at Smith, who placed a miniature tape recorder on the tabletop, and said, "Do you know any reason why the deceased would have been in Falmouth last Monday?"

Without elaboration or emotion, I replied, "No."

He then tried, "Am I correct in my understanding that the deceased was treated for a mental disorder with both prescription drugs and therapy at the Eastern Cape Mental Health Clinic located in Eastham? Also were you his therapist, and if so, how long had you know him?"

"Yes on both counts," I answered. "Jim had been a client of the clinic before I was hired; and I was his primary therapist for almost three years."

We went on in this desultory fashion for about ninety minutes until both McGuire and Smith gave up. I honestly had no real information to give them about Jimmy's behaviors and anything like a lead into who killed him. Sure the stuff about Kevin Turcotte and the missing case files was puzzling, but who knew whether he was connected or not to Jimmy's death. After what happened this morning, I wasn't about to finger anyone from either clinic to be grabbed and interrogated by the likes of Smith's goon squad. Smith sighed heavily leaning over to shut off the tape recorder, a good sign that the interview was over.

"Ok," Smith started, "you want to play hardball, hide behind a dead man's rights or whatever, go for it; but right now without any contradictory information from you we're looking at one of the clinic's characters as the perpetrator. How's that grab you?"

"What? Who? You need motive, means, opportunity; you can't just make this up as you go along!" I was indignant.

"Sure Knight," Smith continued, "right now I'm looking hard at one Leonard Rutkowski of Eastham as a person of interest. From what I gather, he'd had a rocky relationship with Farnsworth. Apparently they've come to fisticuffs more than once."

"You're shitting me, right? Lenny's not a killer; it was Farnsworth who used him as a punching bag," I responded.

"So for the record, you concur that Rudkowski and Farnsworth have had fights in the past?"

"Oh stop with the BS!" I was ripping. "You can't be serious about Lenny as a killer."

"Oh I am, and I haven't heard anything from you this morning to make me move in a different direction," Smith had the stage. "From what I've learned, Mr. Rudkowski has quite a collection of baseball bats—and they are all wooden ones. Farnsworth died from blunt force trauma. The ME found wood splinters embedded in his skull, identified as being ash in nature. Want to bet they came from a wooden bat?"

Now I had thought long and hard about Lenny Rudkowski last night and this morning. I had gone over and over everything I knew about him from the last several years. It was time to mount an emphatic defense.

"Come on, Smith," I implored. "Lenny was a good baseball player in high school and his couple of years at a junior college; even good enough to play in the Cape League one summer. He was a heck of a fielder and even better at the plate. He had his first psychotic episode at the end of the season. He's never has been in his right mind since. The bats are his only link to normalcy; he cherishes them. They're all wooden because the Cape League only uses wooden bats. That's not enough for an indictment. Why would either of them go to Nobska Point in the first place, and how would Lenny even get back? He doesn't drive y'know."

"So you agree that Rudkowski had access to materials similar or identical with the murder weapon? And just how many wooden bats do you think are around these days when everyone from Little League to the college level uses aluminum or composites?" ADA McGuire re-entered the fray.

"Just to answer your other questions Knight," Smith said as he unfolded a piece of yellow legal paper from an inside pocket. "Rudkowski's first residential placement was a Department of Mental Health facility over on Martha's Vineyard. He had relatives living in Tisbury, so he qualified for placement there."

"Yeah, so what?" I didn't like the flow of this conversation at all.

"That's easy; he had to take the island ferry to Woods Hole in order to get psychiatric treatment at the DMH facility in Pocassett. He had to sail past Nobska Point twice each trip, twice each month for the four years he was on the Vineyard. Yeah, I'd say he knew about it pretty well." Smith said smugly. "We have information leading us to believe he could drive a car even though he didn't have a license—don't we Dr. Knight?"

Smith's taunting aside, I realized that he was getting his information about Rudkowski from Rudkowski's missing file at the clinic. One of my bigger gaffes according to the clinic tyrants was that I helped one of the guys get his driver's license back a couple of winters ago. Like Rudkowski, he'd had a psychotic episode when he was at college and ended up spending years trying to claw back from Planet Remulac. After almost a decade, he had aced the written part and was ready to take the road test again. Sure I guess he could have paid to attend a driving school and get some behind the wheel experience; but in reality, he still wasn't real good interpersonally so explaining why he'd let his license expire in the first place would have been difficult. Instead, I volunteered to give him some time behind the wheel of my old SUV on a couple of Saturday mornings in the winter. I had picked him up at the halfway house only to find him accompanied by Rudkowski and one other that I knew from the day treatment program. So there we were—me, Toby, and three mental cases in the parking lot at Nauset Beach. For over an hour, the guy trying to get his license ground the gears of my Explorer driving up and down the parking lot. He even practiced parallel parking for good measure. After he felt comfortable, we headed for the real roads and ended up navigating the rotary on Rt 6 in Orleans. Once we got back to the parking lot, Rudkowski asked if he could drive. I said sure, and Rudkowski got behind the wheel doing a credible job of wheeling around. Couple of hours on a Saturday morning in the winter wasted; one guy ready to get his license; and the other feeling much better about himself and his abilities—we call that self esteem in the trade.

Wouldn't you know it, by the time I got to the clinic the following Monday, the driving episode was all over the place. MaryBeth and Jen were waiting to thump me for a whole list of professional infractions. Probably I could have co-opted them if I'd billed my time as group therapy; but I didn't so I had to listen to their nattering. Bottom line, I had to write the episode up for inclusion in each of the client's folder. That's where Smith was getting his info.

"If I don't get some usable stuff from you and soon, I'm going after Rudkowski as a likely suspect, y'hear?" Smith's voice was firm, and I swear his green eyes flashed jade.

At this point ADA McGuire seemed to lose all interest in the conversation and excused himself leaving just Smith and me to finish—uninterrupted, unobserved, and uncorroborated. Smith had baited the hook with Lenny; how he had gotten access to that file, I didn't know, but I knew I was the fish he planned to land.

"Look Smith," I started. "I don't know how you got any of this information, but you couldn't have gotten it legally. Therefore, you can't use any of it in court. What are you going to do, go to a judge and ask for a search warrant for Lenny's room citing what as evidence—a stolen clinic file? Yeah, I know that Rudkowski's file is missing from the clinic; what I don't know is how you got it. All your so-called evidence is contained in that file so don't bullshit me."

Smith snorted and leaned back, "Who said anything about a file—not me, not ever, doesn't exist. All I have to do is tell the judge that I have a CI providing me the who, what, and why. Game, set, match, good night Irene, unless you can come up with something to move me in a different direction."

I dug in; I'd be damned if he was going to set up a guy like Lenny, but I wasn't going to sing like a canary because frankly I didn't have squat to sing about. Instead, I confronted Smith. "If you bothered to read your entire purloined file, you'd know that Lenny is under guardianship which means he can't speak for himself, his court appointed guardian must do that. Even if you get some bogus search warrant and then pick him up, you can't even read him his Miranda rights. Oh, you can read them all right, but Lenny can't agree, disagree, or even state he understands them because the court has determined that he cannot make decisions for himself due to his mental illness. There's no way you're going to be able to question him."

"Who said anything about questioning him?" Smith rejoined. "Given Rudkowski's mental status, his pysch meds, his long history with the mental health system, I'm sure the judge would agree to an evaluation at, oh say, the State Hospital for the Criminally Insane in Bridgewater."

"Oh I get it, you bastard," I was hot now. "You've got this all figured out, don't you? Rudkowski is mentally ill; we all know that. When he gets to Bridgewater, the shrinks there will agree that he's mentally ill and not able to stand trial because he can't participate in his own defense. That means he stays in Bridgewater until he's no longer mentally ill which for him is a life sentence."

"Hey, Knight, I've seen the little cemetery just outside the wire at Bridgewater, it's touching, but I've a case to close."

"So that's it, right Smith?" I knew where this was going. "You plan on closing the case whether or not you've got the real killer. You can frame Rudkowski, and he never ever gets to a trial to challenge the evidence you've manufactured. You plan to go back to your Boston boys telling them how you solved the case in less than a week. You'll say it's not your fault that one crazy guy killed another and how he'll spend the rest of his life locked up in a prison for the insane. Case closed, bring me home to Beacon Hill; you're one sorry excuse for a cop."

"Whatever Knight, whatever," Smith didn't bother to deny his plan to railroad Rudkowski for life or his motivation for doing so. "You don't have to say anything more, but you've got until Monday to bring me some credible evidence leading elsewhere or I make application for a warrant in Barnstable Superior Court. Now give!"

I had to get Smith moving in a different direction, so I tried changing my own tack.

"My turn," I said as I moved on the offensive. "What about Jim's car? Have you found it yet; have you figured out where he was and how he got to Nobska Point? I asked you Tuesday when we first did this in the Bourne barracks. What's been your progress?"

Smith answered. "We've a BOLO out for the car—we pulled the info about the plate number, make, and model from the DMV—but as of now nothing. For all I know it could be at the bottom of a pond somewhere."

"Here's a freebie that's perfectly above board, Jimmy's car is parked in a driveway on Thorndike Drive off Monument Road in Dennis. I found it last night before it got dark. I didn't want to have to hang around for half the night while you guys got your shit together, so I figured I'd tell Manny about it today. Your stunt at the clinic just wasted another three hours in getting it processed and finding the real killer instead of the fairy tale you plan to spin."

Smith just stared at me, then got up and stomped out of the room. In his place, McGuire poked his head into the room. "Time to leave Knight. Hope you have a cell phone to call for a ride otherwise it'll be a long walk back to Eastham."

He stepped into the room and ushered me out into the receptionist's area where he said to the Statie on duty, "Please escort Mr. Knight off these premises."

I wanted to leave on my own terms with one good zinger at him, but words failed me; I couldn't think of anything weighty or pithy to say. I allowed the trooper to walk me in silence to the property line and headed for the Barnstable Tavern across the street where I'd have a beer and call for a ride.

-17-

Sitting at the bar with a draft Harpoon in hand, I debated whether to call Chris or MaryBeth. I knew Chris would drop her real estate stuff to pick me up, but on the other hand, maybe I should let MaryBeth come for me. It'd give us a good half hour to talk privately about what happened this morning and more importantly, what had been happening with Jimmy and the clinic. Let's see, call Chris, have another beer and kick back, or call MaryBeth, show the flag, and be a team player. I wanted to call Chris but called the clinic instead.

I finished my lone beer along with a bowl of chowder and waited patiently for MaryBeth to pick me up. After about forty minutes her mint green Prius, that figured, turned into the Tavern's parking lot. I hustled over and got in to start the journey back to my car. The first ten minutes or so were surreal as MaryBeth seemed more interested in whether or not the trees would bud early this spring or when the perennial road work on Rt 6A would get started or if we'd have more than the usual number of tourists this summer with the economy and all. Jesus, she asked about everything except when the swallows would come back to Capistrano—avoidance behavior, y'think? Halfway back to Eastham, I finally interrupted her rambling monologue and asked, "Hey MaryBeth, did everyone make out OK after the incident in the driveway this morning with the cops?"

"Dave," she replied in very measured tones, "we need to talk about how the state police knew to be there right when we were having our celebration for poor Jim."

"You told Smith about it Tuesday in the conference room. That's why he left a stack of his cards for us to pass out. I even mentioned it at the end of my stuff about Jimmy," I said as nonchalantly as possible. "I'll admit I went a bit further and got the cops off my back yesterday by telling them where and when the service was. Come on, there was nothing confidential or privileged about the gathering in the parking lot. I told them to observe who we were and with whom we worked. My thought was that both of them could figure out how futile it'd be to try to get information from any of our clients. What they did freaked me out too. And, I must add, I'm the only one who was hauled away in all of this."

"I should have known in advance that they were coming," MaryBeth insisted. "Furthermore you should have discussed this with Jen and me before discussing anything to do with the clinic with the police."

"Sure, but hindsight is always twenty-twenty," I retorted. "How could you or Jen, much less me, have seen this mess coming? Both of you threw me to Smith on Tuesday afternoon about what was in the notes and left me to communicate with him our findings. Jen specifically said to share whatever 'common' information I had so we could fend off his getting a subpoena for our records. I did that to the best of my ability. Telling them that we were having a service for Jimmy didn't seem to be out of bounds."

MaryBeth just sighed heavily and gripped the wheel in the ten-two position even harder. "Dave," she started, "it's all about attitude, and let me tell you, you just don't seem to get along in our clinic. When this is all over I think you, Jen, and me need to sit down for a review of your performance and discuss your future with us."

Aha, I thought, this mess would make a perfect smoke screen for the old dump-a-rooney. But as Tom Paine first said: "These are the times that try men's souls." Instead of bitching and moaning, I shut up in order to keep my job for a little while longer.

"Ok, MaryBeth, if that will work for you and Jen, I think we should plan on something," I tried to sound contrite, but wanted to scream otherwise. "Let me ask you something; is everything copacetic in the day treatment program these days?"

"Why do you ask about the day treatment program, Dave?" she parried.

"Mike Pitts didn't look too happy with me this morning. I haven't had anything to do with him since you made the program off limits for me almost six months ago. Besides which, Jimmy had asked me a couple of weeks ago how come I never dropped in on the program. Any problems with my guys?"

"No, not that I've heard," she said. "Mike does seem to be under a lot of pressure, but it isn't coming from the clinic; he's snapped at me too a couple of times, but I thought it was just the strain of working with all of our clients plus that new thing he's doing."

"What new thing? Did we get a new contract or some new clients?" I asked.

"Actually both. Maybe Mike's a little upset that he hasn't gotten any recognition for his new work. That's my fault, I'd better fix it—thanks for bringing it to my attention, Dave."

"No problem, but what's the new gig over at the day program?" I persisted.

"Oh it's not too much more except Gerry, who's responsible for all of us, encouraged Mike to go after a grant and pulled some strings to make sure he got it. Now Mike is providing some day services to dual diagnosis clients. He's added two more staff positions and taken over the third floor space in the same building where the day program is now. I really haven't had anything to do with it—you know how I feel about keeping the therapy side apart from the day treatment component."

"Where did Pitts get the new clients from? A lot of our clients have several diagnoses—what makes this group special?" I pressed.

"Dave, I've told you I don't know much about this at all; not my business. I suppose that the clients Mike has funding to service are the developmentally delayed who also have mental disorders. Mike's probably integrating the new clients with the old ones who feel their space has been violated. Let me talk to Mike and see if he'd like some help getting the old timers to accept the new clients. I will talk to him, not you; the day program is his and not your office away from the clinic. Am I clear on that?"

"Sure," I knew when to quit.

We finished the remainder of the ride in silence until MaryBeth pulled into her parking space around in the back of the clinic. I thanked her and told her that I had to get to the post office before it closed to pick up something they were holding for me. I'd be back tomorrow to see my regulars on Friday morning. We parted amicably enough, and I headed back down the driveway, out to the street where I'd left my car in the morning.

-18-

All things considered, I got to the South Chatham post office in plenty of time. Handing over the yellow "You've got a package" card to the clerk at the window, I gave her my box number and name, and then waited as she rummaged through the bin to find what was mine. What she gave me was a small box wrapped in what looked like a paper bag scotch taped together at the ends. I looked at the label—handwritten, actually scrawled, in what looked like pencil:

Doc Dave Nite
Box ? Post Office
South Chatham 02633

Huh? There was no box number, and the zip code was for Chatham not South Chatham. There was no return address, and the package wasn't even stamped. I looked at the cancellation mark and saw that the package was mailed to me last Friday. I asked the postal clerk who said that the package had to have been dropped into the outside mail bin before the five pm pickup. The mail staying in South Chatham gets separated first and the remainder shipped off Cape for further sorting. Knowing me by name was the only reason that she was able to put the card into my box. She also said in a snarky, but self-satisfied, tone that there was postage due, which I paid without hesitation.

As I stared at the label, I realized I'd seen this handwriting before. In the past, I would ask Jimmy to make lists of what bothered or frightened him and rank order them, the writing on the label looked a lot like his handwriting especially when he was agitated.

I carried the package out to the car and without even thinking pulled the tape loose and pulled out a used cigarette box. Opening it, I found a wadded up envelope that was still sealed addressed to "Joe Danneo" with a PO Box in Orleans. There was no return address on it, but at least it had postage. The cancellation stamp was blurred. I made out a "New," but the last part could have been anything from "York" to "Timbuktu."

What the hell, I ripped open the envelope and shook out a single piece of paper with just two lines of print:

Fishy Joe5985
0508 PLdcx6

What was this nonsense? Who was this guy, Danneo? Was he nicknamed "Fishy Joe"? What did Jimmy have to do with him? What did I have to do with any of this shit? Why would Jimmy send this, and why would he send it to me in the mail? Great questions without any answers, I thought. First, I figured I should get back to the clinic to see if the handwriting matched, but I was afraid that it would.

I burned up Rt 137 and onto the mid-Cape to get to the clinic. Good thing MaryBeth wasn't watching, or she'd have chided me for enlarging my carbon footprint—not my priority. It was just before four when I pulled into the clinic and headed toward the record room to pull Jimmy's file. I didn't make it past Deb, the receptionist, who called out to me in a singsong voice.

"There he is, our birthday boy. I didn't know it was your birthday, Dave, or I'd have baked you a cake."

"Duh, it's not!" was all I could say as I pushed into the record room determined to pull Jimmy's file.

Deb followed me into the records room and said, "Come on Dave, how old are you really?"

I shook my head and said," Deb, what makes you think that it's my birthday, because I'm telling you it's not."

"Here," she said. "A guy came in just before you got here and said to give this to you." She held out a small package bag festooned with birthday greeting glitz to me.

"Deb, there's got to be a mistake here or a joke. Trust me, I know my birthday; and it's not today, this week, or even this month. Who was this person? Was it someone from the clinic?" I asked.

"No," she said. "He was a big dude wearing a long leather coat, jeans, and cowboy boots I think. He talked funny too."

Taking the bag from her, I commented, "How do you mean he talked funny? Did he have an accent or a lisp or what?"

"No, he just sounded different than people from around here." She thought for a moment and added, "He sounded like that guy Tony on the HBO show about gangsters. He had greasy hair just like he was Italian."

"Deb, now I know something's fishy—I don't have any 'gompah' friends."

"Uh-huh, so maybe he could have been Greek or Armenian for all I know. I mean he didn't have a Portuguese accent; he sounded like he was from Joisey," she parodied the pronunciation of Jersey to make sure I got the point.

Just then, the phone rang on her desk, so she put the gift bag on top of a filing cabinet and headed back to her receptionist's cubby. First things first, I thought, as I fished Jimmy's folder out of the file drawer and found the notes where I'd had him list those things that frightened or angered him. Out of my pocket I pulled the envelope with the writing on it from the package wrapper and compared the two—a match. Either someone was good at faking Jimmy's hen scratching, or Jimmy sent me the letter addressed to Joe Danneo. I'd bet on the latter.

After putting the envelope back in my pocket and Jimmy's folder back in the filing cabinet, I sat down to open the gift bag and find out what it was all about. Inside the bag under some tissue paper was a small jewelry type box. Lifting it out, a hand printed note was beneath it. It simply read, "GIVE IT BACK"

I opened the jewelry box and was startled. There was a man's watch and a large college ring. The watch was nondescript and didn't ring a bell; but the ring was unmistakable. Last time I'd seen it, it was on Fred Dorfman's left hand ring finger at school. I didn't know anyone else who'd gone to a state university in a suburb of Buffalo except Fred. He had his degree on the wall at school along with other stuff, and he always, I mean always, wore that hunk of costume jewelry. He wore it on his left hand as if it were a wedding ring, then again who'd marry Fred? Looking down at it, I had a queasy feeling in my gut that something wasn't right.

I went back to Deb's desk and asked for the phone book while fending off her questions about what was in the bag. Finding an empty office near the conference room, I made myself at home and called Fred's extension at the college. Not there, I only got his away message stating that he was head of the department and his office hours. Although it was late afternoon, and Fred almost religiously left the college no later than three o'clock, there was the off chance that some meeting had kept him there later than usual. Now what? I looked in the phone book and found that Fred lived at 124 Greenleaf Circle which was somewhere in Dennis. Should I call and see if he were home; what would I say to him if he did answer? I'm sure Fred wasn't feeling good about me lately. Maybe I could pretend to thank him for covering my classes for me today. Maybe I should just drive by to see if his car was there, and if he was all right.

I dropped the phone book back on Deb's desk, gave a wave and a conspiratorial wink holding the gift bag aloft, sprinted for my car, and headed toward Dennis. Stopping at the end of the driveway, I realized that I didn't have the foggiest notion of where in Dennis

I was going. Fishing under the seat, I pulled out a dog-eared street atlas of the Cape. I always carried it because there was no rhyme or reason to half the roads down here. I found the long oval that was Greenleaf Circle on the map and figured the fastest way was to go back down Rt 6A. I'd stay on it through Brewster and then turn left onto Airline Drive (never did know why it was called that maybe it had had a grass strip back in the twenties or something) and then right onto Indian Trail Rd which T'd at Greenleaf. Looked less than fifteen miles and there wasn't going to be much traffic headed in that direction at this time of day and year.

I took the left onto Airline and pushed the envelope as I lugged along the two-lane road. Two miles later, I had to slow down as the road hooked to the left to go around Cedar Pond. Indian Trail was the next right, so I was getting close. Just then, something caught my eye off the road in a field leading to the pond. It looked like it could be a car, and it looked like it could be that weird mustard yellow that Fred's Subaru was painted. There was no place to stop until I got to Indian Trail, so I took the right and pulled a U-turn to get back to Airline. More slowly this time, I pulled in and parked on the right hand side.

Running across the road, I noticed the shoulder was torn up. Either someone lost control of his car and plowed into the brush or, I thought, maybe the car was cut off and forced off the road. Pushing aside the brush, I could see the car more clearly. Yup, it was Fred's Subaru, mustard color and all, including a series of parking stickers from the college going back at least a decade. As I got closer, I could see that there were parallel lines of a dark color, green or black running the length of the driver's side. It sure looked as if someone had forced Fred's car off the road. Walking around the car, I saw that the right front tire was flat and rolled off the rim. Next, I saw that the rutted tread marks stopped at least 30 yards from where the car was semi-concealed. Someone apparently had moved the car deeper into the woods than where it originally had stopped. With the doors closed and locked, it looked like Fred had pulled his car off the road. If it were anyone but Fred, maybe he'd be casting a wooly bugger in hopes of landing a bigmouth bass down at the pond. Fred's briefcase embossed with his initials was on the backseat, stuffed to the brim with student papers to read along with a couple of arcane psych journals just in case he needed stimulation. The queasy feeling in my gut became a sick one as the realization of what had happened dawned on me. Fred had taught all my classes today, I'd asked him to take the morning one only. Fred would have done all of them as I hadn't shown up, and he had no classes of his own on Thursdays. Somebody probably followed him out of the lecture hall and to his car. That somebody mistook Fred for me.

Fred ran off the road right here by Cedar Pond, and it was no accident. He could have easily proven he wasn't me, but instead of being let go, he was kidnapped. Whoever grabbed him probably thought up the gift bag ruse knowing how Fred's ring and watch would get my attention. When the swarthy guy delivered the bag to the clinic, Fred had to have been stuffed in the trunk. It was clear that someone wanted a trade—Fred for whatever I had. All I had was the letter that Jimmy sent me with two lines of gibberish. I didn't even know how or who to contact. Jesus H. Christ, this was a mess—first Jimmy, then Toby, now Fred. What was I going to do? I sure as hell wasn't going to the state police. If these were the same badasses, alerting the cops would only lead to Fred's death too. I had to do something to get Fred back, then I could figure out the how and why of all of this.

-19-

I took a careful look around then got back to my car. With hardly any traffic on Airline and the weekend coming up, I would bet if anyone even saw the car back there, they'd figure someone was out fishing. It'd take at least week or so before the cops even looked twice at it. I knew Fred didn't have any family locally and really no friends to speak of at all, so who'd miss him? Maybe after he didn't show up at school for a whole week, someone in the Dean's office would file a report. I had the jewelry and the letter with the numbers, but not a clue about what to do next. I pulled a U-turn and headed to Chatham the back way. I crossed over into Brewster and then past half a dozen kettle ponds until I got into Harwich. After taking a left onto Main, I got through the center of town; worked my way down to Rt 28, and finally back to my place in South Chatham. I kept one eye on the rear view mirror all the way, but didn't see anyone following me. Just to be safe, however, I went past the lane to my house and pulled into the driveway leading to an old abandoned cranberry bog adjacent to my place. I picked my way around the edge of the filled in bog through a lot of overgrown underbrush and found the path leading up to the back of my house.

As sunset wasn't until almost eight that night, I had to make my way carefully toward my house in case someone was lying in wait. Working around the line of brush with the sun at my back, I figured I would be hard to see until I got right up to the back deck. Hugging the side of the house, I peered around the corner, but no cars were in the driveway or turn around. I climbed the back steps gingerly and let myself into the house. I listened for a moment—it was silent—no Toby with his stump of a tail wagging a mile a minute, eager to be petted. The whole house felt dead. I crossed from the kitchen into the living room to see if anything had been shoved under the door, but there was nothing. Opening the front door, I looked around the porch, but again it was empty. After Fred's disappearance, I certainly had no interest in spending the night down at the end of this lonely road. I went upstairs to stuff a gym bag with enough clothes for a couple of more days and left going back around the old bog the same way as I came in.

I headed for Chris's place. It's funny how a couple of turns and less than two miles can significantly change a neighborhood. I live in the last of the rural Cape, and although Chris doesn't live amongst the McMansions and starter castles, her neighborhood is definitely more upscale. Still concerned about being followed, I passed the turnoff to her house, took the next right, and pulled into the Hill's driveway. Wending my way through the connecting backyards brought me to her back door and welcoming smile. I'd forgotten to stop for some dinner or more wine; but Chris had those details taken care of. I was just glad to get inside and hidden away.

Going over the details of the day took a full bottle of wine, but I had to get it all out. I still couldn't put the pieces together, but it really helped to have someone just listen to my ramblings and allow me time to decompress. Chris was bothered about me finding Fred's car and having his stuff delivered to me at the clinic. Both of us agreed that the key to the who and what was in the two lines of text I'd gotten from Jimmy; but what was it? There was no context; it meant nothing.

Chris, however, was nothing if not a code breaker or puzzle solver. Whether it's a jigsaw puzzle, Sudoku, or a crossword, she's aces. I asked, "Hey Chris, do you think there is something encoded in these two lines?"

Not batting an eye, she answered, "no, this isn't a code or even a cipher, it's something else altogether."

Not knowing the difference between a cipher and a code, I shut up and contemplated my wine glass waiting for her to continue.

"You know what I think," she went on. "I think it's a logon and password for a protected computer file. Look at the combination of numbers and letters, there're textbook examples of what logons and passwords that nobody could guess should be. I mean numbers with upper and lower case letters. The only thing wrong is the space on both lines. Spaces, slashes, dollar signs, and stuff like that aren't usually allowed. Best bet would be to try and find this guy Joe Danneo to ask him how or why Jim got his letter."

"Hmmmm," I muttered, "it can't be that simple."

Chris was on the hunt. "Use my laptop and Google him; let's see if we can't get an address for him to start with. Maybe he's on Facebook, and we'll find a listing of his friends who might be connected to you or Jimmy."

My Google search was short but not sweet. I had several hits, but the only one that stood out was from the police blotter of the local paper back on the third week in April. Opening the link, I read that the cops had found Joseph Danneo, with an address in Brewster, dead in his car in Harwich of a suspected drug overdose. There wasn't any further information; and checking the obits didn't help as I guess there wasn't anyone to mourn the loss. Still no connection, however, to Jimmy, and I was even more frustrated now than before.

"Chris, I've got to give this a break," I told her about the dead end with Danneo and suggested we drive into Chatham for dinner somewhere decent.

As usual, she was one-step ahead of me saying, "I picked up some cod down at the fish market this afternoon; how 'bout having it baked with some grated cheese? That and some veggies with a salad on the side sound Ok?"

"Why not?" I was relieved not to have to venture out.

"Let me get the fish in the oven, and if you'll make the salad—use that avocado, it's almost past; then if you want, I can call my friend Tommy. If anyone knows about ways to get into computers, it'll be him. Why don't I ask him to come by?"

Nodding my approval, I started to make the salad while listening as Chris called Tommy, who lived not far from her. She told him that she had some nerdy college professor over and invited him to join us for dinner saying that we needed to pick his brain about computer software. Putting the phone down, she said, "Not a problem, Tommy'll be over in about twenty minutes. He's a big guy, Dave, better double up on that salad."

Even though Chris had said Tommy was a big man, her use of the diminutive nickname as well as someone knowing about these little electronic devices made me think of a pudgy guy, sort of geek-like, whose idea of a good time was reading tech manuals. Was I wrong when Tommy walked through the back door without even knocking—not his style and being about six-four and two thirty-five meant he rarely stood on ceremony. After Chris introduced us, Tommy pulled out a twelve pack of Bud from the backpack slung over one shoulder and drained the first can in one long chug. Not, I thought, what I'd imagined, but if he knew his stuff, maybe I could feel comfortable with someone that big watching over me.

"So Dave," he began without preamble. "On the phone Chris said you've got a weird logon and password and want to know to what it belongs. Let me look."

"Why don't you have another beer; Chris and I are having some wine to go with the fish. You're having dinner with us first and then we can take a look at it later." I offered trying to buy some time, as I really wasn't sure that I wanted to share with this guy what Jimmy had sent me.

"Naw, no time like the present," he said. "Give it over; let's see what you've got."

I handed over the note with the two groups of letters and numbers on it and briefly explained what Chris and I thought it might mean.

Tommy studied it for less than a minute and shouted, "Bingo!"

From the kitchen, Chris joined in singing loudly, "…and Bingo was his name-o!"

I drank more wine; Tommy pounded down a second Bud, belched loudly, and continued, "Don't get fooled by what looks like a name 'Fishy Joe' with some numbers after it. What you got here, Herr Professor, are four separate messages. The two on right of the space are indeed a logon and password. 'Joe5985' and 'PLdex6' are right for perhaps a bank or email account. What the stuff to the left of spaces, the 'Fishy' and '0508' represent, I don't know yet."

Chris announced that dinner—let's call it supper after all we were eating in the kitchen—was ready, and we should help ourselves to fish, veg, salad, and more wine or beer. As Tom and I headed into the kitchen to fill our plates, Chris leaned over the coffee table where we'd been sitting and studied the two-line scrap of paper.

"Dave," she said tentatively, "why couldn't the '0508' be shorthand for a date, say the eighth of May? What happened today that we should know about? I mean today is May 8 after all."

Looking up from his meal, Tommy added, "Why not a date? That sounds believable. And if the right side stuff really is a logon and password for something like an email account, then the 'Fishy' could be code or shorthand for the email server."

"Sounds right, good work," I chimed in, ever the cheerleader. "But how do you get Google or Hotmail out of 'Fishy'?"

"Time-out," Chris interrupted. "Let's take a break, have dinner, talk about something else, then tackle this over coffee."

"Or another beer," Tommy said with a grin.

Making small talk, I asked Tom what he did for a living. I figured he managed a Radio Shack or something just as technical.

"I run a tree cutting business," he said. "You should see my chipper; it'll take a whole pine, trunk, branches, needles, and all. I just mess around with this computer stuff for fun. It's what I do in winter when there's no work, and my boat is on the hard."

"You've got a boat too?" I asked hoping to find something in common with Tom, maybe he sailed, which was my passion.

"Yeah," Tom said nodding his head with a heaping plate in front of him. "It's a center console SeaCraft with a pair of honking Mercs hanging off the stern. I've got it all tricked out for fishing. I mean everything from blues to tuna with stripers as my specialty. And yours?"

"Nothing much, just an oldie but goodie, classic plastic sloop from the sixties. I try to get away for a week during the summer mostly down the Sound and out to Cuttyhunk."

"Sounds good, seeing the Cape and South Coast at five knots. Personally, I like jamming the throttles open and hitting forty or better. That SeaCraft can literally fly out of the water when there's a swell running. Sweet."

"The never changing disagreement between rag-baggers and stink pots," I shook my head and pointed a finger at Tom seeking a rebuttal.

"Ok guys, that's enough who's got the bigger, better boat for now, let's eat, and then get back to solving the riddle of the note. Come' on there's plenty more on the stovetop!" Chris settled the discussion for now. I drank more wine and sat back as Chris and Tommy caught up on the local gossip.

-20-

After dinner Tom and I headed back to the living room, where he dug into his backpack and pulled out a well used laptop computer. After setting it up, he called to Chris who was stacking dishes in the sink, "Do you have an Internet connection here that I can logon?"

"Sure, click on the connection called 'my home' and the password is 'TERRIER' all caps," she answered.

"What's the game plan?" I asked.

"Oh I'm going to Google freebie email accounts to see what names come up," Tommy told me.

"Talk about a futile fishing trip, but hey, I'm a hooked, so let's do it." I didn't think much of the strategy.

"Drum roll please, I've got a list of the top eighteen free email services. Here take a look at the list," he said as he turned the laptop toward me.

I scrolled down through the names from the familiar Gmail to something called Zoho and didn't see anything close. Shaking my head, I turned the laptop back to Tommy.

"Okeydokey let me scroll down and try another site—here what do you think?"

I didn't see anything that looked right, but then Chris who'd come into the room looked over my shoulder and started to laugh.

"There, Dave, look at the last name. It's Sushmail— think sushi for fishy—and it works. Get it? Am I the crossword cue queen or what?" Chris leaned over and fist-bumped Tommy in triumph.

He took back the laptop, typed in the URL Sushmail.com, and hit enter. In a nanosecond, the computer brought up a logo with a dialogue box asking for a logon and password. He entered 'Joe5985' followed by 'PLdex6' and hit enter. A pause and then up came a screen labeled inbox with one message logged.

"Come on Tommy," Chris prompted. "Open it, no suspense; you don't need another drum roll."

On April 22, almost three weeks ago, "Joe5985" had sent the email to "me." It had no subject line or text. Instead, there was a picture attached with "sent from my iPhone." The picture displayed was of nothing. The entire screen was black; it was useless.

"Now what?" I said disappointed as the three of us stared at the black image.

"We find out more about this picture, if it really is a picture," Tommy said. "Let me download it, and then we can read the stored data. There's a file embedded on the picture itself and has all kinds of good stuff like when it was taken and where."

"You've got to be kidding," I blurted out. "Pictures taken with an iPhone have secret stuff stored on them? You're kidding right? Sounds like big brother to me."

"No, it's true," Chris broke in. "I've read where they've been able to catch burglars who posted pictures of their loot on Facebook and even have rescued kids when their parents were sent pictures of them for ransom."

"Here Dave, go ahead," he continued turning the laptop toward me again. "I've downloaded the picture, so now right click on it. Open Sesame, and *shazam*, look there are the details of the picture. Now just scroll down!"

I started to scroll down and went through a bunch of stuff stopping immediately when I reached the GPS information. There were two entries with data:

Latitude   41:38:496
Longitude   69:37:168

"Hey, I've got it, whatever this is supposed to be, it's got to be pretty close to right here. If I remember correctly from last summer, these are almost the lat/lon numbers for Stage Harbor."

Tom swiveled the laptop back to him, hit a few keys, moved the mouse on the finger pad, and sat back with a satisfied smile on his face.

"I've got this program called 'Offshore Navigator' that has all the charts for the East coast on it. Looks like you were close, Dave, saying it was Chatham; the Lat/Lon numbers put this picture only fifteen-twenty miles out due east of here."

I got up to look over his shoulder, as did Chris. Tom had marked a spot right on the western edge of the outbound shipping lane from Boston headed south toward New York smack dab on the forty-fathom curve. He moved the mouse to the top of the screen and left clicked, identifying the spot as a waypoint for future reference.

"How far is that off Chatham?" Chris asked writing down the coordinates on a pad. "Is there a name I should call these numbers?"

"I don't know, maybe something like Boston Traffic Lane," I offered.

"Naw, too difficult, call it Waypoint Alpha. I've been out there fishing before, there are a couple of wrecks and a pile of boulders just this side of it," Tom answered. "Here I can create a route from the waypoint back to the Chatham buoy—you know the one you can see off Lighthouse Beach."

Tom quickly hit the keys and up popped a box detailing the route—it was just shy of fourteen nautical miles and south of east from the Chatham buoy—no more than twenty miles all told from the inner harbor near the fish pier.

"What's do you think this is supposed to mean?" I asked him.

"If I were a betting man, Dave, I'd say you've just found the coordinates for a drug drop; the goods were heaved overboard in the middle of the night and their picture taken," he replied. "This is damn clever."

Reaching for the wine bottle to ward off the uneasiness I felt growing, I said, "A drug drop, how do you figure that?"

"I've heard lots of stories about guys picking up buoys with drugs attached that were dropped from tankers or freighters coming up the coast. I mean you just have to go out to fish or haul your own lobster traps and grab hold of one of these buoys—five minutes hauling, a short run to the shore and you've made a big score—rumor has it that half the new pickup trucks in town are bought with drug money."

"Yeah but," I persisted, "why do think it's clever?"

"The Coast Guard monitors the inbound lanes pretty closely, with satellites and whatnot just to shadow boats coming up the coast from South America or one of those shady southern ports. They'd be able to detect according to the stuff I've heard if a ship slowed down or if a small boat made a habit of hanging out around the eastern side of the traffic lanes. But check this; the mark is on the western edge of the outbound lane—neat huh?"

"No, I'm not getting it," I complained.

"Who's going to shadow a ship coming from Portland or Boston toward New York or farther South? It's only logical to get rid of the drugs going in, not coming out, but I'll bet that's exactly what's happening. The drop is made after they leave port."

"Why take a picture of nothing with the GPS data stored on it? If you're dropping drugs overboard why not just call someone on shore and tell them where to make the pickup."

"Haven't you ever entered a waypoint, like a buoy, as you sailed past it?" Tom asked. "Well, I'll bet what they did was throw the drugs along with a weight over the side snapping the picture at the same time. Next send the picture to this email address and bada, bada, bing, someone's all set to make the pickup."

Come on Tom, you're making this way too complicated," I protested. "Why not just call someone using a cell phone and give them the numbers?"

"This means you have to have a hand held GPS or GPS app on your iPhone to mark the position. Now you have to call in the numbers. How good's your cell phone down here in South Chatham?" Tom asked.

"Hmmm, not good, I get one bar maximum."

Tom popped open another beer and said, "See there wouldn't be enough power for a cell phone twenty-thirty miles out to sea. Sure, you could use a ship's radio or a satellite phone, but they're too easy to listen in on. Just look at the size of the antennas on the towers at the Coast Guard station right by Chatham light, they'd hear that chatter easy. Besides, calling someone on the phone at any hour of the day or night to give him a bunch of numbers is a perfect recipe for error. You get one number wrong, and you could be miles off. Sending an email with the exact coordinates embedded in the picture is way slick."

"All right, I've got it," I agreed. "But isn't it a big risk for them to drop overboard the drugs attached to a buoy; then have to wait days or even weeks before the numbers get sent to the pickup guys?"

Tom shook his head while chugging another Bud. "Nope, it's an old lobsterman's trick from back when they all used wooden buoys. Dropping pots in the harbor channels caused all sorts of trouble because they beat the shit out of props when hit. Today all anyone uses are those foam buoys—not a problem, so they're all over—ever been to Maine? Jesus, you could walk across the harbor in some places.

"Anyhow, the old timers used to set their traps with a burlap bag filled with salt or sugar around the buoy to weigh it down. After a couple of days, the stuff would dissolve and up popped the buoy. All you had to do was get the timing right, and the buoy would surface right before you were out there to haul the trap. Tell me that's not slick!"

"It's neat," I conceded. "So the crew on the freighter dumps the whole shebang over the side including a big bag of something to dissolve, records the lat/lon coordinates with the camera, and waits until they get close to the next port to pop it in the email."

"Now the question is," said Tom, "what are you going to do about it? Besides, I never asked how you got it in the first place."

Chris, who'd been sitting quietly with a mug of coffee, spoke up, "Hey Dave, you ought to just give it all over to the cops. You have a dead patient who probably was murdered; your house has been torn up; your chairman at the college is missing; and now you've found a drug drop—this is way too scary. Just lay it in their laps, go teach tomorrow, or go to the clinic and shrink heads."

"No way," Tom interjected. He reached for Chris' pad and ripped off the sheet with the numbers. "This is a golden opportunity for us—it's like finding gold or diamonds—all we have to do is make the pick up!"

"Come on Tom," I said disgusted with the whole thing. "Chris is right! I'm in way over my head. Besides, you don't know the half of it. Somebody knows or thinks I know about this position out in the ocean. That's number one. Number two, I've spent a lot of the last three days with the state cops who are all over this thing. Number three, what would I do with a barrel full of dope even if I went to pick it up? Number four, I don't want to spend the rest of my life looking over my shoulder for some mobbed up hit man. Add to that the chances of getting caught selling the shit and spending ten years in jail on a mandatory sentence for drug trafficking—no thanks!"

"Well," Tom replied. "I'd like the one big score. You think I want to be a tree cutter and yard raker all my life? Jeez, it's like a dream with someone offering you big bucks free. I'd go for it."

Chris came to my rescue saying, "Tommy, it's not that. If there're drugs out there, and if you can find them, and if you can sell them, and if you aren't caught, then what happens? You buy a few toys, a new boat, a new truck; but you won't have changed, and if you don't work for a living, you'll end up swilling that Bud for breakfast."

"Hey I could buy a restaurant and run for office, but I guess that's been done," Tom conceded. "Maybe it isn't so much a get rich quick scheme as just the thrill of it all. I know you're right, but what are you going to do Dave?"

"I got to think, and I got to do it cold sober; right now I'm up for one more glass of wine, here you grab another Bud. I can sleep on it while I'm sleeping it off," I tried to end the discussion.

"Fine, I understand, it's crossing a line. So let's drink to the thought of an adventure, and you can think about it in peace," Tom answered. He added, "Don't forget I've got that weather beaten SeaCraft with a pair of 150 Mercs ready to go. Just give me a shout, and we're off. I've already got her down in Ryder's Cove all rigged up—hey even just taking a run out there to see if we can find the buoy would be a kick."

Tom's enthusiasm was infectious, but I didn't bite. I thanked him for his help and suggested for his own health given what had happened in the last couple of days that he keep quiet, real quiet about talking to me. He knew I was serious when I held out my hand for the return of the sheet with the waypoint coordinates on it.

We said good-bye, and I turned my attention to Chris thanking her for the cod casserole she'd baked. I was still pretty wound up, and even the better part of second or was it a third bottle of chardonnay, didn't take the edge off. My clean-up help was to unload the dishwasher, and then I told Chris I was ready for a shower and bed. She suggested that I didn't have to sleep in the guestroom and the exercise might help relax me. No dummy me; we spent the night together; I slept like a log.

MAY 4: FRIDAY, MAY 9TH

-21-

Chris and I slept in together until her terrier started his tippy-tap, I gotta pee dance. As we freed ourselves from each other and the bed sheets, I took a hot shower while she began the breakfast coffee. I was late starting my day, but I really wasn't all that eager to get to the drug clinic much less the mental health one. Chris sensed that I was upset or distracted and said she'd be at the real estate office all day in case I wanted to talk or share my thoughts. A quick hug and kiss later, I stuffed the waypoint coordinates into my shirt pocket, was out door, through the backyards, and into my car heading for the drug clinic. Something still didn't connect; I just didn't get it; but the best I could do was to keep plugging.

In my box at the drug clinic, I found I had two new referrals for the alcohol group. Usually I like to see the offenders for a one-on-one first, but this morning I was going to have to leave a note with the dosing nurse for them to show up at Wednesday's group meeting. On my way back to the office I was using, I stopped for coffee in the conference room and ran into Pete, the clinic's director. Pete was a good ol' boy, sort of the aging hippie type, who really wanted to make a difference in the lives of those who'd got addicted to hard drugs. I don't think there was any secret that he'd been a pot smoker as a kid and probably drank peyote tea or swallowed some 'scrooms.' All of this gave him street cred and a better way of dealing with the hard drug users who seemed to believe that they were entitled to do whatever they pleased. Anyway, I liked Pete and respected his up-through-the-ranks achievements. In addition, he and I were of one mind when it came to paperwork so maybe that was why there so much secretarial help available.

"Hey Pete," I said as I lifted my coffee mug toward him in acknowledgement. "What's new in our world of drugs?"

"You heard that we're going to be adding a new treatment program next month?" he was positively chipper in response.

"No, what now, something that works for a change?"

"Oh stop it; you're our resident cynic, y'know. Seriously, we're going to pair up with the hospital to do methadone detox using a naltrexone implant. All of the follow-up and therapy takes place right here. It'll be a life saver and a money maker for sure," Pete explained.

"Great, Pete, really great," I said. "We addict them to methadone on the government's dime, and charge the government a dollar to detox them. Why detox them, I thought you were convinced that methadone was the magic bug juice?"

"I am, but we've got some real problems with our census. I mean that in a good way, I guess," He continued. "We've got a limit to the number of addicts we can treat with methadone from both the state and the town. Right now, we're almost twenty-five percent over capacity with more addicts in the pipeline. The wait list is three to four weeks long. So we have to innovate!"

"Pete, listen to yourself. You're excited because there's so much dope on the street that when a junkie wants to quit you've got to tell him to keep shooting up and wait a month. Isn't this bad news? I mean isn't our goal to not be needed anymore?" I needled him.

"I'm the realist and you're the academic in the ivy tower," he retorted. "Demand for treatment is up all across the Cape and SouthCoast; the clinics in Wareham, Plymouth, and New Bedford are all bursting at the seams. Somehow the supply of dope has just blossomed, I don't know how or why."

"All hard stuff—coke and opiates?" I was suddenly seriously interested.

"Yeah, I'd have thought that pot would be big now that it's been decriminalized, but no, it's the hard stuff and apparently it's pretty pure and pretty cheap."

"ODs must be up too then," I added.

"Oh yeah, we've lost a couple of our guys in the last couple of months," Pete said with a sigh. "The latest to leave us for a better place was Joe Danneo a couple of weeks ago."

"I've heard that name, but not here in this clinic. How would I have known him?" I asked trying to be coy.

"Oh, Joe was part of that new program we've got going over in the Eastham clinic's day program. You know the one that works out that unused office building down from the rotary in Orleans. Talk about a sweetheart deal for all of us," Pete answered. "You should be interested in this program. You heard about us getting a new clinic administrator, Gerry Pence?"

"No, I must've missed that memo; but is this the same guy who's running the Eastham clinic?" I asked.

"Yeah, apparently he's got a contract with Ramparts and the parent agency that owns the mental health clinics to coordinate services and regionalize just like school systems do to bring together the billing and administrative parts of what we do. He's pretty sharp— he did a deal with both Ramparts, they're the Boston company who owns us, and HarborBay Collaborative out of Middleboro who owns Eastern Cape—so now he's the head honcho here and at Eastham as well as our drug clinics in Falmouth and Wareham. He has the mental health clinics in Hyannis and Bourne too. It's a pretty consolidated model that will cut our costs"

"How did Joe fit into all this?" I was getting fed up with Pete's cheerleading.

"Well Gerry's set up a demo program for guys at our clinic with psych issues to get help over at their day treatment program. Remember you're the guy who's always saying that the addiction comes after the mental illness, and how we need to treat the mental disorder first. So now we're treating both at the same time."

"Hey," I perked up. "Is this the new dual diagnosis program that I heard about from MaryBeth?"

"Yes, I set this up with Mike Pitts at the day program with all the funding coming from Gerry. In fact, he's using this as a demo double D program to show how much savings our cooperation can generate. Plus we've shipped out at least a dozen clients freeing up some new treatment slots."

"Gee," I interjected. "She never mentioned that it was for addicts with mental illness; I bet she thinks it's for the mentally retarded with mental disorders."

"No way, and they're called developmentally delayed, get with today's jargon," Pete retorted.

"Who's handling the paperwork and client files?" I started to get interested.

"Gerry is. I mean it. He's taken all of our records, creates the treatment plans, files the paperwork, and, get this, pays us in cash—can't beat that!"

"Whoa, slow down a minute, Pete," I said. "What do you mean he's taken the records? Do you mean the file folders themselves? If someone was getting his bug juice here and psych services at another program, there should be two sets of files. Why take all the files from here? They're still our people getting our methadone. And cash, who's kidding whom with this scam?"

"Yes to the first. Gerry's also found overlap with clients at the Eastham clinic but dosed here. He's taken both sets of files and put them together for this new program. No, to the second, this is no scam. Gerry's getting reimbursed from the feds and state for the program, but right now he doesn't want to show it as a separate income source for both clinics, so he's paying us with cash for continuing to dose these guys so they don't show up on our books. I know he's picked up part of Mike's salary directly as well as paying rent and hiring some new staff at the day program. This is a win-win-win situation—so stop being a cynic," Pete said with a hard smile.

"Hey, I said I agreed with the premise. It all sounds great," I backpedaled. "Tell me; is Kevin Turcotte, I think he's one of ours, in the double D program?"

"Yeah, he's been part of the program for the last couple of months," Pete affirmed. "Why do you ask?"

"Oh, he was here in my alcohol group a while back, and then I thought he was in my men's group in Eastham. When I looked for his records, I got nothing but empty file folders at both clinics. I should have asked you or MaryBeth what was going on, but hey I'm busy."

"Yeah that's right; that's how it works," Pete said. "Check with Mike at the day program. I'm sure he's got all the files coordinated. I think most of the double Ds come from us; but, and that's the point, clients like Turcotte overlap with us and Eastham."

"Sounds good, Pete. It really does. Good luck with it," I conceded. "I've got to scoot and assign some new guys to the alcohol group for Wednesday's meeting. I'm glad you brought me up to speed."

I refilled my mug and headed out to the receptionist's office feeling less reassured than I hoped I had portrayed to Pete. Now I had a link between the two clinics in general and between Jimmy Farnsworth and Kevin Turcotte in particular. There was something going on between them, and it took place at the day treatment program. I needed to smoke the peace pipe with Mike Pitts over there and see what had happened between the two of them.

-22-

Instead of driving back to the mental health clinic, I took a detour at the rotary and headed down Rt 28 toward the center of Orleans. On a little side street sandwiched behind a bank and hardware store was a three-story building designed to be subdivided into office condos, but given the business downturn, it was leased out to the Eastham clinic for the day treatment program. Orleans was the business center for the lower Cape and a magnet for many of the lower Cape's disadvantaged. Instead of wasting time with the endless cup of coffee at the Compass, a local diner, the day program offered these lost souls a refuge as well as a treatment option. People like Jimmy needed a home—sure he had a place to sleep and eat, but these were just boarding houses—he needed more than that; he needed a place to call home. Some place that when he needed to go there, they had to take him in. I stood up for Jimmy more than once as he didn't get along with or trust most everyone, but throwing him out of the day program wouldn't have helped him or the community, which would have had a hard time tolerating his psychotic foibles.

I started to think about when my relationship with Mike Pitts, the director of the day program, first hit the skids. I liked seeing some of my guys over at his place just because this was where they hung out, and where they got into trouble. Sitting in an office in the next town wasn't the same. I wanted to see them in their environment not mine. At first Mike was cool with this arrangement, and on a couple of occasions called me to help defuse situations especially with Jimmy and his paranoid tendencies before they escalated into something violent. I mean think about it; what if Jimmy waving that bowie knife of his freaked someone out enough to go after him with a knife or worse a gun.

Everyone would have ended up a victim. Add to that how quickly the good citizens of Orleans would have called for the closing of the day program, and the victim list would have grown exponentially. It seemed to me that the Mike pulled in his welcome mat about six months ago. That was right around the time he'd started to set up the double D program.

Well, I knew that Mike had gotten MaryBeth to agree to limit my participation in the day program, but this was going to be just a friendly informational chitchat. Hey, who better than me? As Pete pointed out, I worked both sides of the double D street. Maybe I could help with therapy sessions under Mike's auspices instead of under MaryBeth. I pulled into the parking lot of the day program and headed for the back door.

The door to the vestibule was propped open, and camping out there was a couple of my mob sneaking a smoke. I knew that the program prohibited smoking in the building; but smoking at the open door was probably an acceptable compromise. I waved hello and started for the stairs when Max reached out and grabbed my sleeve.

"Hey doc," he said, "Don't go up there. We've all been thrown out for the day for doing nothing; Mike's really pissed at everyone."

I stopped and replied, "Come on Max, I know you better than that. You and your buddies could get even MaryBeth riled, so don't give me that crap."

"No doc, it's true," Craig, another member of my group, said. "There's something really strange going on up on the top floor. You haven't been here for a while; now they're using the top floor; but they always keep it locked. Today there was a bunch of guys in Mike's office. I've never seen any of them here before. They all went to the third floor and locked it. Mike came out of his office while we were just watching. He screamed at us to get out. We didn't do nothing, honest."

Max and Craig were two of the most sincere psychotic individuals I'd ever known. Max who claimed not to be psychotic, just brain damaged, while Craig's hallucinations hid him from the reality of being abused throughout his childhood. Something was up, but maybe nothing more than a bad day for Mike as program manager—it happens!

Before dismissing their concerns as over the top, something struck me as odd. In group on Wednesday, both of them agreed that they'd seen Jimmy talking to Kevin Turcotte after our session two weeks ago. I had just found out that Turcotte was at the drug clinic, now he was part of the new day program too; yet neither Max nor Craig had mentioned seeing him at the day program.

"Hey," I asked, "have either of you seen that guy, Kevin, who was at group with Jimmy when they started arguing here at the day program?"

Both shook their heads no. This didn't compute. I was torn between running up the stairs to confront Mike Pitts or just running back to Manny to hand over the drug drop coordinates and tell him about Fred's disappearance along with the "gift" I'd received yesterday. Yeah right and have Smith decide to tank Rudkowski because this was all unraveling too fast. Talk about being between a rock and a hard place. If I went upstairs and found out something I didn't want to find out about, then I could end up like Jimmy, or Toby—not good. Going to Manny might just cost Fred's life too—not good either. I ended up going to clinic in Eastham just to think.

The ten-minute drive helped settle my nerves but didn't help me resolve my dilemma. As soon as I entered through the main door into the waiting room, Deb, the receptionist, waved me over to the counter where she sat.

I smiled weakly saying, "Hi Deb, you haven't got any more presents for me I hope."

"As a matter of fact I do. Here this was left for you; I found it this morning when I came in," Deb wasn't at all as teasing as yesterday when she first gave me the bag with Fred's ring and watch in it. She handed me a plain envelope with my name printed on it.

Saying thanks, I carried the envelope down to the conference room where I planned to sit and have a cup of coffee. The door was closed, so Plan B was to camp out in the alcove to the records room where the coffee pot was located. I leaned the desk chair back on two legs stretching out to savor the cup of wretched coffee and postpone opening the envelope. When I finished the coffee and couldn't delay the inevitable, the hallway door to the conference room opened allowing MaryBeth and a neatly dressed man whom I didn't recognize to head in the direction of the coffee pot. Seeing me, MaryBeth stopped and turned toward me.

"Gerry, I'd like you to meet our clinic's psychologist, Dr. David Knight. Dave, this is the new area administrator for clinics like ours, Mr. Gerald Pence, he's a social worker so he understands our issues with therapy," she made the introductions.

I responded first, "Mr. Pence, a pleasure to meet you; I've just finished talking with Pete over at the Ramparts clinic about your dual diagnosis initiative. Neat concept."

"It's pronounced 'Pensay,' but please call me 'Gerry,'" he said affably. "I'm pleased to meet you too. Both Pete and MaryBeth here have had nothing but good things to say about you."

I knew right away that Gerry was as phony as the proverbial three-dollar bill, an empty suit—probably would have made a great politician or used car salesman. No clinical supervisor had ever said anything good about me! I looked over to MaryBeth and winked, but she just rolled her eyes. We all smiled and nodded while they filled their coffee cups and went back to the conference room firmly closing the door. I, too, needed privacy and found an empty office to open the envelope.

It contained only a single sheet of paper with a message written in bold letters, "Use yesterday's gift bag to put what's ours in the trash barrel next to the town landing at the bottom of Cove Rd by 10 am tomorrow. Don't and your friend goes bye-bye."

The coffee I'd just finished churned in my gut. I felt as if I was trapped; I had no answers; I had no out. I wanted to run, but where to?

Turns out, I didn't have a chance to escape into a fugue state as my cell phone started to chirp. Looking at the screen, I didn't recognize the incoming number at all. Being the trusting soul that I am, I answered with a tentative, "Yes?"

"Is this Dr. David Knight," a strident female voice demanded.

"Yes, it's me," I answered quickly.

"Dave, it's Rachel, you know, the Statie who picked you up at the college on Tuesday and drove you down to Woods Hole."

"Oh," was the best I could muster. "How did you get my cell phone number, and why are you calling me?"

"I remembered that you kept talking about a Lieutenant named Manny from the Bourne barracks, who you thought was playing a trick on you, so I called him. He gave me your cell number, but also said he'd deny it if you got pissed."

"OK, that's part one, now why are you calling?"

"This is a lot harder, but I need your help," she said and her voice softened noticeably. "I'm on duty through the weekend; on Sunday, I've been tagged to be part of a SWAT team that's going to take down Leszek Rudkowski. They want to charge him for murdering Farnsworth, the one whose body you ID'd on Tuesday. You've got to do something, Leszek couldn't have done this."

"Wait, you mean Lenny?" I responded. "Your fellow Statie told me just yesterday that he wasn't going to move on this until Monday the earliest. What gives?

"No, I got briefed this morning at roll call by CJ." she explained. "He's decided that pulling Lech in on Sunday will make it easier to get him to Bridgewater. He figures all he has to do is sign the pink slip for commitment to the state mental hospital; their screening team won't want to admit an accused murderer, so Lech gets shipped to Bridgewater probably for the rest of his life."

"Why is this an issue for you? How do you know Lenny? And what's with calling him by some other name?" I was suspicious and wondered if I was being set-up with Smith recording the call.

"Dave, I'm putting my career on the line here. I've got to trust you because there's nobody else I can turn to for help right now," Rachel became soft spoken. "It's a long story, hope you've got enough battery on your phone."

"Rachel, I hear your concern, but as a psychologist I have privilege like a doctor or lawyer. Nobody not even the courts can force me to testify or disclose anything you tell me. You've called me for a consultation, and here I am in the mental health clinic; my lips are sealed forever."

"Good, the thing is I grew up with Lech, short for Leszek, that's his real name not Lenny. My real name is Ruta, but I changed to Rachel when I went away to college. Lech and I are the same age; we grew up together in Dennis in winterized bungalows off the state highway. Being poor didn't bond us; being Polish did. Try going to school where nobody bothered to learn your name. Dombrowski and Rudkowski, we were a pair of 'skis' to everyone from the principal down. It was worse in the summers when Dennis became the damned South Boston Irish Riviera."

There was a hitch to her voice, but she continued to pour it all out, "Lech was my protector all the way through high school. He even took me to the prom when no one else asked me. I used to go to those Cape League games to watch him play ball the summer before he got sick. After that, we lost track of each other. I went to UMass, became a Statie, got married, had kids; and Lech went to one mental hospital after another in between spending years at a halfway house on the Vineyard. Sure, I know he's back living here on the outer Cape, and I've seen him a couple of times. You know he doesn't even remember me; it's all the damn drugs they've pumped him full of; he's practically a living zombie."

That was it, the floodgate opened, and I could hear Rachel sobbing into the phone. I tried to comfort and console her, but she wanted action not words.

"Rachel, trust me on this, I am working on finding who killed Jimmy independent of the cops. I don't trust your lead detective, Smith, or his motivation any further that I could throw him. I hear you and am sorry for the pain you are carrying. I can't make a promise to save Lenny, but I can promise you that I will call you before you have to pick him up on Sunday. Keep your cell phone on, I'll get back to you on it."

She said, "*Dziękuję i niech cię Bóg błogosławi*" softly in Polish, and hung up. I don't speak Polish, but there's just something about "thank you and God bless," that transcends the language barrier

I had to do something; I didn't know what, but I had to get into action. The list of victims kept growing from Jimmy, to Toby, to Fred, to Lenny, and now Rachel. I was under the gun and knew it; time to get my sorry ass in gear.

-23-

I wheeled out of the parking lot, headed back down Rt 6 into Orleans, and then followed the road along Pleasant Bay back to Chatham. I kept going straight at the lights onto Shore Road and past one of the greatest views on the Cape. Coming over the rise leading to both the town's fish pier and the Chatham Bars Inn, my eyes wandered across the vista. It was just beautiful. I could see past Tern Island, over the sand flats to the barrier beach island all dappled in sunlight; and then beyond that, the Atlantic Ocean stretching all the way to Europe. The spring fog bank lying offshore considerably foreshortened the view. I just felt better. Checking to see that I didn't hit anyone in the crosswalk at CBI, I noticed on the shore side, a new boat moored just outside of the channel. It was more than fifty feet in length and totally different in design from CBI's Hinckley built motor yacht moored just behind it. The Hinckley was a traditional powerboat from a traditional downeast boatyard, but the new one was sleek and swoopy. She screamed Mediterranean—French, Italian, or even Spanish—and expensive. She also screamed drugs! Talk about being out of place in Chatham Harbor side by side a fleet of inshore draggers, lobstermen, and longliners. She might not have stood out in Newport or Nantucket in the height of the season; but early May in Chatham, she was different.

I turned down Claflin Landing toward the water to get a closer look. Although the early afternoon breeze was out of the southwest, the tide was running out so the yacht was swinging on her mooring in a wide arc. I was curious about where she was from. Parking with my front wheels in the soft sand, I pulled the binoculars from under the seat and focused in on her transom. "Peaches 'n Cream" was written in a golden arched script with a hail port of "Johnston, RI" underneath. Johnston, Rhode Island, who's kidding whom, Johnston is about ten miles inland; it's on the west side of

Providence; it's a little less salty than Cranston; and it's reported to be home to the New England crime family. I felt suddenly cold again. First Jimmy is found dead with my business card halfway down his throat—even the cops thought it that looked like a mob hit. Next my house is ransacked by persons unknown but driving a black caddy with smoked windows. Then Fred, standing in for me in the classroom, gets scooped up right off the road on the way home. I get a gift of his ring and watch from someone who talked like a *paisano*; and now the floating equivalent of a pimp mobile anchors at the mouth of the harbor. I needed to know who owned this scow.

Putting down the binoculars, I fished out my cell phone and cursed loudly at the buck surcharge I incurred dialing 411 to get Chris' number at work. After telling me the number, the system automatically dialed her and a couple of rings later, I got through.

"Chris," I said, "it's Dave. Things are getting more squirrelly with this drug drop thing. I really need to find Tommy, but I don't have his phone number or know where his office is. Do you have his number handy?"

"Sure, I've got him on my cell's speed dial," she answered. "Let me look it up now for you. Tom has one of those bays in the metal buildings in Commerce Park. I don't know which one he uses, I've never been there. I don't know the real name of his business either, but he's got 'Stump Dog' lettered on the doors of his truck. Just look for that—it's huge and usually is towing a trailer with a chipper on it."

After getting Tom's number, I thanked Chris, promising her that I would be careful and back in South Chatham for supper. Next, I called Tom who answered on the first ring. He said I was lucky to find him in his shop. Usually he knocked off early on Friday because his crew got antsy if kept from the Squire, Yardarm, or any of the half dozen places where the crews gathered to hoist a pint after a week's work. Probably a good strategy I thought as nobody got hurt cutting corners trying to get out early to wet his whistle. Tom told me to come by; his place was the third building on the left at the very end.

It took only ten minutes this time of year to get from Shore Road down Main St to Commerce Park. Try doing that in July—it'd take a good half hour at least. I pulled into Tommy's place right next to this oversized Dodge 4x4 with "Stump Dog" on the door and huge decal of a pit bull wielding a revved up chain saw on the front fender.

I knew Tom was a working man, but I was unprepared for the inside of the bay. The ground floor was what I expected—chainsaws, parts of chainsaws, a chipper, a workbench with all sorts of gear strewn about—but the loft astounded me. Tom used it as his office; he was standing at the top of the stairs and waved me up. I entered a completely different world—not a chainsaw in sight, but lots of computers, flat screens, and sundry high tech gear.

"Tom, great to catch you in," I started. "How come you're not standing the crew to a round at the Squire?"

"Hah," he laughed, "my gang of hollow legged beer mutts would bankrupt me in an afternoon. What I do is pay the lot of them for Friday afternoon and let them go wherever to do whatever. It really guarantees that they'll be ready to work on Monday morning, and I don't have to worry about them buying me a round. With three crews of four buckos each, I'd be looking at belting back a dozen brewskis or more. No way, this is cheaper and safer, trust me!"

I'd have loved to spend the afternoon shooting the breeze about Tom's work and all of his computer toys, but I needed information, so I said, "Tom is there any way to find out who owns a boat on one of these computers?"

"Sure, the state has a database for excise tax purposes; just give me the MS registration numbers," he replied without hesitation.

"There weren't any numbers on the bow, and the hailing port was out of state. This one's probably federally documented," I told him.

"That's not a problem; I've got the Coast Guard's database online with a link from NOAA," Tom was a pro.

"Sit here, and I'll use the flat screen TV on the wall instead of the monitor, it'll keep you from having to read over my shoulder. What's her name?"

"She's "Peaches 'n Cream" with an apostrophe n," I gave him the information.

"That's fine; I'll just enter Peaches and see what comes up."

With just a couple of key strokes, a list popped up of all the vessels documented by the Coast Guard beginning with the name "Peaches." There were over twenty listed including a handful of "Miss Peaches," a bunch of "Peaches," a "Peaches Delight," and four varieties of "Peaches 'n Cream."

Each entry on the screen was linked to a page that contained all the information about the boat—size, who built it, when it was built, where it was used, previous names and owners, and current owner and address among other things.

The one I wanted was toward the end of the file—whew, what a beauty, she was a twin diesel, 65 footer, built by Antago Yachts out of Italy—but what stymied me was that her owner was listed as a corporation, "Tight Lines" with an address in Johnston, Rhode Island.

"Tom, can you print out that listing for me?" I asked. "Also can you figure out who owns 'Tight Lines, LLC'?"

"Here are the details on the boat, want to look it up on Yachtworld to see what she's worth?" Tom was getting into it.

"No, but I'd like to find out more about 'Tight Lines,'" I replied. "Can you get on any websites that would tell who's involved in the company?"

"Yes and no—I mean yes there is a way to get the info from government websites, but no I can't. You've got to see Diane over at the library for help." He answered. "I had some problems a couple of years back with summer people from Connecticut. They wanted some tree and shrub work done on their summer place up off Old Wharf Road in the ritzy section. I did the work at the end of the summer like I was asked, but got stiffed on the bill. The place wasn't owned by them, but by a LLC or corporation or some tax dodge. I tried to bill the company, and that didn't work either. I was left out in the cold as I'd paid the crew for the work and paid Eldredge's to dump the slash."

"So how'd the library help you out?" I was more than idly curious.

"Diane was able to look up who owned what in the town records, and it was in a corporation's name all right. Next, she searched around for who owned the company using some government websites. It took about five minutes and my credit card to get the address for these pukes in Connecticut. The rest is history."

"Come on, Tom, don't leave me hanging. What happened next, did you file a mechanics lien or something?" I asked.

"Too complicated, I just sent a registered letter to their Connecticut home asking for my money within 10 days or else."

"Or else what?" This was getting to be like pulling teeth.

"Oh they found out when they didn't pay up 'cuz I sent them a picture of their front yard with a huge cherry tree chopped down. Yup, you can call me George Washington, but their check was in the return mail." Tommy grinned in satisfaction at the memory and no doubt the check.

"So it's off to see Diane at the library, thanks Tom." I got up to go, but not before Tommy reminded me that the library was only open two afternoons a week for a couple of hours. I was in luck, one of the days was Friday; it was time to get on down the road.

After thanking Tom for his help, I briefly told him about the note that had been waiting for me in the clinic this morning. I left out Rachel's call as irrelevant, and as I had promised her, privileged. Walking down from the loft, Tom went from being the incredibly computer savvy techie to a hulking lumberjack. He grabbed an axe propped up on a stump and motioned for me to follow him around to the back of the construction bay. A 4'x8' sheet of plywood with the outline of a man painted on it was nailed against a tree. Standing about thirty feet away, Tom raised the axe over his head and flicked it toward the target. The axe whirled and struck the silhouette square in the chest area. Tommy just smiled.

"Dave," he said. "Need someone to watch your back?"

"Thanks Tom, but I can't afford to get anybody else mixed up in my mess."

"Seriously I can help with the heavy lifting, and if you want to check out the water at Waypoint Alpha, give me a shout. I mean it; I can get my SeaCraft moving at a moment's notice."

"I appreciate it Tom, I really do, and I will call you—trust me!" I conceded and left him to perfect his tomahawk toss albeit with a twelve-pound axe.

-24-

Looking at my watch, I realized that time was getting away from me—it was already quarter to two—I had time but barely! I headed for the library but first stopped at the village deli for a quick ham and cheese, chips, and coke to wash it all down.

Parking on the side street behind Diane's old, red Toyota I walked across the lawn to the front door. Now this wasn't a library with all of the trappings of the digital age, it's a one room, twelve by twelve, unheated relic from the 19th century. Entering the front door—the only door—there were books stacked to the ceiling on all four walls with short shelves to the right and left. A narrow aisle like a nave lead to the altar, the oak librarian's desk. Behind it the high priestess sat, the librarian. As formidable and riveting as the desk was, even more riveting and formidable was Diane, the librarian.

How old is Diane? I didn't know, but I'd bet she's over eighty. She's an octogenarian and a feisty one at that. I know she walks every day about four miles no matter what the weather. What did she do before becoming the librarian? I didn't know that either, but she could have been the CEO of a Fortune 500 company or a third grade school teacher—my hunch is the latter as she seems battle tested! There's something Slavic about her features, her accent isn't Cape Cod, so she's another washashore. But boy can she read! I make my living reading and then telling others what I've read. Diane reads for the sheer love of it. There probably isn't a book in that tiny crammed library that she hasn't read. We often talked about books, characters, plots, and writers' idiosyncratic behaviors. If anyone could penetrate the labyrinth of corporate filings, I knew she could. Sitting down across from her, I told her about the boat in the harbor.

Reaching into her desk drawer, Diane pulled out a sheaf of 4x6 file cards and the ubiquitous #2 pencil. Must have been a second grade teacher—I'd bet there was a ruler made for the knuckles in that drawer too. She spent a few minutes dividing the file cards into piles and labeling the top card for each pile, finally she looked up at me with a set to her jaw.

"Let's take a closer look and see if we can't penetrate the corporate shield for this boat," she said reaching down into a canvas bag by the side of the desk pulling out a laptop. Leaning back, she swiveled slightly in her chair as she typed on the keyboard.

"Hey, Diane," I interrupted her clicking. "What are you doing with a laptop, you don't have an Internet connection, and even cell phones don't work well enough down here?"

"Don't worry," she said with a savvy smile. "The good minister next door has a router set up in his study so he can use his notebook and iPhone anywhere in the church. I just borrow a bit of bandwidth whenever I need to; call me the reincarnation of 'Thoroughly Modern Millie.'"

"Diane, that's stealing and from a church too," I said in a mockingly rebuking tone.

"Heaven helps those who help themselves," was her sly rejoinder. "How much do you know about Internet resources?"

"Enough to catch a few students every semester plagiarizing," I answered. "Other than that, I use email and have a cell phone."

"Dave, I hate to break it to you like this, but your cell phone isn't twenty-first century much less Wi-Fi enabled. Plus email is for old people; I've my own Facebook page with a thousand friends, I'm on LinkedIn with ninety connections, and I have a Twitter handle—want to see my latest hashtag?"

Holding my hands in the air, I said shaking my head, "You've got me there, Diane. You lead, and I'll try to follow, but go easy on me, I'm no teenager!"

"Agreed, but once we're on the Internet the rest is easy. All I have to do is Google the Secretary of State office for Rhode Island. You did say that's where 'Tight Lines' was incorporated, right? Once there I hit the link for the Corporations Database, and I'm in." she said as an official looking form with the seal of Office of the Secretary of State for the State of Rhode Island and Providence Plantations popped up on her screen.

"Is this available for every state?" I was a bit amazed.

"Sure why not, it's the twenty-first century out there Dave," Diane was ragging on me. "Now I just have to type the name into the first box here and hit 'Search.' There I'm into the database—got your credit card handy, Dave?"

"Are you charging me for the search?" I teased.

"Not a bad idea, but that'll have to wait until tomorrow. I could plug one of those card reader apps right into my iPhone. Know what an app is Dave?" She volleyed the banter.

"Enough, enough, let's get on with it."

"Here's how it works. Right now, I have to create a temporary account with your credit card to download the corporate information like who's on the board and their addresses. If we cross state lines, I'll have to set up accounts in each state. Don't worry; I'm building a dummy account with a phony name and address. The only real stuff is the credit card number, but I'll close out anything I set up this afternoon."

Glumly I handed over my MasterCard to Diane. While she was entering data and clicking all over the keyboard, I busied myself reading dust jackets from Loren Estleman's and Robert Parker's latest contributions to the genre—jeez where was Hawk when I needed him?

"Gotcha!" Diane announced, "Tight Lines, LLC on the screen. Now let us go look at the corporate structure. I'm going to look at all of the filings for this LLC, and you're buying a copy of the latest Annual Report to find who the owners are."

"How do I get the copy? Is it mailed or emailed?" I asked worried about the time.

"No you Luddite," she laughed. "Once you have an account each transaction is billed to your credit card, and the results are displayed to copy, print, or save."

Almost immediately, the results were posted, but for each of the officers, there was exactly the same listing. It was another corporation, "XYZ, LTD."

"Hey Diane, what's this, a shell game?" I stared at the name on the screen.

"Yes, of course," she said. "Someone's trying to hide ownership of the boat, but let's just keep digging."

I couldn't believe that there were multiple companies in Rhode Island named "XYZ," but there were. Clicking on the entry "XYZ, LTD," Diane pulled up the records page and then downloaded the summary screen listing all of the details. *Voila*, and there it was, Tight Lines, LLC was owned by XYZ, LTD, which in turn was owned by Fruit Hill, Inc. of Providence.

In just under two minutes and about twenty bucks, Diane had gone from the name of a boat through half a dozen screens to her real owner, the owner of Fruit Hill, Inc., John "Peaches" Ianello. I knew that name from the days of working in the drug clinic in New Bedford.

"Peaches" Ianello was part of the northeast crime family headquartered in Rhode Island that controlled literally every illicit activity from drugs to protection racket shakedowns throughout New England. Ianello got his nickname because, unlike most rather swarthy Sicilians, he had no beard at all, just "peach-fuzz." Ianello was big into running a sports book for the mob as well as making sure that the drug dealers in New Bedford bought their stuff from the right sources.

So that was it, I thought, those bastards from the Pallatroni crime family whacked Jimmy, killed Toby, and snatched Fred. They must of gotten something from burning Jimmy and breaking his fingers—me! Now they knew that I had the frigging location of the drug drop. Either I gave it back not knowing what it was all about, or if I did know and tried to pick up the junk, they'd follow me. I had painted myself into a corner—going to the cops was out if I wanted Fred sprung, and as much as I couldn't stand him, I wasn't going to let him die too. If I turned over the offshore location as instructed, I'd have no leverage to help Fred. If I tried to grab the dope and do a deal, I'd have to outrun this sleek 60 footer that did better than 25 knots according to Tommy who'd found a sister ship on Yachtworld and regaled me with her stats.

Suddenly I had a plan, not the whole thing, but at least a direction for action. Leaning over the desk, I said to Diane, "You've been a great help. This really is what I need, but hoped not to find."

"Want to tell me something about what's going on, Dave?" Diane offered to listen if I wanted.

"No, it would be better for you not to know, but I promise I'll be back here next time you're open to spill the beans," I stepped around the side of the desk and gave her a hug of appreciation.

-25-

Half an hour later, I headed down the mid-Cape highway toward the canal. I planned to cross over the Sagamore Bridge to stay as far away from the State Police barracks in Bourne as possible. I called Chris to tell her that I was going off Cape for a while and wouldn't be back in time for dinner. Thanking her for her help and understanding, I said I'd call when I got back on Cape. I drove over the Sagamore Bridge, navigated the flyover's cloverleaves, and headed along the Scenic Highway before connecting with I-195 headed west. Less than an hour later, I crossed the Acushnet River, took the exit onto Rt 18, and sped down on the New Bedford side of the river. At the first set of lights, I took a right onto Elm and a quick left onto Water. I was near New Bedford's famous Whaling Museum on Johnny Cake Hill when I parked and made my way into a dive named the Cross Rip Café. New Bedford's waterfront is home to some truly scummy bars, and I just entered one.

The place was dark, dank, smelled of a mixture of urine, stale beer, and tobacco smoke. Fishermen and fish lumpers continued to smoke and drink in the waterfront bars, but that didn't seem to concern many in this tough town. I bellied up to the bar and pushed a Jackson in the direction of the barkeep.

"I just need a number, Ok?" I said making it clear I was willing to pay for the information. "I'm back in town, and I want to call my old friend, Tiny Macedo. Got his number handy?"

Tiny was the owner of this bar as well as having an interest in at least a couple of other waterfront joints. He was a tough cookie as they say, who would extend credit to any fisherman down on his luck; but beware, you either settled with Tiny before shipping out, or he'd be the first person you'd see on the dock when you landed.

He was a little guy whose family was from either the Azores or Cape Verde but tough as nails. He'd made his mark as the dockside union rep for Jorge, "the Shiv," Souza who ran the local longshoremen's union hall. Tiny organized the lumpers, the roughnecks who grunted, sweated, and unloaded by hand the fishing boats, some thirty years ago. He'd held his own whether down in the hold or stacking the one hundred twenty pound fish boxes four high. After hurting his back followed by a couple of failed operations, Tiny eased the pain with heroin and ended up being one of the biggest drug dealers on the waterfront. At first he smuggled the dope in from a supplier in New York City, but after a sit-down, and an offer he couldn't refuse from "Peaches" Ianello backed up by a couple of heavies from the Pallatroni family, he saw the error of his ways and only distributed heroin that had been mob approved.

Fast forward twenty years and Tiny was finishing a stretch in the state prison. He'd had the bad luck of being busted when his car was rear ended on the highway with a load of dope in the trunk. I was working in the drug treatment program in New Bedford and running an out-reach program for addicts in the Dighton Correctional Facility. Tiny and I hooked up there.

I couldn't do much about his sentence or desire for heroin; but I was able to help his son who'd gotten on the spike when dad was in the slammer. Tiny's kid, like the old man, was bright and ambitious; but unlike his dad, he wasn't half as tough. Long story short, I got him into the treatment program and then facilitated his application to a minority enrichment program at the university where I was teaching. I don't think Tiny had graduated from eighth grade much less college, so a few years later when his son walked across the stage to get his degree, Tiny was prouder than his tough-guy macho veneer would let on. We'd kept in touch a bit over the years, as Tiny wanted me to know how well his son was doing at a real job in a big city. Today I wanted to call my marker in.

The barkeeper sneered and said, "Who wants to know?"

"Hey just call Tiny, say '*bem vindo*' for me and tell him Dave Knight needs a favor. And keep the change." I noticed that the twenty-dollar bill had disappeared into his paw.

He went behind a beaded curtain at the end of the bar and punched out a number on a hand held phone. After listening to it ring a couple of times, he started to speak, probably in Creole, the patois favored by Cape Verdeans. Saying "*sim, sim*" and nodding, he came back to me and handed me the phone. Tiny was on the other end. I told me I needed his help, and what I wanted. He told me to sit still, have a glass of *vinho* and give him forty-five minutes to meet me. I passed on the wine.

Only about half an hour later, Tiny pushed his way through the beaded curtain having entered the bar from the rear. He was dressed in a suit complete with a tie and matching hankie in the breast pocket. He looked like a successful businessman.

Coming around the bar, he gave me a hug and said how glad he was to see me. Noticing that I didn't have anything to drink he told his bartender to bring a couple of glasses of the special *vinho vermelho* which I wasn't going to be able to refuse.

"Dave, Dave, what's it been four-five years now?" he asked. "You're looking well. Life away from us must agree with you."

"Most days that would be true, but not right now," I responded. "But first tell me about your son, Joe. Has he made you a grandfather yet?"

"My son Joe married an incredibly beautiful woman who's given us two children both even more beautiful." I could hear the pride in his voice once he got started.

"The only regret is that Joe is still working out of state in the mid-West. He is head of the human resources department, and the company likes him so much that they sent him to get his MBA at the University of Chicago. Can you believe that my Joe has an advanced degree?"

"Tiny, I'm glad for you. It's a shame your wife wasn't able to see all the good that has happened to her boy," I said softly.

"No Dave you're wrong. My Rose knows everything and is watching over him and her grandchildren every day. Besides I go to up to Sacred Heart cemetery every week to talk to her about him." Tiny's wife had died a number of years earlier when he was in prison and had not lived to see or share in her son's achievements.

"Do you think you can help me out with this problem I've got?" I asked.

"Dave, I owe you more than you'll ever know, and I am a man who pays his debts," Tiny replied. "I've reached out to Roberto and asked for this favor. One of his sons will meet with us at Belle Sera on Atwell Avenue at seven tonight. Do you know it?"

"Wow, is that place still around? I remember going there back in graduate school. It was a mob hangout back then. There were nights when they wouldn't let us in or even better when they simply picked up our plates and told us to leave. I guess some things don't change. But seriously, Tiny, you don't have to go with me. I don't want you to get mixed up in this any more than I've already got you," I protested.

"Dave," he lifted a finger to caution me, "I've got this arranged, and it is important to me that this be done correctly."

I realized that Tiny wasn't wearing his best suit for nothing. This for him was a presentation. Lucky for me I was wearing the prototypical human services worker's uniform—blue blazer, grey slacks, blue button down, penny loafers (no socks), and striped tie. I looked at my watch and figured it would take close to an hour to get to the Federal Hill part of Providence, so we'd better get started.

Tiny and I chatted amicably on the drive to Providence like old friends catching up on the news about each other's kids. I crossed the Washington Bridge taking the left hand lane for I-95 at the split, and then made the exit onto Atwell Avenue. As I was driving due west, the setting sun was squarely in my eyes, but I couldn't help but notice the garish statuary that was Carmine's Roman Garden on the corner of Atwell and Bradford St. Some things never change—I thought that phony Neapolitan stuff was an eyesore when I hung out here back in graduate school. The street became more familiar as we lugged up to the top of the hill. I passed Belle Sera on the right, and sure enough, the old sign was the same as were the plaid café curtains across the front windows. Finding a spot on Atwell, I pulled in, and we got out making our way back to the restaurant.

"Dave, you're not carrying are you?" Tiny's asked in a serious voice.

"Sweet Jesus, no! I'm dumb not stupid," I answered, but Tiny's admonition made me realize how I might be doing the most stupid thing in my life, not counting my first marriage, if I was getting set up. As we climbed the steps with Tiny holding the door open for me, I really, really knew how the Christians felt entering the lions' den.

-26-

Along one side of the restaurant was the bar with tables on the other. It was Friday night, there was standing room only at the bar; all of the tables were full with families enjoying huge portions of pasta, salads, and that braided sourdough bread, which was still a favorite. I stood looking about, gawking actually; Tiny pushed past me and strode purposefully toward the opening to a back room. Before he could enter, a man swiveled his bar stool around and shot his arm out effectively barring the doorway.

"Private party," he snarled. "Wait for a table to clear out here. Check with Antonio over at the cash register. Got it?"

"*Prego*, tell Mr. Roberto's son that his company has arrived. We'll wait here until it's convenient for him to meet with us," Tiny said announcing our presence.

Without a word of response, the minder slid off the barstool and disappeared into the back room. We stood and waited silently for only a couple of minutes until he returned and with a jerk of his chin motioned for us to enter. The room was the width of the restaurant and lined with booths along one side. We followed him as he walked down the aisle past half a dozen empty booths stopping at the last. As we came even with it, a young man sat with what looked like a martini in front of him. He motioned for us to sit down. We did.

"Mr. Macedo," he said nodding toward Tiny, "and Dr. Knight," nodding to me. "I'm James Pallatroni, Roberto's youngest son. I understand that you, Dr. Knight, want to consult with me and my family on an urgent matter."

"Well, yes," I began, but James cut me off holding up his hand.

"Let's do this my way," he said interrupting me. "Mr. Macedo has been loyal to our family and business for a number of years. He had the opportunity to, how one says, 'rat us out' but acted with honor; what the old timers would call with *omerta,* the code of silence. For that he has earned my father's respect; and I'm here to answer your questions if I can."

I just shook my head knowing how horrible it must have been for Tiny to turn down a deal from the DA, never to see his beloved Rose again and lose contact with his son during the teenage years. Worse, here I was calling in his markers. Tiny was tough.

"I appreciate both your offer and Tiny's willingness to be an intermediary," I started. "Why don't I just ask my questions and then leave you here to dine without our intrusion."

"You've just come all the way from Cape Cod, that's at least a two hour drive," was his response. "Why don't we have a drink first, maybe some dinner, then there'll be time to talk?

I guessed this wasn't really up for discussion, so I joined Tiny in ordering a glass of wine allowing the knowledgeable waiter to bring something decent.

"Good," James said amicably, "I've taken the liberty to order an antipasto and brochette. They serve family style here, so I hope you like my choices for the soup, salad, and pasta."

Although I thought Tiny and I had made it clear that we wanted just a glass of wine each, the waiter brought three glasses and a large carafe of red wine. He offered it to James, who tasted it and nodded his approval. After filling my glass, I thanked the waiter and took a sip—outstanding, what a great tasting wine. If it were just Chris and me out for a dinner, we could have really enjoyed this spread. I just hoped this wasn't the prelude to my last supper.

I must have been staring inadvertently at James because he cocked his head to one side and said with a smile, "So Dr. Knight, I don't fit your preconceived notion of a mobster?"

"No, I mean yes, I mean you're not exactly a ringer for Brando in the *Godfather*." I tried to make light of an embarrassing but accurate observation.

"That's not right; I think I look a lot like Brando especially when he played Johnny in *The Wild One*. He was only twenty-nine when he made that movie; that's my age now!" James said somewhat triumphantly.

"Point well taken. I remember only Sonny and Michael Corleone," I apologized. "You don't seem to fit in with any of those images, I'm glad to say."

"You'd have liked my grandfather—he was really from the old Sicilian mode—always a fedora, black suit with a vest, and you should have seen his wingtips." James was laughing at me and my discomfort.

"Even my father and his brothers were more old school," he said. "Look at Mr. Macedo here, he's dressed to the nines; and that was just what the older generation did. I don't even own a suit and don't know the last time I wore a tie."

"Was it just the times that made the 'older generation,' as you call us, so formal?" I asked.

"Perhaps, and perhaps it was a sign of respect to wear one's Sunday best; but I think it was to compensate for their lack of a formal education. Certainly my grandfather, but as I said my father too, all held priests, doctors, and teachers in respect, maybe even awe because of their titles, degrees, and professions that weren't really businesses."

"What about lawyers, haven't they been part of the 'family?'" I continued the conversation.

"Well the term *Consiglior* has always been around and means 'counselor'; it didn't have to be a lawyer, but I think it's evolved over time into being an attorney. But here's the rub, in granddad's time, lawyers didn't have to graduate from law school to take the bar exam. That's why I think lawyers weren't in the same category as the others."

"What about you, may I ask?" I said respectfully.

"Sure, I graduated from PC with a BS in business administration, and then picked up a MBA from Fordham in finance. I'm not only a well educated businessman, but I am also well schooled in the ethics of the Dominican as well as Jesuit orders," James said with a modicum of pride.

"My son's got his MBA, too," Tiny chimed in.

"See that's the point," James went on, "We're the next generation and will adapt to the style of our peers, a bit more casual and a lot more educated."

"But Tiny's son runs a human resources department for a company in the mid-West. No offence, but he's moved on from his father's type of business, but you?"

"Ah, I get your point, but I'm a business man not a gangster. I run several businesses providing different opportunities for interested people. That they are illegal seems to me to be a technicality."

"I'm a little more than confused here," I admitted giving James a chance to expound. We were his guests, so why not?

"Well take gambling, stuff like the numbers. It used to be a mainstay in our business, but now every state has a lottery with bouncing balls or scratch tickets with instant winners. We used to have gambling parlors with poker games, crap tables, and one-armed bandits. Now they have casinos in Connecticut, and even the old dog track in Lincoln has become an upscale venue for slots. What's left?"

"Sports betting," I said.

"Absolutely—unless you go offshore through some online system or get to Vegas—there's no legal sports book if you don't count the off track betting shops in New York. Where do you go to play the ponies, put some money on your favorite team, or even bet on who wins the coin toss at the Super Bowl? Answer is: you come to me."

"So you see this as just a business venture?" I said and then exclaimed, "Hmmmm, this is great!" with a mouthful of some outstanding Caesar salad, made with raw eggs, as it should be.

James smiled and said, "This is when my grandmother would say, '*mange, mange*'; but really, lots of people want to gamble, and I provide the service. I also provide some help when people need money to pay their debts whether to me or anyone else and can't get help through the banks. Compared to what rates I've seen on credit cards, I don't think of myself as a loan shark."

"Should we add drugs and prostitution to the list?" I asked.

"Yes, why not? People want to take drugs for all sorts of reasons—just ask Rush Limbaugh! Once again we provide a service to those who want a particular product, that's all; it's just business. The same can be said for prostitution, we're not white slavers, and we don't violate the Mann Act. You know if abortion were illegal, then we'd be in that business as there'd be a need for the service and a willingness to pay. It's all economics—just supply and demand."

By now, the main courses had been served, and we passed around the bowls and platters commenting on the food and not the business at hand. About forty minutes later, filled to surfeit, I accepted a cup of coffee and looked over to James who seemed ready to get down to business.

"So Dr. Knight, why did you ask to speak with me tonight?"

"It's about Jimmy Farnsworth's death, ransacking my home, kidnapping Fred Dorfman, and Peaches Ianello's boat in Chatham Harbor. You're after me, and I want out."

"No, we're not after you; we're after a cache of drugs, that's all," He said.

"What about Jimmy or Fred?" I protested.

"I've never heard of either of them, just as I hadn't heard of you until Mr. Macedo called this afternoon," he answered.

"I can't figure this out, something is happening, and you have to be involved especially as it involves a drug drop off the coast of Chatham."

"Look, we're in the business of distributing drugs. I mean that's what we are paid to do. Two things have happened. First beginning about six months ago, we were pushed out of the Cape Cod market for coke and heroin. We sell to the middlemen who cut and package the product for distribution on the street. We really don't care where they get their stuff, but if it's not from us, then they have to pay to play. After all the goal of any capitalist enterprise is a monopoly—just ask the Rockefellers."

I leaned forward gaining interest saying, "What was happening on Cape Cod?"

"I don't know, and frankly it really didn't bother us. With access to the Cape limited to those two bridges, the Cape was a pain. Once you factor in all the summer and holiday traffic, the demand for our product was too variable to predict. We just wrote it off and let it go."

"And then?" I prompted.

"And the second thing a couple of months ago happened," James continued. "The battlefield moved to New Bedford. All drugs in an arc from just over the Rhode Island line down to the Cape and up to Brockton come out of New Bedford. It's the hub. Now we have competition from the Cape moving onto our turf in Wareham, Plymouth, and even New Bedford itself. Trust me; we can't take that lying down."

"What type of money are we talking about here, may I ask?" I was inquisitive.

"Let's use round numbers, but there're all in the ballpark so to speak," James said warming to the task. "Right now in Southeastern Mass we supply enough product for over forty thousand bags of heroin a week at street level. That means we service around a thousand users if each had a four to five bag a day habit. At twenty-five bucks a pop, the take is over a million dollars a week on the street. Of course, that's retail, and we're wholesale, so we're taking in a bit less.

"Normally we cut our stuff with a mixture of quinine and lactose, until it's only forty percent heroin. But the guys from the Cape have raised the heroin content to sixty percent for the same twenty-five dollar bag."

"Doesn't that mean they'll sell fewer bags? I mean an addict will get just as high off two bags of their skag compared to three bags of yours," I asked.

"Doctor, it doesn't work that way. An addict who has a five bag a day habit will shoot all five bags. If he gets higher than expected, he's a happy camper; but for us it means he's not buying again from our dealers," James replied with a bit of ire in his voice.

"Now our cost on a single bag basis to raise the dope from forty percent to sixty percent is only four bucks, that's all. On a weekly basis, however, that's almost a hundred seventy thousand, and yearly it's almost nine million. No way am I going to lose almost nine million bucks to a bunch of yahoos from Cape freaking Cod."

"Ouch," I said. "What about cocaine, are the numbers the same?"

"No, not really," he shook his head. "Coke for us is a loss leader; the profit margins aren't as high. Sure, we double our investment, but the main idea is to let those who want to 'party hearty' use cocaine at a reasonable rate. The withdrawal afterwards gets them. What can you treat a cocaine addiction with besides more cocaine?

Heroin, that's what; it's the only workable alternative, and presto we have another long-term customer. Right now we're not in the oxy or meth business; but we're thinking of having to diversify if we can't knock out the competition."

"Do you have any idea who these Cape guys are or where they're from?" I tried to refocus the conversation on my problem not his.

"The origin of the drugs is one of the Columbian cartels. I don't know the top-level players from Cape Cod. The street level pushers seem to be all users from what we've found out, and what's weird is that the mid-level distributors, you know, the guys who supply the product to the street vendors seem to be nuts. We've tried talking to one or two, boosted some of their product, and rousted their butts from our turf; but they're fruitcakes or retards. We got nothing from them at all," James threw up his hands in disgust.

"Yeah but Jimmy was one of those fruitcakes as you put it; and he was mixed up in something. The cops know his death Monday night was a murder; he was clobbered with something like a baseball bat and thrown off a cliff," I began. "Add to that Fred Dorfman getting kidnapped out of his car on Thursday—someone sent me his ring and watch to let me know they had him. I also got my house trashed as well as my office at the college. Who could've done this, and again I have to ask, why am I being targeted?"

"I really don't know. The word of the street is that these yahoos from the Cape are promising a big spike in the availability of their junk soon. They're taking orders for blow and horse at prices and purity we can't match. We are going to stop this, period. The reason Ianello is down in Chatham is that besides thinking he's Captain Ahab or something, he believes that the drugs have to come in off the water, so he's down there watching. I mean it'd be a twofer, score the drugs to put the competition out of business and as a bonus pick up at least ten million bucks worth of product."

"You are being straight with me when you say I'm not on your radar screen?" I was still not convinced.

"No, Dr. Knight, we don't know you or any of the other names you've mentioned. We're making an educated guess here about the drug drop with the Cape gang being imminent. With summer coming on, demand really peaks on not only the Cape but also Nantucket and Martha's Vineyard. Everyone wants to party and not everyone drinks Bud Light."

"Ok, I believe you, thanks, I appreciate you seeing me and setting me straight," I said lightly. "Somehow I'm at the epicenter of what has happened, and I don't like it, but at least I'm not being pursued by wise guys with their MBAs."

"That's the good news, Dr. Knight," James said. "Remember this, if we wanted Mr. Farnsworth dead, he'd have had two in the hat, as my grandfather used to say. As for Mr. Dorfman, we would send you his ring, but it would still be on his finger. We've sophisticated our act in many ways, but there are some aspects of our business best left 'old school.'"

Although he said this with a smile, I couldn't help but notice his eyes. They were dark brown as one would expect to see in a second-generation American with Sicilian grandparents, but they were deep and cold. I shuddered at the implication of his words backed up by the deadness of his eyes. This was not a man to cross.

Pallatroni nodded to me and Tiny, slid from the booth, stood and then made his way out of Belle Sera. I looked over to Tiny who just shrugged and signaled to the waiter who brought the check. I noticed that I was paying for our meals plus the bar tab of the Praetorian Guard. I was paying for the information received; it was all business to James and the Pallatroni family. The tab was hefty and padded with the lost revenue from the empty back room booths. Good thing I had healthy credit limit on my Visa card. Only a couple of minutes later, Tiny and I left the restaurant to begin our trip back to New Bedford and for me all the way back to Chatham.

I left Tiny at his bar begging off from the invite to drink more red wine with him. I thanked him for his help and asked if I called his bar would they be able to reach him 24/7? He said he'd make sure that I could get through. Finally, I told him to say hello to his son for me and headed for the Cape knowing more than when I left it, but still not enough.

Crossing back over the bridge, I tooled down the mid-Cape making two calls. The first was to Chris to tell her that I was on Cape, but I'd sleep at my house because I needed to get going early Saturday morning. She said she understood, yet the tone of her voice was one of disappointment. I promised I would see her Saturday and even take her to the Land Ho for their roast beef special. We had a date!

Next, I called Tom. Although it was now after ten, he was still up playing computer games or surfing the web or something. I told him that I had found out from Diane who owned the boat sitting in the channel leading out of Chatham Harbor. I also said wanted to make the run to the waypoint in the morning—early! We agreed to meet down at the Ryder's Cove boat yard about an hour before sunrise. Just after eleven, I pulled into my driveway and parked next to the house. I doused the lights and listened—nothing but the sound of peepers from the marsh and the hoot of a horned owl as it sought after prey. Going up the stairs and in through the back way, I kicked aside the debris still scattered on the floor making my way to the bedroom where I just flopped down and was asleep in minutes.

DAY 5: SATURDAY, MAY 10TH

-27-

I woke up with a start and listened, but there was nothing to hear. I got up, turned the lights on, and changed into some warm work clothes; I knew it was going to be chilly offshore with the water temps still in the low 40s. Looking around, I found my foul weather gear hanging on a peg near the rest of my boating gear piled in a corner. I rummaged around through a couple of cardboard cartons until I found my hand-held GPS and a couple of new batteries. I put the batteries in and turned on the GPS. To get the satellites loaded after a long winter in the house, I had to put the unit on the back porch rail while I dug out the lat/lon coordinates that Tommy had dubbed "Waypoint Alpha." After a couple of minutes, the GPS was ready to go, but it took me at least five more minutes to remember by trial and error how to load in the numbers to create a waypoint.

Grabbing my wallet and cell phone, I stuffed them and the GPS into my pockets and climbed into the car. I felt under the seat for the gift box containing Fred's jewelry and put an envelope containing the letter Jimmy originally had sent me next to it. Looking up, I could see that the sky was lightening to the east, but I could feel a damp wind coming off the ocean. I had to meet Tommy down on the dock at four-thirty and figured I had time to grab a couple of cups of coffee along with some doughnuts at the gas station in East Harwich then circle back to the dirt road leading to the boat yard.

I pulled in and parked next to Tom's truck. In the dark, all I could make out were the running lights on his boat tied to the dock. Grabbing the coffees and doughnuts in one hand and fishing out the GPS with the other, I picked my way down to the dock and called out. With a flick of a switch, Tommy lighted the boat up like a Christmas tree and waved me aboard.

"Tom, Jeez why all the lights?" I asked. "You're calling attention to us."

Taking a swig of the coffee I had passed over to him, he said, "That's the point. We're just a couple of mugs headed out to jig for cod or some other dumb ass fish. Think about it, it's a Saturday morning in May; so what could be more natural than going fishing even in this muck?"

"It seems thick, is this mist or fog?" I asked as I swung myself aboard. "How are we going to handle this? Let's get a game plan together."

Seeing the GPS in my left hand, he said, "Just give me the coordinates from your GPS for the waypoint, and I'll plug them into the one on my boat. We'll run out to the mark using both, plus the radar, and our eyes; we'll find the buoy. Simple enough." Tom was confident. He thumbed the starter, and the twin Mercs started with a roar and then settled down to a throaty burble.

"No, here's the problem," I said. "If we come out past Tern Island and through the mooring field to cross over the Chatham bar, we'll have to pass right by that boat I told you about yesterday. I heard last night that the owner, a real Mafioso named Ianello, is looking to highjack whoever tries to bring the drugs in. Oh and add to that we'll be right in front of the Coast Guard station. I mean they've got webcams and some pretty high powered radar too."

"I thought of that," Tom said dismissively. "With the tide almost full, we're going to be able to run the new cut in North Beach. I went through there just last week. It's dicey with no markers and the sand spits building up all the time, but I can take it slowly, watch the depth sounder, and listen for breakers. There's a rock about the size of a pickup truck on the south side of the cut. Something left over from the glacier, gotta be careful there. Do you think the skipper with a boat worth more than a million bucks will follow us through that mess even if he sees us on his radar?"

"After talking to his boss last night in Providence, I'll bet a call to watch out for me was made. I was told that whatever's out there may be worth ten million or more, so my bet is that he'll be ready to go at a moment's notice."

"Let's do this then," Tom started to say as he cast off the spring line holding us fast to the dock. "I've a buddy who's got a Boston Whaler with a whopping fifty horse Evinrude on her. He's off Cape for a while, so why don't we take his boat along with us? If we could see in this muck, she'd be right over there on her mooring. That way we make the pickup, and if your Rhode Island friend comes after us, you can take the Whaler in with the prize while I take off toward Monomoy. I'm a bigger radar target, so chances are he won't see you and will end up chasing me all the way to Nantucket."

"Yeah but," I started, "why won't he be able to see me out there too?"

"No reflection, the only thing that can make a blip on his screen is the engine housing, and with what, like a foot of freeboard, it's practically submerged with the swell that'll be running out there. He'd have better luck with Sonar," Tommy laughed at the thought.

"But if the fog breaks won't we be sitting ducks?"

"Look, we're going to get out there and back within a couple of hours of sunup, our prize is going to be smack dab in a fogbank lying right offshore with this east wind we've got." Tom's answer was definitive as he backed out of the slip and gingerly threaded out of the mooring field.

"Wait," I protested. "What about me? How am I going to get the Whaler back here through the cut in all this fog?"

"Easy, we're going out using both GPSs, so all you have to do is follow the track on the screen back to the harbor. Going out I'll show you how to zoom in for more detail so you won't miss the inlet and put her up on the beach. Here get in the Whaler and start it up. Make sure we've got enough gas," Tom said as he pulled alongside the low-sided open boat.

"Where's the key for ignition?" I asked as I climbed aboard.

"Mark always leaves on a hook underneath the center console. Lower the engine first and then fire it up," he answered.

After fumbling for the key, I worked it into the ignition and turned the battery switch to "Both." I pressed the trim button and waited until the engine hit the upright stop; finally, I opened the choke and thumbed the starter button. It caught after grinding for a couple of seconds. I backed off on the throttle and let the engine settle to an idle to warm up.

"Hey Tom," I called, "there's no fuel gauge, where do I look?"

"I think there's a tank under the deck, see if there isn't an inspection port to unscrew just under the console."

There was, and I unscrewed it to reveal a fuel fill plus a mechanical gauge showing less than a quarter of a tank of fuel.

"Tom, it's almost empty on the gauge. Will that be enough?" I asked having no idea about the size of the tank and how much fuel the engine burned.

"Yeah, it's at least a hundred gallon job, and the engine burns five-six gallons an hour at running speed. Figure we'll be only about fifteen miles off shore and add another couple to get back to the dock. It'll be fine if you don't miss the cut and have to fart around trying to find it. I'll have to remember to tell Mark or next time he takes her out that he'll be running on fumes."

I shut down the engine and raised it; tied a towing line to the bow cleat; cast off the mooring line; and hopped back aboard Tom's boat. We headed out toward the cut in North Beach that had broken through back in 2007. It was a dangerous stretch of water with no buoys to mark the shoals. I was just a passenger watching as Tom threaded his way around the shallow spots and into deep water. I couldn't see the beach on either side of the opening, but I knew when we crossed from Pleasant Bay into the Atlantic because a long swell replaced the chop, the fog thickened, and the air got a lot colder. I could barely make out the Whaler riding at the end of its painter no more than a hundred feet astern.

Tommy opened up his big Mercs and the SeaCraft rose swiftly onto a plane.

"Tommy, how fast are we going?" I shouted over the engine noise.

"Maybe fifteen knots, I don't want to lose the Whaler if the line parts. Here Dave, take the helm while I enter the coordinates from your GPS to mine. Head southeast about one-twenty degrees magnetic, and we'll be Ok for a bit. I figure at the rate we're hauling right now, we should be at the waypoint in about forty-five minutes, so let me get tracking here."

As Tom turned on my handheld GPS to get the latitude and longitude to set his own GPS, I kept one eye on the compass and the other on the radar, which was set on the twelve-mile range. I could see that we were leaving the shore quickly behind us, and there didn't appear to be any boats around us. The only blip on the radar screen was the Chatham Buoy a couple of miles southwest of us. Soon Tom had the data loaded into his boat's GPS, and both sets were showing the waypoint clearly. In fact, the LED target in the GPSs was the only thing we could see as the fog still hung heavily over the ocean's surface. The rising sun had brightened the gloom but hadn't penetrated the fog.

"Hey Tom," I shouted. "What's the accuracy of these things? The old one from my boat can be off by as much as fifty feet."

"That's about right for your Garmin, but the one on my boat has a real antenna and is supposed to be accurate to within three meters—think ten feet max. Our problem isn't going to be the accuracy of the waypoint, but where the buoy is relative to the waypoint," he said.

"Don't we just go to the waypoint and look for the buoy?"

"That sounds right, but you've got to figure that the ship was moving when the buoy was thrown overboard. Now someone could have snapped the picture, then thrown the stuff in the water, or it could have been just the opposite—gear and buoy first, then record the location. Either way there's an error based on the ship's speed from what's plotted as the waypoint and where the buoy really is," Tom called out.

"Won't that mean we'll have a harder time finding the buoy?"

"Yeah, and you've got to figure the good news is that nobody can see us wandering around in the fog, and the bad news is that we can't see the buoy in the fog," Tommy commented with a shrug of his shoulders.

"How 'bout setting the radar down low, like to an eighth of a mile, that's only two football fields, and try to pick up the buoy's reflection," I offered.

"Good thought for a smooth sea, but with this swell running, there'll be way too much clutter. That's why nobody would ever see you running away in the Whaler." Tommy said flatly. He continued, "What we'll do is get to the waypoint, then start a box pattern working from that position farther and farther out. You're the professor, can you figure out a search diagram for us?"

"Now, let's just talk our way through this. I mean if the ship was making ten knots—how many feet in nautical mile, Tom?"

"Figure about six thousand and change, it's around that I know," He shot the number back to me.

"At ten knots then the ship is moving something like six thousand feet an hour. There are sixty minutes in an hour and sixty seconds in each minute. What's that come to—sixty squared—call it thirty-six hundred. Ok, now divide the two, and the ship is making about twenty feet through the water every second. Sound right?"

"Hey not bad for an academic," Tom said. "Let's figure at most a minute between shooting the waypoint and having the gear hit the water or vice versa."

"All right, then the buoy could be anywhere inside a circle with a radius of up to twelve hundred feet. Assuming the waypoint is actually at the center. How are you going to find it in visibility like this?" I was getting skeptical.

"Once we get on station, we'll box the compass. I'll head due north for twelve hundred feet, then east for another twelve hundred, south for twelve hundred, and finally west for twelve hundred; that'll bring us back to the starting point. We'll make a second box by going south first. We just have to do all four sides in a logical order. If we don't spot it, then we'll do the whole thing again, but this time only go eight hundred feet depending on how thick the fog is. This could take some time. Try figuring out how long it'd take us to cover twelve hundred feet at five knots."

"Sure," I was pleased to be able to be useful. "Let me talk through it. Five knots figuring six thousand feet in a nautical mile is just over thirty thousand feet in an hour. Dividing that by the number of seconds in an hour is a little less than ten feet a second. Twelve hundred feet at ten feet a second means that'd take us two minutes plus to cover the distance."

"Good, we'll give ourselves a cushion," Tom said, "and go three minutes each leg. Then we can redo the box cutting our run time by thirty seconds each leg. Damn but that's almost an hour for the first box alone. After that, they'll go more quickly. Let's hope we find that buoy on the first pass."

"Let me take the Whaler to cover half the search area. That means we'll cut our time in half," I offered. "I can use the little Garmin to monitor my speed."

"Sure, that'll work. See we've a plan after all," Tom seemed pleased with himself.

-28-

We honed in on the waypoint and watched as the GPS counted down the distance to go. Tommy's big GPS had a built-in alarm that went off as we closed to within the ten-foot error zone. We didn't see a buoy floating on the ocean's surface. Tom took the boat out of gear and fiddled with the radar's monitor as I hauled the Whaler alongside eager to get started.

"Hey Tom," I called, "did anyone follow us? Can you see the shoreline on the radar?"

"Yeah, the harbor opening shows up pretty clearly because the cliff by the lighthouse is high enough. The two big radar reflectors forming the range marker to get through the gut light the screen up something wicked. I can pretty much spot where the entrance to the harbor is, but the beach on one side and the island on the other don't really show up at all—too flat," Tom responded. "There's some action; it looks like more than one boat is coming through the main channel. Probably a couple of workboats at this hour; but to be safe, I'm knocking the range down to two miles and setting the watchman."

"Tom, I've had a Furuno on my sailboat for over five years now, and I've never heard of a watchman, what are you talking about?"

"I'm building a buffer ring around us; if the radar detects something entering the zone an alarm goes off. It'll be our warning that we've got visitors," Tom answered as he adjusted the controls next to the radar screen. "If someone is targeting us, I'll get a head's up in time to head toward Monomoy Point and draw them away from you. I know that the Whaler can't be seen on radar until they're on top of you. And who'd think someone could be dumb enough to be fifteen miles to sea in almost zero visibility in something as dinky as that skiff?"

Feeling vulnerable but determined, I climbed over the rail and lowered myself into the Whaler. I called to Tom, "How am I going to let you know if I find the buoy? Think I should send up a flare?"

"Get real, and using the radio is out too. Is there one of those horns onboard—you know the ones that screw onto a can of compressed air?"

I rummaged through a gear locker on the front of the console and found an airhorn. I gave it good blast; it worked. Next, I got the engine started and was good to go.

"Ok, you go north, I'll go south, and we should cross paths back here in about ten minutes. Good luck!" I called casting myself off from Tom's boat.

Looking at the GPS, I advanced the throttle until the display showed my speed as five knots. According to its internal compass, I headed south as planned. I glanced at my watch to set the time for the three-minute run and looked over my shoulder to see when the fog swallowed up Tom's boat. I wasn't surprised that it took less than thirty seconds before I lost sight of him. We were moving apart at ten knots, I guestimated that Tom was about six hundred feet or so from me. Great, I said half out loud, one tenth of a mile visibility, fifteen miles at sea, and me sitting in a seventeen-foot open boat.

Looking right, left, ahead and astern, I saw nothing as I made my turns having run my time and distance out. I heard Tom's boat before I saw it, then it loomed out of the fog at right angles to my course. He hadn't had any luck either. We waved and slipped back under the blanket of fog. Ten minutes later, we completed the first box. My spirits were flagging, but Tom just grinned as we started down the track for a second, shorter pass. Just six minutes into the new course, I heard the screeching of an airhorn. It was Tommy; he'd found the buoy!

I gunned the engine and whirled the steering wheel to turn the boat in the direction of the horn. Even over the engine noise, I could hear Tommy blasting the horn right straight ahead. In a couple of minutes, the SeaCraft loomed large in front of me, and I throttled back. Tommy was pointing to the stern where two bright orange buoys, each about the size of a basketball floated about fifty feet apart. Wowee!

I pulled up alongside Tom's boat and made fast. He surprised me by climbing down into the Whaler saying, "It'll be easier to lift the gear into the Whaler with its low side. Besides if we've got to separate on the way in, it'll be faster if the stuff's already loaded in here."

"Are you just leaving your boat here? Aren't you going to anchor it?" I asked.

"Not a lot of wind out here, just some swells, so I don't think it'll drift too far," Tommy said confidently. "We ought to be able to hear the engines even if the visibility shuts down. Besides who wants to have to haul an anchor up if the Watchman alarm sounds?"

I cast off and backed down on the buoys. Tom used the boathook to snag the line that attached the buoy to the prizes below. As we started to pull in the line together, I pointed out to him a burlap bag wrapped around the line. He'd been right, what a simple solution; just fill the bag with salt, heave it overboard, and after whatever time, the buoy pops to the surface. Although the water was over two hundred feet deep, we had to haul up only about sixty feet of line before two stainless steel canisters broke the surface. They looked a lot like a cross between a beer keg and a scuba diver's air tank. Tom tied the line to the bow cleat and fished under the canisters for the anchor line. With a slash of his knife, the canisters were free and hauled aboard. Next, he cut the top line off coiling it on deck. We did the same thing with the second buoy. I maneuvered the Whaler back alongside the SeaCraft, shut down the engine, and we both clambered back aboard. Looking down at the four shiny canisters on the deck of the Whaler, Tom and I high-fived and started to laugh out loud. Talk about a release of nervous energy!

"All right," Tom said to me. "We did it; we found 'em. Are you sure, you don't want to look for a buyer? Those suckers must weigh over fifty pounds each; I mean they've got to be worth millions."

"No, that isn't part of the plan," I replied. "Let's just haul ass back to Ryder's Cove. I have to be in Orleans before ten o'clock, where things are going to happen quickly, I hope."

"I'm going to keep the radar alarm at two miles. I should be able to see a boat on the scope farther out than that; but if I miss, and it gets close, this thing will screech. It'll give you the time you need to get away in the Whaler. Did you leave the GPS in the Whaler?"

Yeah," I nodded, "all I have to do is follow the course line back from the waypoint to where we left the inlet. I can do that."

Tom slipped the engines into gear and headed back to Chatham as fast as we could go towing the Whaler. We were about halfway back to the inlet when all of sudden there was a piercing electronic siren coming from the radar display. A boat had come within the two-mile alarm range.

"Shit, there it is! It's almost five miles off the Chatham buoy, see it?" Tommy was pointing at a blip just inside the innermost ring of the screen. "I didn't see it at first; bleeping tub was lost in the background clutter."

"Has he seen us? Is he tracking us?" I asked nervously.

"I think so. He's headed toward our track, but we're also closing the angle heading for the beach. We're on a collision course for sure and can't wait until he gets any closer," Tom was eerily calm and continued in almost a monotone. "You take the Whaler back to the cove, and I'll sweep down toward Chatham Harbor to pull him off if he's looking for us. I can make this baby hum better than forty knots. No way can he match that speed. I'll take it around Monomoy with one foot on the beach. Tell you what, when you get in, come over to Stage Harbor, and I'll be tied up at Brad's marina."

Tom pulled back on the throttles, and the SeaCraft came off the plane while I pulled in the slack on the line to the Whaler. Getting into the Whaler and casting off took less than a minute. With the SeaCraft's outboards idling, I could hear the whump-whump of big diesel engines coming through the fog.

Tommy called to me, "Dave, keep down and steer northeast for a couple of miles, that'll minimize your profile and give me time to pull him off. Then come back to this course line and get back to Ryder's."

Leaving me no time to answer, Tommy punched the throttles and the fog swallowed up the SeaCraft. I could hear his engines roaring in the distance, and then they went silent. Oh no, I thought, what if Tommy had fouled his props on a lobster pot marker. To make matters worse I still thought I could make out a deeper, diesel like throb, which chilled me more than the damp fog and forty-degree ocean temperature. I just sat still and in shock for at least half a minute when the reassuring roar of the twin Mercs rolled through the fog to me. Tommy was on the move. Then the engines cut out again followed by their re-firing.

What was Tommy doing? Was he trying to get us caught? I couldn't wait any longer and as soon as I fired up the Whaler's outboard, the only sound I heard was its engine screaming over the churning wake. Staring straight ahead into the fog was like looking into a bag of cotton balls. No way was I going to futz around for a couple of miles out and back when I had hardly any gas. Besides, my best chance lay in getting inside the inlet as quickly as possible where I couldn't be followed. I balanced the GPS on the lip of the console and zoomed in on the display screen to be able to see if I was running the course back to the beach cut and hung on for dear life as the Whaler skimmed the ocean swells.

I must have looked at my watch every couple of minutes in anticipation, but in reality it was twenty minutes before the fog lifted considerably, and the wave action changed dramatically. I was nearing land—the GPS said so too! The tide was ebbing and running hard through the inlet kicking up a horrible chop. The long swells of the Atlantic had given way to a short, choppy sea that threatened to swamp the Whaler. I could see pretty well now, but what I saw was frightening. The opening into Pleasant Bay was full of cascading whitecaps. I could see the land on either side of the cut, but I didn't see any smooth water at all. Working the Whaler toward the north shore, I hoped to be able to run into the inlet on a diagonal keeping the worst of the seas just off the bow. The good part of this little rugged Whaler lay in its unsinkable design; the bad part was the low freeboard, which made it more easily swamped. Resigning myself to getting wet, I pulled the drain plug from the transom so the boat would automatically bail if I shipped a sea onboard and eased back on the throttle. As I slowed down, the Whaler pitched and yawed; she stuck her nose into a couple of big ones and took them green over the side; before I could panic in this maelstrom, I shot through the rip into calm water. I laughed aloud at my good fortune, and began my run into Ryder's Cove shouting, "Home is the sailor from the sea!"

The rest of the trip was uneventful, the water finally sloshed out through the drain hole, and I could see both shorelines all the way in. Not having a dinghy, I couldn't put Mark's boat back on the mooring, so I beached it just to the right of the boat ramp. A bunch of fishermen's skiffs were hauled up on the beach, and I made fast the Whaler's painter to a tree trunk at the water's edge. Next, I realized how good terra firma felt under my feet. My plan was to leave the canisters along with the buoys and line lying on the deck of the Whaler in plain sight. Anyone looking would think some boater was getting ready to set out his moorings for the summer season. For the time being, they'd be safe enough, I hoped.

I'd gotten wet out by the inlet, but my foul weather gear had protected me pretty well. My feet though were soaked and cold; I had an extra pair of socks and my old workboats in the SUV, which made all the difference. With the heater on full blast, I pulled out of the parking lot and turned left on Rt 28 heading back into Chatham. I stayed straight at the lights and continued down Shore Rd just as I had done yesterday. The fog had lifted enough for me to see Tern Island and the anchorage off Chatham Bars Inn. Peaches 'n Cream wasn't in the harbor, so it had to have been her that was trying to intercept Tom's boat out there. Farther along I pulled into the parking lot opposite the Coast Guard station and Chatham Light. I could see out to the line of breakers, and sure enough, there was Peaches 'n Cream picking her way through the channel back into the anchorage. Backing out, I headed for Bridge St and the marina knowing that Tom had outrun the competition.

Crossing over the Mitchell River Bridge, I could see on my left Tom's boat pulled into a slip at the marina. I parked between a couple of sailboats still under their winter tarps and made my way around to find Tom. He walked up the dock and was all smiles.

"We did it," he called to me. "We made one hell of a run out there."

"I just got a glimpse of Ianello's boat off Lighthouse Beach. It looks like she's headed back to the harbor empty-handed," I was in a gloating mood too.

We got into my SUV for the ride back to Tom's truck at Ryder's Cove.

"Did you have any problems getting away from him? What was all that starting and stopping for?" I asked.

"Naw, piece of cake," Tom said. "Ever go out into the National Seashore in the spring and flush a quail that's got a nest on the ground to protect? Well she staggers off leading you away from the nest with a great imitation of a busted wing. I did the same thing with the SeaCraft. Ran it up and then shut it down as if something was wrong just to make sure I had his attention. I turned into him after you took off in the Whaler and ran just under his stern. I think I caught a glimpse of the hull as I passed, but I know I was off the stern because I jumped the wake. He came around and tried to catch me, but wide open he probably can't do more than twenty-five. No busted wing for me 'cuz I kicked ass to at least forty."

"Weren't you worried you run into another boat especially off Monomoy?" I asked.

"Oh yeah, but I put her right up on the beach and just hauled ass toward the buoy off Bearse Shoal. Ever been there? Ever been caught in the rips? I started to pick up blips just inside of the shoal and figured they were guys looking to land the first striper of the season. I slowed down when I got into them and worked my way around the point and lost the big boat. I don't think he dared get into the rips; I mean he's gotta draw at least five feet or more, and when there's a swell running you can have breakers even at high water in spots. Last time I saw him on the radar, he had turned back off Bearse and looked like he was trying to find his way over to the channel through Pollack Rip, but good luck with that." Tom explained.

I parked next to his truck, and said, "Tom, I really appreciate you putting it on the line for me today. Now

I've told you about them wanting to trade Fred for the numbers that'll tell them where the drug drop is. I've only got 'till ten o'clock to get them what they're after. I'm going to have to leave Mark's boat tied to that tree over there. Want me to help you move your boat back here, maybe later this afternoon or tomorrow morning?"

"Dave, I can leave my boat at the marina for a while without a hassle. Maybe I can get you to go striper fishing with me next week."

"Sounds good, I'll give you a call as soon as all of this nonsense is over. I'll bring the beer and spring for a fill-up too. This afternoon, if all goes well, I can grab a dinghy and take care of Mark's boat. Thanks for the help, man, you've been a life saver." I said and meant it too. Tom shook my hand, slapped me on the arm, and headed for his truck. I watched him cross Rt 28 onto Old Comers before I slogged back to the tied up Whaler and wrestled two of the cylinders into the back of my SUV.

-29-

The clock on the dash read just past nine-thirty giving me over twenty-five minutes to get to the town landing at the bottom of Cove Rd in Orleans. It'd be close, but I thought I'd be able to make it if I wasn't stuck behind some ancient crone determined not to drive within ten miles an hour of the speed limit. Being still early in the morning and still early in the spring, I made the turn off Rt 28 onto Cove Rd with time to spare. I parked past the public landing ramp and dock in one of the spaces reserved for the Orleans Yacht Club whose clubhouse was adjacent to the landing ramp. The trash barrel I planned to use was between the ramp and dock.

I took a moment to turn on the GPS and found the screen containing the waypoint. Remembering what Tom had told me, it took only a couple of taps on the screen to delete the information completely. Pulling up the menu called "Tracks," I hit the delete key. If it worked then the tracks I'd used to get out there and back this morning would be erased. Finally, I opened the back of the unit and pulled out the batteries in the hope that all information would be lost. Reaching under the seat for the gift bag, I exchanged the envelope with the original note, for Fred's ring and watch. Putting those in my pants pocket, I shoved the tissue down hard on top to wedge the envelope in the bag more securely and walked over to the trash barrel. With what I hoped would look like a casual toss to anyone watching, I dropped the bag into the barrel, got in my car and drove back up Cove Rd taking a left onto Rt 28.

Pulling in to the parking lot of the Yardarm, another watering hole favored by locals, I reversed directions and drove toward Cove Rd. There's a museum on the corner with a good sized parking lot and a great view of Town Cove, the dock, the landing ramp, and of course, the trash barrel. I leaned forward over the steering wheel and scanned the area looking for anyone headed toward the barrel. A few minutes later as the ten o'clock deadline passed, I watched as a middle-aged man with a distinctive gait walked down Cove Rd past where I parked and toward the trash barrel. I knew him; I knew that he had been sent to pick up the gift bag; and more importantly, I knew where he was going to take it. As I watched his progress, I called Tiny on my cell phone and told him what I'd done and what I now knew. He said he'd make a call and get back to me. I watched and saw the gift bag lifted out of the trash and disappear into a coat pocket. By the time he had walked back up Cove Rd and crossed over Rt 28, I got the return call from Tiny.

Pulling a U-turn in the parking lot, I drove up Cove Rd, took a left through the bank parking lot, and then headed toward the rotary. I parked in the pizza joint's lot prepared to wait. Fishing around in my pants pocket, I dug out a scrap of paper with another set of coordinates on it. I put the batteries back into the hand held GPS, turned it on, and recreated Waypoint Alpha. About ten minutes later the same character with the unique loping stride was cutting through the parking lot. Getting out I feigned surprise and called to him, "Jeff, hey what are you doing here? Long time no see!"

He looked quizzically at me with a smile and waved hello in a child-like fashion. Jeff was another of my motley crew from the mental health clinic whom I'd lost to the day treatment program over time. In this case, it wasn't too bad because Jeff was more mentally challenged than psychotic. He lived in a group home sponsored by a local church and worked part of everyday in the local supermarket breaking down produce boxes and bagging groceries. The rest of the day, he spent in the day treatment program where he actually was learning how to improve his social skills and gain proficiency at those activities needed for independent living. It didn't matter that he was in his early forties; he still had a shot at making it on his own.

"Doc, doc, how are ya?" Jeff called to me. "I haven't seen you forever, but I'm doing good, real good."

"You're looking good too Jeff," I replied. "I'm glad to see that you're getting some exercise and not just chowing down on the doughnuts at the day program."

"No, no, I walk all the time." He said.

"I see you're headed over to the day program now." I added. "I'll bet Mike had you pick up a package for him, and you're taking it there now."

Jeff's eyes opened wide and he gasped, "How did you know that?"

"Remember Jeff, I've told you before that I'm a psychologist, and I know everything," I teased him. "Tell you what, I'm on my way over to see Mike right now, so why don't I take the package to him for you?"

"Oh no, no, no," Jeff sputtered. "Mike said it was real important that I get the package and bring it right to him. He'd be upset with me if I didn't do what he said."

"Come on, Jeff, I know that you're doing this for the money Mike promised you. I'll double what he's giving you and throw in some money for lunch at the Dairy Queen too."

I think lunch at the DQ won him over because his smile went from ear to ear. Jeff fished out the gift bag from his jacket pocket, and I dug a twenty-dollar bill out of my wallet and gave it to him.

"Fair enough?" I asked.

"Yes, are you sure Mike won't be mad at me?"

"I'll fix it with Mike, don't worry. I'm going there right now." I said swinging the gift bag by its handle as I started over toward the day program. Looking over my shoulder, I saw that Jeff had turned around and was hoofing it back to the Dairy Queen on the double. Now things could get dicey.

Pulling into the day program's parking lot, I removed Jimmy's note from the gift bag and tore it up. In its place, I put the GPS. Looking around the lot, I saw a couple of cars. I recognized Mike's old pickup, and I knew where I'd seen the black caddy with smoked glass windows before. I walked closer and saw that there were a couple of long scrapes on the passenger's side tinged with the same yellow as Fred's car. In addition, there was an almost new Lexus right by the door. Climbing the back stairway, I listened at the landing to the second floor but didn't hear any voices. I tried the door—locked. Figuring all or nothing, I headed up to the third floor that had always been vacant and locked. Now apparently it was being used for the double D program or at least that's what I'd been led to believe. I pushed on the door and entered a large open area with two doors at the far end. The room itself had what looked like several picnic tables and benches set up. Each table was littered with plastic envelopes, heat sealers, digital scales, and bright clip-on lights. Three men sat at one of the tables; I recognized only one, Kevin Turcotte.

Ignoring him, I moved directly to the doors at the far end. The one on the right had a padlock on it, but the left one seemed simply closed. Shoving it open, I found both Mike Pitts, the day treatment program's director, and Gerry Pence, the clinic's administrative guru, seated at a desk working on a computer. Both looked up and did a double take.

Throwing the gift bag on the desk, I said, "Here Mike, here's my GPS with all the info you want. I cracked the code and downloaded the picture with all the details."

Mike grabbed for the bag, pulled out the portable GPS, and toggled the on/off switch. After about a ninety-second warm-up, he pushed the page and program buttons then hit the "Go To" key. Looking at the screen showing the location of Waypoint Alpha, he screamed, "What the fuck have you done Knight?"

"Don't worry Mike; those coordinates put you right on top of the Provincetown monument, got your climbing shoes on?"

"You're a fool, asshole, you'll be sorry you screwed with us," he threatened.

Of the five men, I knew Mike Pitts was the one who'd stand and fight. He didn't like me at all, and he was scrappy. Pence, on the other hand, was the type who never got his hands dirty—figuratively or literally. He always had others do the heavy lifting. I had to get to him before the others got to me.

"Hey Pence—I wasn't going to pronounce it 'Pencay' as he had corrected me on Thursday—tell your boy to be nice or else you won't get your drugs back."

Pence looked aghast, he had paled at the sight of me; Pitts looked steamed, his face was red; and behind me, I heard noises letting me know that Turcotte and the others had entered the room.

"Hey Mike," I heard Turcotte say. "Want us to correct this jerk's attitude? He's led us on a wild goose chase too long; I've got just the thing." He poked me in the back with what probably was the same baseball bat that had bashed in Jimmy's head.

"Let's get some things straight first," I asserted. "Number One, there are no drugs offshore anymore; Number Two, I have the canisters of drugs; Number Three, you'll get them as soon as Fred's freed; and Number Four, poke me with that bat again, Turcotte, and I'll make you eat it!"

"Oh yah Knight, what makes you so tough?"

"I'm not so tough," I answered. "It's you who's got no stones. You bitch and moan about life screwing you as an excuse to shoot up. You've spent the last dozen years on the nod, so don't try to talk tough to me. It's time to call off your running dogs Pence." I'm in trouble, I thought, Could I bluff my way through?

I was standing off to one side so I could see everyone at the same time. Besides Turcotte, the other two had the same wasted look of drug addicts about them. One was sallow, thin, and could've been HIV positive, the other was bigger, had slicked back hair, but his eyes were somewhere else. I'd bet he was the one who'd acted as if he was a New Jersey gangster when he first handed the gift bag to Deb at the clinic. Right now, knowing what I knew and confronting the five of them gave me back a little of the wiseass swagger that'd been missing for most of the past week. Would Pence cave under the pressure?

"Guys take him down," Pence ordered. Clearly, he wasn't a visitor to the operation; he was the head of it and was in the know about what had been going on all along.

Oh holy shit, Batman, I was in for it now. I was so pumped up from having found the drugs and sniffing out Pence's scam, that I'd forgotten these guys had killed Jimmy and kidnapped Fred. Not only that but they'd tossed my office and home where Toby died trying to fend them off. Once more, I'd fucked up.

Turcotte hit me across the left shoulder with the bat sending me sprawling into Pence, who tried to get distance between us. I grabbed his blazer's lapels pivoting him so his back was to Turcotte who couldn't check his swing. Pence howled as he got cracked a good one right in the ribs. The skinny kid got an angle on me and kicked me in the thigh. It burned but didn't have any real weight behind it. Then the swarthy, heavy set, Elvis look-alike, landed a roundhouse right to my right temple. I went back into the wall with a thud letting loose my grip on Pence. Seeing nothing but stars, I felt my knees buckle as Turcotte brought his bat to bear on my kneecap. I was kept upright by Turcotte's buddies as they pinned me to the wall.

"My turn," I heard Pitts' voice hiss as I tried to clear my vision. He slammed a couple of hard rights into my side and then a vicious left hook into my spleen. I struggled to get free and broke away from the skinny kid holding on to my left arm. I managed to club a left to Pitts' head when Turcotte using the bat as a spear knocked the wind out of me. I collapsed to the floor. Now, I thought, I'm in over my head.

I saw past the next kick to my kidneys when the door to the program room flew open. Tommy burst into the room, all six feet four inches of him, carrying his axe. I got kicked again but winced more as Tommy lowered the lumber on the first thug—Turcotte. Using the handle of the axe like a hockey player, he crosschecked Turcotte into the wall behind me, then using the flat of the axe he knocked the bigger guy into tomorrow. The little one raised his hands in surrender while Pence grabbed at Pitts' arm to restrain him.

Turcotte half turned looking glassy-eyed from having hit the wall hard, and the skinny guy bent over to help the heavy one sit up from the floor where he was trying to shake the cobwebs out of his head. I scrambled to my feet and taking one step forward planted my size ten work boot with as much force as I could muster into his back.

"How'd you like that, big guy," I wasn't feeling charitable at all. "That one's not for me but for my dog you bastards let die."

I whaled away at the three of them with my boots and fists. Drawing my arm back for another salvo to Turcotte's head, Tommy pulled me off with a heavy hand on my shoulder and roughly shoved me into a chair. Waving his axe menacing, Tommy lined all five of my assailants up against the wall and then cleaved the desk chair in two for good measure. Nobody moved.

-30-

Sitting in the chair I was aware of the pains up and down my body and realized how close to joining Jimmy I'd come. Looking up at Tommy as he stood there with his axe across his chest like a rifle at the ready, I said with labored breath, "Thanks man, but how did you know to come here?"

"I was worried about you, especially after you told me you were going to return the GPS coordinates. Do that and you'd have been dead. I looped back around to Rt 28 in time to follow you. I met that mutt Jeff in the DQ parking lot and got him to tell me where you were going. I was outside on the landing for a while when I heard the fight break out. I gave you enough time to take 'em all; but I got antsy, good thing huh? Looks like you needed help."

"Tommy, Tommy, I owe you big time, maybe even more than a couple of beers down at the Squire," I tried to make light of what had just gone on and how lucky I was to be alive.

"Now that we've had our fun," I said to the group up against the wall, "it's time to get down to business. We are going to start with Dr. Dorfman. You need to know that I've pulled up the two canisters of dope, and we can play let's make a deal only after I hear from Fred that he's home safely."

Leaning across the desk, I picked up my GPS and pocketed it. Out of the corner of my eye, I saw a frown pass across Tommy's brow when he heard me say there were only two canisters.

"So why don't we start now? Here," I said, "tossing his watch and college ring on the desk top, he'll want these."

At first, nobody moved, but after a moment's pause, Pence reasserted himself saying to Kevin and the other two, "You heard the man, go get him and bring him in here."

He then held up his hand stalling his workers while he said to me, "I don't know what kind of shape he'll be in. He's been, ah, how you say sedated for the last forty hours or so."

"What you bastards do, shoot him up with some of your dope?" I demanded

"No, nothing like that," Pence elaborated. "When they found out that he wasn't you, they calmed him down with a shot of valium. We've been keeping him in La La land ever since. He's probably more than a bit unstable on his feet, and I'll bet he won't remember much after he got snatched."

"Where is he? Over there in that locked room?" I pointed. "Open it up, I want to see him, and then you take him home once I make sure he's able to function. You'll have to call someone to get his car and make sure you pay for it too."

Pence nodded his assent to the three workers. Kevin unlocked the door, went inside, and came back a minute later holding Fred upright. As much as I didn't like Fred, he was pathetic—all rumpled still wearing his suit from the college three days ago and barely able to stand. His eyes were unfocused, his speech slurred; he was in a semi-coma not knowing who I was, where he was, or what day it was. He was a pitiable rag doll.

Turcotte half-pushed Fred toward me in a "you want him, you've got him" gesture. Close up Fred was even worse with a three-day stubble, rank breath, and an awful odor emanating from his suit pants. His had soiled himself more than once as he'd been left to rot in that locked room. I was pissed big time.

"Easy Fred, just take it easy," I tried to be reassuring. "Need some water?

"Turcotte," I fixed my eye on him, "get Dr. Dorfman some water, and you two," gesturing to the others, "lie him down, take off his tie, and clean him up.

"This sucks you bastards. What's wrong with all of you?" I hissed. "Your screwing around with IM benzos could have triggered a heart attack and killed him. Besides, you didn't even know if he was taking any other meds that could have wiped him out. You're lucky he's still alive.

"Forget taking him home; he's going to the hospital to get detoxed. With what you've pumped into him, he could easily have a seizure to boot," I added.

I looked over to Pence and asked, "How do you want to play this? I can call 911 for him, and an ambulance along with cops will show up; or you can have your 'A' team take him to the emergency room to get him admitted as having accidently OD'd."

"Let's have the guys take him to the hospital, will that work for you?" Pence asked.

"Yes, but he's not to be dropped off on the steps of the emergency room. I want that one," I said gesturing toward the swarthier looking punk, "to go with him and stay there answering the triage nurse's questions about how much benzo you shot him up with. And stay with him until he's admitted, because I'll call patient information to confirm he's all right before we even talk about turning over your drug cache."

"What if the cops get called?" the big fellow didn't sound too happy.

"Then, my friend, you take the fall, and either dummy-up or rat out all your buddies here," there was no sympathy in my voice. "Get going now, and be gentle with him down the stairs.

I watched as Fred was roughly helped out of the room and down the stairs by the two guys whose names I never got. Leaning over the table, I grabbed Fred's jewelry and re-pocketed it. No way was I going to trust these bozos with his stuff. From the corner of my eye, I noticed that Kevin had sidled to the far side of the desk during the commotion and picked up the baseball bat. He had it at his side and remained behind in the room.

I looked at him and laughed, "Hey asshole, didn't anyone ever tell you not to bring a bat to an axe fight?" Without waiting for an answer, I said, "Tommy take that bat from Turcotte, but grab it with a towel to keep your prints from getting on it; it's probably a murder weapon.

"Turcotte, you're not needed here. Go get Fred's car back on the road even if you have to call a tow truck. Change the flat tire and get it back to his house. Dr. Dorfman lives at 980 Greenleaf Circle in Dennis. Call me on my cell, the number's 518-239-4606, when his car is back in his driveway. Take Pitts' truck and maybe save a towing charge."

Looking over at Pence, I said, "Write down the number for Turcotte and stick it in his shirt pocket or else he'll forget what he's supposed to do. Get me his number while you're at it."

Shifting my attention back to Turcotte I finished, "When you call I'll have instructions for you. Right now, I have things to discuss with your bosses. Just go, and we'll keep the Louisville Slugger."

-31-

"Well boys, it's just after ten-thirty, and we've got about half an hour before they get Fred to the hospital, and maybe another hour before he gets admitted. It'll take Turcotte that long to haul Fred's car out of the thicket next to Cedar Pond where they stashed it. So we've plenty of time for you to tell me your tale of woe, and we can make a deal for the two cylinders full of dope I've just unloaded."

Tommy looked at me askance as if I had planned all along to trade for the dope and cut him out of the deal with my highfalutin moral talk. Even more menacing, Pitts looked at me as if he was sizing me up for an attack. I said, "Mike, it's two on two, but you've got Pence on your side with his hanky stuffed in his sport coat pocket while I've got Tom here with his axe. You're out numbered, but if you want to bring it on, I'm still in the mood for some payback."

I think Mike actually was mulling over his course of action when I said, "Don't even think about it, Mike. If you clobber me, I'm not telling where your precious stuff is. Hey, let's go out into the main room so we can all sit down and figure out how to divide up the booty."

Pitts scowled but followed Gerry's lead as he walked out of the small office and sat down at one of the picnic tables. Pence started by saying, "What do you need to know, and how much of a cut are you interested in? We can work together on this; it's just the cost of doing business. There's something here for both you and your friend."

We squared off with Tommy keeping a watchful eye on Pitts who seemed to be itching for a fight while I went over to first picnic table with Pence.

"Yeah right," I said surveying the tabletop. "What do we have here, a production line for dope?"

"That's exactly what we've built," Pence answered somewhat proudly. "It's a state of the art assembly line for processing and packaging heroin and cocaine. Look we've taken all of the guess work out of cutting the heroin down to the sixty percent purity we need using these blenders. All we have to do is drop the heroin in this side and the filler on the other. The system is programmed to weigh, drop, and mix exactly four hundred grams of sugar, or whatever we're using for filler, to every six hundred grams of heroin. If we wanted to recalibrate and cut the heroin higher or lower we'd just program it in here."

"Then what, once you step on the junk and weigh it out, can you automatically bag it?" I asked.

"Close, this thing pretty much runs itself, and Mike here put together most of the pieces," Pence continued. "Take a look at this Ferris wheel gadget with all of the little cups on it. He got half of this stuff from a candy shop in P-town where they used it to mix and weigh out some sort of granola mix. Each cup holds exactly one bag of dope. The dope falling into the cup moves it forward where it drops into these aluminum foil precut squares on the circular frame. All someone has to do is pull them off and fold them together. Result—a dime bag, which of course with inflation sells for twenty-five dollars. We use these little zip lock type bags to presort and then fill a bigger freezer bag with each dealer's order. Yah, I'd say it's an assembly line all right."

"And I suppose that table over there weighs and bags the coke?" I pointed to the picnic table on the left.

"Yes, but I never did know why cocaine is sold by the half sixteenth of an ounce. We just make up fifty bags per ounce of coke and call it even. I mean it's not as if our users are going to complain to the Better Business Bureau that they've been short changed," he laughed at the irony of his own remark.

"Right now we're pushing about two pounds of heroin a week mostly here on the Cape, but our goal is to double or even triple production by moving off Cape big time. Our profit per pound is just under fifty thousand dollars, but if we ramp up the volume, we can cut way down on the bite taken by the fixed costs. Ideally, we want to make a quarter million bucks a week profit for ourselves. Ain't America a wonderful country?" Pence grinned at me.

"Your costs have to be squat," I responded. "All you have to do is use guys like Jeff, from whom I got the gift box by the way, as coolies and hope as you've said he doesn't sneeze on your production line. I'll bet you pay Turcotte and the others you've hired with dope. How do you plan to expand your racket?"

"Well, I've become the field administer for half a dozen mental health clinics all owned by HarborBay Collaborative out of Middleboro. That gives me access to a mentally disturbed population from Brockton to New Bedford to Plymouth and the Cape. Even better, I'm doing double duty for Ramparts that has drug clinics in all of these places too. "

"Yeah so?" I wasn't getting it.

"Oh, it's all about our ability to distribute our products and contain our costs" Pence was gloating. "First we use this day treatment program to process and package the coke and heroin. In a couple of months, we'll have at least a couple of more production plants like this to spread out our risk and shorten our supply lines.

"As you put it Dr. Knight, we've got a ready supply of workers at real cheap rates unless they sneeze a lot. In addition, I use my people to deliver the product to the street dealers. I mean nobody, but nobody, wants to see the mentally ill around. They're invisible and of course they're nuts so even if they get tumbled who'd believe anything they said."

"What a model, using the mentally disabled as slave labor. You're a regular cross between Fagin and Simon Legree," I snorted in derision.

"I need the dopers from the Ramparts clinics to work the streets; they're the ones who make the contacts, cut the deals, and collect the money. I pay mostly in dope, but I also need a few workers like Pitts and Turcotte to be the glue for the whole operation so I throw in some cash too. The best part is that I'm able to go from clinic to clinic with a week's worth of dope in my briefcase and nobody's the wiser. No, I take that back, the best part is that I've the final pass at the books for all the clinics so I get to launder the money. Folks have to pay for their treatments at the clinics, and if they pay in cash then it's untraceable. I'd say we've got a tiger by the tail on this one."

"That's pretty slick, I'll admit, who'd go looking for a dope ring inside a drug rehab clinic? What about Pete at Ramparts or Jen and MaryBeth at the Eastham clinic, are they in on this scam too?" I asked.

"No," Pence admitted. "Pete's just a wonderfully naïve warrior who's never met a drug addict he didn't want to treat. The more bodies coming through his door, the happier he is. To add the frosting on the cake, the more drugs we distribute, the more addicts we get seeking treatment, and the more money the clinic makes."

"What about the mental health clinic?" I insisted. "You can charm the Birkenstocks off MaryBeth, but Jan's way too savvy for you to cook her books."

"Ah well, you're right there. It's more complicated at the Eastham clinic," he admitted. "I was able to get Pitts here hired, we go back a long time together. Then I was able to get him to convince MaryBeth to isolate this program from the rest of the clinic. I understand you had quite the reputation for hanging around here and being involved with the clientele. By stopping that, I've built a firewall so MaryBeth has no idea what's happening over here."

"And Jen?" I persisted.

"I do have to worry about Jen because she's sharp enough to double check and find out I've been cooking their books. Soon I'm going to try to get her kicked upstairs to the corporate level and out of my hair. Right now though, I'm able to pay for this program at both clinics with drug money and funnel the state's money into our bank accounts. I've set up a non-profit just to be able to deposit legit checks and pay expenses with tainted bucks."

"And I suppose," I interjected, "that you've already set up an offshore account to stash the profits."

"But of course," Pence was expansive as he wanted to explain the value of his growing empire.

I had to admit that Pence was probably as close to a classic anti-social psychopath as I'd encountered in quite a while. For him, being right was what made him happy and being wrong just the opposite. There were no morals, scruples, or even adherence to the law; just what got him what he wanted. Sure, he could be charming and talk a good game, but at the end of the day, whatever lined his pockets was the right choice for him to make.

The trilling of my cell phone broke the spell. I checked the screen and saw it was the number Pence gave me for Turcotte. Contrary to instructions, but typical, he'd gone to the hospital with the others in the Caddy. According to him, Fred had been admitted for a drug overdose and was being treated. Apparently, everyone in the ER thought he'd be all right; that's all he knew. The three of them had just left to retrieve the car, and that he'd call me when they dropped it off in Fred's driveway in Dennis. I told him that they had no more than an hour to get the job done and hung up.

"Fred's been admitted to the hospital," I told Pence. "I'll tell them where the drugs are stashed when they let me know his car has been taken care of."

"Well, there's not much we can do about that now." Pence picked up where he had left off as if Fred being in the hospital was meaningless to him. "What we have to do is bring you onboard as a therapist here. Your friend can make big money with us too. That way you'll both be able to prevent any more tragedies."

"Do you have any specifics or is this all in the realm of the hypothetical?" I asked wanting to know more about Pence and his thought processes.

"Well seeing as how you've come to us, we need to find a place for you in our business model and convince you that working with us is the best alternative," Pence was delusional; he truly believed he was the center of the universe.

"How are you going to take care of both of us, now that Tom here is in the mix?" I asked.

"Well we don't have the cash reserves to pay you both off, and quite frankly, having you two walk away leaves too many loose ends." Pence was nonplussed and slick. "Why don't I clear it with MaryBeth so you get to work out of the day treatment program like you used to. It would be good for all of us because you could screen for potential trouble spots like Farnsworth, and we'd be able to isolate them from the get-go. I'm sure we could find a good way to sweeten the pot; I mean it wouldn't take much to beat your hourly rate at the either clinic."

"And me?" Tommy was still a little bit pissed thinking that I was selling him out.

"Depends on what you can do for us," Pence replied. "What's your gig, and how can we use it?"

"I run a tree cutting business and general landscape work on the lower Cape," Tom answered with flat affect.

"That's great, we can use you easily," Pence was expansive. "What a transition, sending our day treatment crew out to do real jobs for real money. I can see it now; we'll get you a contract from our non-profit front to provide some on-the-job training. That way we can handle more clients and further confuse the clinics if they try to locate someone."

"And what would I have to do with your drug running business?" Tom pressed.

"Small risk, big reward," Pence was winging it now. "Think about it, who'd ever look in the bed of a truck for a bag of dope buried under a bunch of branches and leaves. It's a perfect cover. We can expand your business all the way off-Cape by getting you contracts for landscaping services at the drug and mental health clinics that I now control. You in?"

"Sure, why not?" Tom sounded less than enthusiastic.

"Now that you both have joined up, anything else needed to clear the air?" Pence said with a smug smile.

"I've a couple," I said. "Tell me about the missing session note for Jimmy at the clinic? Was that your work or do you have someone else inside?"

"No, I pulled it to keep you off track about any link between Turcotte and Farnsworth. Didn't work did it?" Pence said with a shrug.

"One more thing," I went on. "What made you decide to throw that kid, Rudkowski, to the wolves? I've heard that the cops are planning to bust him for Jimmy's murder."

"Another misfortune of war," Pence replied smoothly. "Mike knew of Farnsworth's dislike for the kid, so I figured who better to take the fall?"

We'll see about that, I thought but said aloud, "That's all I've got, looks like we're all members of the board."

Pence and Pitts solemnly nodded and looked resigned to the partnership. I'm sure, however, they figured they'd get a chance to use my skull for batting practice by Turcotte just as soon as Tommy's back was turned.

-32-

Before anything else could be said, my phone rang again. It was Turcotte telling me that they had pulled Fred's car out of the field by Cedar Pond and changed the tire for him. After driving the car to his house, they dropped the keys through the mail slot.

"Now we've done our part, where'd you stash the drugs?" Turcotte was insistent and had a nasty tone to his voice.

"I left the canisters in the boat at Ryder's Cove, do you know where that is?" I kept my anger in check.

"Is that the place at the end of Old Comers Road across Rt 28 by the town landing?" Turcotte asked.

"Yes, that's the place, and look for a Whaler tied to a tree just to the left of the ramp at the landing. There's a bunch of dinghies pulled up there, and the Whaler should be aground at the far end. There are two canisters onboard. Just bring them back intact, and we'll open them here. If anyone asks you, just say that you are working with Mark, it's his boat, to set out moorings." I said and cut the connection.

Turning to Pence I asked, "So how come in this glorious scheme you had to torture and kill Jimmy Farnsworth?"

"No, no, that was just an unfortunate accident" he protested.

"It was no accident, nobody gets all their fingers broken, their arms and chest burned, and whacked over the head with a baseball bat by accident." I was getting angry again.

"No," he protested. "I don't know anything about torture. I wouldn't have condoned that, that's not my way."

"Ok, have it your way and tell us your story."

"Farnsworth was driving clients from the clinic in Wareham to New Bedford. We distributed the product

215

to the local dealers using the mentally ill from the Wareham clinic and not from here. This gave us some separation in case someone wanted to talk or was pressured to talk. Farnsworth was a little spacey, but he really loved to drive around especially the highways, so for gas money we had someone to move the product and people too. But then the system fell apart."

"How so? And you haven't got to killing Jimmy yet." I wanted an answer, not a description of Pence's business model.

"We knew we were pushing off Cape to get a foothold in the New Bedford market and anticipated some resistance. We lost some product, and a couple of our boys got picked up by the competition and shook down for answers. But as I said, the best part of the operation has been that they know nothing and typically are out of their minds. For the most part, we flew under the radar and were invisible. A couple of months ago in March, Mike got Jimmy to drive a carful to New Bedford. Some street thugs, I mean real goons like out of the Sopranos or something, grabbed one of the runners and beat him up pretty good. Stealing his dope wasn't enough; they beat him so badly that his spleen ruptured along with one of his kidneys. Jimmy found him lying in a pool of blood. The kid who was beaten, name of Dan or Danny or something, died in the ER at St. Luke's. Farnsworth had picked him up, but he just dumped him in the ER parking lot and then came all apart. He just took off without picking up any of the others and was all freaked out. Mike really worked on trying to settle him down, but apparently it was the blood on the car seats that Farnsworth couldn't take."

"Jimmy was paranoid enough without having to find some guy beaten to death practically right in front of him," I insisted. "You've got to remember that Jimmy saw his car as his friend, so the blood wasn't human, it was from his car. In Jimmy's tortured logic, he'd hurt his friend, his car. But that still doesn't get us to the next step. Stop stalling."

"Right, you see that the problem was that he was great for us to use. I mean with his temper and paranoia, nobody wanted anything to do with him. If you were normal, you just wanted out of his way especially with the disgusting pelvis thrusting thing he did. The mistake Mike here made was to rely on him too much not realizing how limited his thought processes really were."

"What you call 'disgusting pelvis thrusting' is an akathisia that comes from the drugs he was given. It wasn't something he wanted to do, but that still doesn't sound like a reason for murder," I interrupted. "Cut to the chase and let me know what happened. After all I'm the one who's spent most of the week getting grilled by the state cops."

"You know the three amigos that escorted your friend to the ER? Well there used to be four of them, but one, Joe Danneo, OD'd and died about two weeks ago" Pence explained. "He was working right over there when he snagged some of our uncut dope. He couldn't wait to get out of here and shot up on the way home. They found him at the park-n-ride off Rt 6 in Harwich. Joe was hooked up with some local fishermen and was our go-to guy for bringing in the dope from the drop site. When the picture with the position for the drop embedded in it was sent to us, it was addressed to him. Problem was that Mike was still trying to settle Jimmy down and having him do small stuff like pick up the mail. Well Joe had died when Jimmy picked up the envelope addressed to him; apparently, he didn't know what to do with it. We figured he talked to you or worse gave it to you. Am I right?"

I nodded in agreement, and Pence continued, "Turcotte and the guys tried to get him to tell them, but when they pushed, Farnsworth went all squirrelly on them. I mean talk about raving. We were sure that drop had been made and sure that the picture had been sent to us; all we needed was the logon information. Farnsworth had to have done something with it. What happened was an accident. They grabbed Farnsworth from behind the drug clinic and took him down to Nobska Point at night to scare him into telling. I guess things got a little out of hand when they tried to get him to own up about talking to you. He broke loose and ran, I mean just ran, straight down the face of the riprap until he got into the rockweed below the high tide mark. He slipped and jammed his foot between two rocks and broke his leg. He went down hard and smashed his head on the rocks. That's it, the guys went down to help him but saw he was dead. They left and tried to track you down after that."

"That's bullshit," I was steamed at this ridiculous story. "First of all, your three goons picked Jimmy up on Friday afternoon behind the drug clinic. He had my card with my hours at the drug clinic on the back. He was watching the parking lot hoping to find me. They held on to him for three days, probably in the same room where you stashed Fred, and hurt him badly just to get him to talk. When he couldn't or didn't, they disposed of the body at the other end of the Cape to keep anyone from sniffing around Jimmy's home territory."

"Believe what you will," Pense argued. "I told you I don't condone torture, and I didn't order his death either."

I turned to the picnic table where the bat lay and picked it up carefully using a paper towel to hold it by the handle. I shoved it menacingly back under Pence's nose. "Look carefully," I hissed. "Tell me what you see on the barrel of this bat."

"I don't know," he stammered. "I'm not a forensic scientist; it looks like some scrapes and brown stuff."

"When this gets to the state's crime lab," I explained, "the brown smudges will turn out to be

Jimmy's blood and the scrapes will match the wood slivers dug out of Jimmy's skull. There was no accident, no falling down the slope, and no 'we're just going to scare him.' It was murder first, followed by dragging his body down the riprap to the low tide mark and jamming his leg into the rocks. They broke his leg, beat his head with a rock to cover the bat's blow, and left him for the tide and seagulls. Some accident!"

"That's not what they told me and Mike," Pence weakly protested. "There's no way that we would have authorized any intervention leading to his deliberate demise."

"Gee," I mocked, "big words for murder, and sending a trio of dopers to convince Jimmy was not only dumb, but it was criminal. When you sicced them on Jimmy, you signed his death warrant."

"Jimmy had choices, Knight; he could have given back the envelope and not let it get to the level it did," Pitts said coming to Pence's defense.

"Right, blame the victim," I countered, "that's like saying the girl raped in Central Park was at fault because she went walking there—that's bullshit!"

-33-

I wanted to come back with something scathing to tell Pence about what I thought of him, Mike Pitts, and the whole stinking operation when the door from the stairway banged open. In came Turcotte and the other two dragging the keg-like canisters full of dope with them. They wrestled them across the room onto the table in front of Pence sending his precious dope production line flying.

With his back to the door, Turcotte pulled a gun out of his waistband. He said, "Ok Knight and your friend, Paul Bunyan, drop the axe and get over to the wall. This thing isn't over yet. I've got a couple of scores to settle."

Both Pence and Pitts looked surprised, but Pence reacted first. "Turcotte don't be stupid, where'd you get the gun? Put it down! This is just a business deal, nobody should get hurt."

"We made a pit stop at my house on the way to pick up those drums of dope. I'm in this too deep to play nice now," Turcotte growled.

I could see that Pence wasn't pleased, but the look on Pitts' face told me that he was more than pleased with this turn of events. But then the look on both of their faces changed to one of surprise and fear.

Walking into the room behind Turcotte were five men, none wearing a white hat. The first one had a handgun and stuck the barrel into Turcotte's right ear from behind. He simply said, "Drop it."

The second one carried what looked like a shotgun, but it had only a short barrel. He moved to the left along the wall to cover the entire room. Behind them came Tiny from New Bedford, James Pallatroni from last night's dinner in Providence, and an older gent who I never had met, but by deduction, it would be Johnny "Peaches" Ianello. The gang was all here.

I nodded to James and mouthed a "thank you" to Tiny for getting the posse organized so quickly. Now it was time to make my play.

"Pence," I said, "these gentlemen are here to relieve you of your canisters and put you out of business once and for all. They're the real deal so I wouldn't even try to sweet talk them into a partnership. You apparently got greedy and wouldn't just stick to Cape Cod. Once you crossed over the bridges you got the attention of the family from Rhode Island.

"First let's open these canisters to make sure they've got the stuff in them that was worth killing Jimmy and kidnapping Fred.

"Turcotte," I ordered, "grab a wrench and undo the nuts dogging down the top on both drums."

It didn't take long for both canisters to get opened, and Turcotte fished a plastic bag holding at least a pound of white powder out of each.

"There's supposed to be fifty or more bags in each of these," he said. "One's loaded with snow and the other skag."

"I don't care," I broke in. "You and your buddies are going to clean out this building. By the middle of the afternoon, there won't be any processing equipment or drug stuff left. I want everything gone and this room so clean that even a dope sniffing dog couldn't get a hit—use bleach."

"Where do you want us to put all of the equipment? In the dumpster?" Turcotte whined probably at the thought of some real work.

"No, the dumpster is connected to the day treatment program. At three o'clock when we leave, there won't be anything in here or on the grounds that's linked to drugs." I was adamant. "You've got that ark of a DeVille out back. Fill it up with this shit and then get it out of town! Get going now!"

Speaking for the first time, James told his underling who still had his pistol trained on Turcotte to stay with us. He sent the other one with the sawed off shotgun down to the parking lot to make sure nobody left without permission. Peaches Ianello casually bent over to retrieve Turcotte's gun and pocketed it. The three amigos as Pence had referred to them started humping stuff out to the Caddie; I took over with a nod of approval from James.

"Now, let's get down to business you two," I said to Pitts and Pence. "There's a computer and printer in that back room where I found you earlier. Pence, you stay here, and Pitts you get on that computer and write a letter of resignation effective immediately to Jen at the clinic. You're done working here on the Cape."

Pitts scowled but got up and retreated to the office; his retreat was helped along by the waving of the pistol in the hands of James' guy.

Pitts was back in a couple of minutes with a printed copy of his resignation letter made out to MaryBeth. I read it; it was simple and to the point; he was done and would not be at the day program on Monday. I told him to sign it and put it in a stamped envelope addressed to the clinic. Next, I had him trade places with Pence; he had some idea what was coming for him.

"Pence," I said, "you need to write your resignation to the President of HarborBay Collaborative in Middleboro with a cc to the directors of each clinic in the system. Also I need your resignation to the head honcho at Ramparts with copies to the local guys too."

"Is that all you want?" Pence was agitated. "You're destroying all I've done for years in this part of the state."

"No," I continued, "there's the matter of your license as a social worker. I want you to write the Licensing Board in Boston and surrender your license.

I'm going to see that you never work in human services around here."

James snorted in derision and broke in, "Ah, when Mr. Pence's suppliers come asking for their money, his ability to work in the state will be the least of his problems."

I was too wound up to process what James implied.

"Look I want to go to the cops and have you both jailed for a minimum of ten years for drug trafficking. That might yet happen; but I can also see the community getting up in arms about the drug clinics and day programs that you've used. Some of the good citizens don't like us in their neighborhoods, so they'd use this scandal to run us all out of town. I'm not going to let that happen even if it means you get away scot free. So start writing! When you've done that, print out the envelopes and rummage up some stamps too."

As Pence began to bang away on Pitts' computer, I pointed to Ianello who was still standing inside the door next to his boss and said, "Tommy say hi to John Ianello, he's the guy you led on a merry chase this morning. Also, there's Mr. Pallatroni, a businessman out of Providence, and Tiny Macedo, a long standing friend of mine from New Bedford. They are going to make sure that the drugs and all the crap in this room gets off Cape."

Tommy started to say hi, and I could see he wanted to talk further with Ianello about the chase this morning; but something in the expression of all three men plus the one with the handgun put a damper on the conversation. Instead, Tommy turned to me saying, "Here's a thought Dave, these guys are just giving you a letter of resignation. They could rescind it later. Why not make a video of them with the drugs here and all of this stuff to keep forever?"

"Tom," I shot back, "do you see any video equipment? We don't have the time to go out and buy the stuff at Staples."

Tom pulled out his iPhone and waved it in front of me. "You can make a video with this and post it to YouTube for everyone to see whenever you want—like if they try to get a job anywhere else."

"I'm not sure what you're saying or how it'd work, but I like it. Ok Pitts," I went on, "let's start with you. Take one of the plastic bags of dope and pretend to pour it into the mixing machine. Can you record sound with the video on that phone, Tom?"

"Sure, just get him to ID himself and say what he's done. I can burn a disc for you so you'll have it whenever you need to dime him out. When I get back to my place, I'm going to set up a Facebook site in their names but make it so you can post this video to it. That way anyone Googling their names will find the confessions."

As we went through the charade of making a couple of videos with Pence and Pitts confessing their sins, I noticed that the others were getting a kick out of the action.

Now that I'd gotten my pound of flesh, I was willing to open it up to the others.

"Show time," I said to James. "Here's the deal. I don't know the value the drugs, but they do have a wholesale cost from the supplier. Based on what you told me last night, if there's about a fifty pounds of dope in each of these two canisters, then we're looking at a total price of eight to ten million bucks. Forget the street value, let's just stay with wholesale. Can you sell this junk back to the supplier?"

"Sure," James said. "I've known for a while which cartel was pushing into my territory. It'll be a pleasure to sell them back their own product. On the other hand, we can keep all of this in-house so to speak."

"No, no," I protested. "I want this junk deep-sixed or out of the country. I don't want to wake up one morning to read in the local news about some eighteen year old who OD'd on the drugs I was responsible for."

Sure Dr. Knight," James said solicitously. "I don't care, as I said last night; it's all business to me. But if the cartel not only loses their investment but also has to buy their product back even at a discounted rate, then I wouldn't worry about your friend here, Mr. Pence. He's a dead man walking."

"You mean they'd kill him?" I asked.

"Well these gentlemen are known to have manners if nothing else. They ask you nicely whether you want the blowtorch down your throat or up your anus. After all they need to make a statement for others."

"I'm not going to deal with that," I shook my head in denial. "Let's divide these spoils of war. I'm willing to split the proceeds seventy-thirty with you getting the seventy. My thirty percent to be divided into three equal pieces. First, a third will be a donation, from an anonymous donor of course, to the day treatment program. Maybe something naming the program in the memory of James Farnsworth would be a nice touch. Second, give another third to the hospital and Ramparts to develop jointly a detox program that would really work. Finally send a third to the college here on the Cape to underwrite a scholarship fund for students who want to learn about addictions and mental disorders. Can we do these Mr. Pallatroni?"

"Sure, I see no reason that your requests can't be honored within a reasonable period of time," he said. "Once the original owners of the product have been contacted and the deal done, then the proceeds can be divided and paid out according to your wishes. If it's Ok with you, we'll make the payments over time in the form of multiple anonymous contributions. That way my bottom line won't be impacted and suspicions about the origin of the windfall to your programs will be minimized. Realistically all of this will take less than a year to transact."

I looked over to Pence who should have been looking as grim as his buddy Pitts, but he was staring out the window with a Cheshire cat like smile. I figured it out—the offshore bank accounts might cover some of the costs and save his hide.

"Oh, another matter of money business," I said to Pallatroni, "Mr. Pence here has one or more offshore bank accounts that he uses to launder money. I don't know how all of that works, but I'm sure you are familiar with operations like his. Would you have a private conversation with him to facilitate moving his funds out of those accounts and into yours? I'd like you to make them available to Tom here as a sincere thank you for his help."

"Not a problem, but of course there will be a handling and processing fee for the work involved," Pallatroni allowed himself a small smile as his take probably would be at least half.

"One more point," I continued. "With the collapse of the Cape operation, I don't want you looking to fill the vacuum and creating a drug ring down here. I can't stop dealers from bringing dope in from New Bedford, but promise me you won't make the lower Cape a drug distribution center."

"I think we've got a deal," James Pallatroni said evenly.

-34-

"Last piece of unfinished business," I added. "There were four canisters we brought up from the deep not just the two you see here. That means the gross take is northward of fifteen million. Get Turcotte and the others to take these two and the two in the back of my SUV to your car, James. You have to follow these three off Cape. I don't care where they go, but go they must.

"And I wouldn't let Pence out of your sight until you've confirmed the transfer of funds from his accounts. Pitts, on the other hand, is just a lightweight flunky; he can be cut loose."

"Well I will need a way to contact your friend here with his share of the money," James said gesturing to Tommy. "I'm not big on sending checks, so we'll have to find a convenient way to transfer cash."

"Why doesn't Tiny handle the exchange for a percentage? Tommy can stop at his bar in New Bedford after getting a call from him?" I suggested. "Hey, Tommy, give Mr. Macedo one of your 'Stumpdog' cards so he can contact you. Oh, do me a favor too and make sure all those envelopes get mailed at the Orleans post office."

I thanked Tiny again for his help; shook hands with James to seal the deal; told Peaches Ianello that his boat was sleek; and headed down the stairs to the parking lot carrying the blood stained bat and a bag of the dope both wrapped in paper towels.

As I approached the Caddy, I saw the trunk filled with drug paraphernalia, as was half of the back seat. Opening the driver's side rear door, I stuffed the bag of dope into the pocket on the backside of the front seat and laid the bat on the floor. Next, I walked to the front of the caddy and asked Tommy for his axe. Sliding the blade of the axe under the license plate, I pulled on the handle until the two screws holding the plate in place broke. I went back to the trunk tossed the plate under a pile of drug stuff.

Going over to Tommy, I handed him back his axe and gave him a heartfelt hug. It was sincere; he'd saved my life and stood tall with me over the last couple of days. I owed him, and the money he was going to get from Pence's offshore accounts was worth only a fraction of the debt I felt.

"Hey Dave, when are we going striper fishing?" was his only response.

He walked over to his truck and waved adios. I climbed into my SUV and wheeled down to the parking lot by the yacht club. Flipping open my cell phone, I punched in the number for Rachel or Ruta or whatever.

After only two quick rings, she answered. I said, "Rachel, this is Dave Knight, are you on patrol?"

"Well good afternoon to you Dr. Knight," she answered. "Right now I am sitting in the middle of the median strip next to Exit 9. How are you doing?"

"I'm going to make your day if not your career, so listen carefully. Get up to the roadside rest area west of the Bass River bridge and wait there until a black caddy with tinted windows blows by. There are a couple of long yellow scratches on the passenger's side door too. It won't have a front license plate, so you can stop it for that," I was serious.

"What's the ETA?" she came right back. "And what's the big deal over a missing front plate?"

"Sometime within the hour it'll come by. You've got to pull it over and do a search."

"Just give me probable cause, and I'll comply," she said.

"How about murder?"

"No, I mean what am I supposed to see that would let me go further than just a routine traffic stop?"

"In the back seat there's a pile of stuff used for drug dealing," I went on. "It's in plain sight. There's a pound of uncut dope behind the driver's seat. On the floor is a baseball bat, which will match the wounds on Jimmy Farnsworth's skull. It's the murder weapon. The three guys in the car killed him."

"Besides the bat, are there any weapons in the car?" she asked. I could hear the excitement building in her voice.

"No, they're not armed, but please make sure you have backup close by because the one riding shotgun is unpredictable." I had a hunch Turcotte would be in the passenger's seat while the big guy drove.

"Copy that. If I can make this stick, and I will, then Lech won't be grabbed up tomorrow," she said.

"That's the point. I told you I'd do all I could to protect Lenny. Now it's up to you to intercept these guys and make the collar. You can arrest them for drug trafficking with all the evidence in the car. After that, CJ Smith and company have to make the murder charge stick. As of right now, I'm out of it, and we never had this conversation."

"What conversation?" Rachel caught on quickly.

Next, I covered my six o'clock by calling Manny at the state police barracks in Bourne. I knew Manny wouldn't be there, so it was easy to leave a voice message telling him to check with Rachel as soon as possible and get CJ to hold off snatching Rudkowski because Jimmy's murderers would be in custody. I reminded him that a murder trumped drugs so plea bargaining or trying to trade up to get off the hook was a no-go.

I hung up and headed back to Chatham. A shower, shave, clean clothes, and a date for the roast beef at the Land Ho would be a fitting end to this day.

DAY 6: SUNDAY, MAY 11TH

-35-

Sunday started as a day of rest but not relaxation as I planned to tie up loose ends. I had thought I was taking Chris to the Land Ho on Saturday night for the roast beef as promised, but she had steak for the grill and more intimate plans. I gave her a lot more information than what I had left on the answering machine for Manny, who of course would share it with Smith. Hmmm, in other words, I pretty much bared my soul to her, but the steak was rare and the Harpoon cold.

Chris and I spent the night in each other's arms, and I felt the tension ebb from my body and psyche. We would have spent the entire morning revisiting the previous evening's adventures, but the terriers had different ideas. After a leisurely breakfast, we discussed the next step in our lives over a second cup of coffee.

"Have you ever thought of giving up your gigs at the clinics?" Chris asked me. "I mean, the pace is grueling what with both clinics and your teaching job; plus the money is hardly worth the effort once you deduct your expenses."

"What possibly would I do with all my spare time?" I asked. "Maybe I could be like Fred and do research."

"Maybe you could take walks on the beach with me and the dogs." Chris said smiling. "Come summer we could leave the dogs with Anita next door and do some serious sailing. Maybe downeast to Maine even."

"I'd like that, but my poor boat is a bit beat up for such an adventure. I can hardly trust it to cross the Sound to Nantucket."

"Well think about it," she continued. "You could always sell your place to finance a bigger, better sailboat."

"And where would I live?" I said as we toyed with the idea.

"Oh, I think I could find someplace for you to put your head." Chris said definitively.

Before the discussion could take a turn back upstairs to the bedroom, my cell phone started to chirp. Looking at caller ID, I sighed as I saw that the caller was Manny DeSilvia. He'd gotten my message I guessed.

"Good morning, Lieutenant," I said off-handedly. "How can I help you now?"

"You can tell me the whole story with no blarney." Manny's voice was tight. "Or I can send a cruiser to bring you down here to sing."

"Come on, it's a beautiful Sunday, don't ruin it for me." I said looking over at Chris.

"Knight, I'm not kidding," he went on. "There are three guys in a holding cell in the Yarmouth barracks who swear that you've got something like ten million dollars worth of drugs stashed. What's the score?"

"Well to answer a question with a couple of questions. Did Rachel get the drugs and the bat out of the back of the Caddy when she busted them?"

"Yes to both," Manny conceded. "But have you been or are now in possession of a quantity of heroin and cocaine?

"Let me plead the Fifth to the former and categorically deny the latter. I can state unequivocally that if such a cache of drugs ever existed, it does not exist on Cape, in the state, and maybe even in the country. Try to think back to your undercover days in New Bedford and the drug connections we both knew about over there," I couched my answer carefully.

"I'm down at the lockup now, and these mugs aren't capable of running a red light much less a dope operation of the size they're describing," he added for emphasis.

"No, Manny, but they are capable of murder, all three of them," I sought to deflect the conversation. "Has Rachel been able to get the ME's opinion of what's on that baseball bat? Whose fingerprints match those on the bat? I'll bet the farm that they're not from Lenny Rudkowski."

"No, you're right there. We've lifted finger and palm prints that match those from Kevin Turcotte, who seems to be the leader and somewhat in charge," he took the bait. "I'm waiting for word from the ME right now; your friend Rachel took the bat down to the hospital in Hyannis for further examination."

"It'll be a match," I said with resolution. "Was it enough evidence to keep CJ from rousting Rudkowski?"

"Yes and no. Rachel got to him yesterday after the bust, and he agree to postpone the raid waiting for something conclusive from the ME. If the blood and fibers match along with fingerprints we lifted, then he'll go after these guys and pass on Rudkowski altogether."

"Remember yesterday what I told you about murder trumping drugs? I guarantee you that CJ will have egg on his face if he deals down the murder charge to chase the specter of fictitious drugs."

"From what I hear, this guy Turcotte is spinning a far out tale involving you, the clinics you work at, and some guy named Pence," Manny was trying to move the conversation back to drugs again.

"Sure and next you'll be saying that the drugs were dropped off a freighter, and I fished them out of the Atlantic. Give it up and book all three for murder. Let them spend the rest of their lives in Cedar Junction."

"If the bat proves to be the murder weapon, then I think we've got a good case. I've separated the three of them; let's see if I can't get one of them to rat on the others." Manny knew that I wasn't going to be leaned on especially if the bat matched. "Bottom line the three of them look as if they're jonesing, so a few more hours in solitary to contemplate their sins and get more dope sick might just loosen their tongues especially if an offer for a hospital transfer is dangled."

"You'd withhold medical treatment to get a confession?" I asked in mock indignation. "Shame on you; but good for you. And I'll bet you'll let CJ take all the credit for solving the murder."

"He's the lead detective," Manny said with resignation. "All right Dave, I'm sure I'll hear the whole story someday but only in the hypothetical. Right now, you're off the hook with us, but only if the bat match is a winner. Got it?"

"We're good Manny; we've only a couple of weeks left in the school year to get a beer, so call me Tuesday," I said and ended the conversation.

-36-

Leaving Chris who had a couple of cottages to show for summer rentals, I promised to be back in time to make it for cocktails at the Land Ho, then headed down the highway to the hospital to check on Fred. The drive was leisurely compared to my burning up the asphalt most of the week. Yesterday's fog had given way to bright sunshine and the promise not tease of spring was in the air.

I asked a volunteer at the welcome desk where I might find Fred. She asked if I was a family member, and when I said no, she started to recite the new rules governing privacy. As if I didn't know them by heart! Cutting her short I fibbed, told her that I was Fred's psychologist, and needed to discuss his care and treatment with the attending MD on the floor. I asked again, where could I find him? Talk about a tough sell, but after showing her my state license as a psychologist and a health care provider, she consented and gave me instructions to Fred's room.

Fred was supposed to be in the critical care unit, but the charge nurse there said he'd been moved to a regular room as his vitals had stabilized. Retracing my steps, I found Fred in the oldest part of the hospital in a six bed common ward, which wasn't at all a match with the type of insurance he had from the college. More than a bit pissed off, I approached the nurse's station to ask why Fred was not in a private or semi-private room. Anticipating a privacy run around, I first asked for Fred's private effects so that I could verify his insurance coverage. The nurse sighed and said that the Bursar's office down on the first level would have logged anything personal.

Back on the first floor, I found the right office and asked if I could add Fred's watch and ring wallet to his possessions. I was still holding on to them from yesterday so just putting them with Fred's other stuff made the most sense. The woman at the desk found a manila envelope with Fred's wallet and some loose change in it. There was also a note that she scanned.

"Seems as if Mr. Dorfman was dropped off in the ER yesterday just before noon," she said holding the note up. "Whoever left him just left him sitting in a wheelchair in the waiting room with no identification. We are authorized in these situations to determine the identity of the patient, but we can't go further without consent from him, a family member, or his care giver."

Can I add his watch and college ring to his envelope as he left them behind accidentally?" I asked and at the same time cursed Turcotte for being a total slime ball.

Reaching over I picked up the envelope and fished in my pocket for Fred's things. Instead of dropping them in the envelope, I pulled his wallet out and began to sort through the variety of ID cards that we all carry.

"Hey, you can't do that!" exclaimed the clerk wide-eyed.

"It's fine; I just want to fish out his insurance card," I answered. "Here I have it. Fred belongs in a semi-private room not a Medicaid ward. Take this card and Xerox it, then get him moved ASAP."

Looking at the card's logo and knowing how critical the bottom line was to the hospital, she took the card and retreated to an inner office to make a copy.

"Ok," she said. "I'll get this to the Admitting Office pronto, and your friend should be transferred as soon as his coverage is validated. You shouldn't have opened his wallet, but I'm glad you did. That note I was reading said that they couldn't get an answer from his home phone, and none of the Dorfmans living on Cape knew him."

"I'm going back to the ward to check on his condition, thanks for your help. I'm sure Fred will appreciate it once he gets back on his feet." I winked conspiratorially.

Back on the ward, I chatted up the charge nurse telling her what I'd done down at the Bursar's Office. She thought it was funny. I left my name and cell phone number with her as a contact in case Fred needed anything, anything at all.

I knew better than to ask for his chart, as it was no doubt sacrosanct, so I approached the question of his treatment from the other end.

"Given the amount of diazepam in his system and its long half-life, is Dr. Dorfman being titrated to lower gradually the level of Valium and detox him without risk of seizure or hyperpyrexia?" I asked in my most professorial voice.

Regarding me as a colleague, she flipped open his chart and said, "We're keeping him on a saline drip and continue to monitor the diazepam level hoping to decrease slowly the concentration to a therapeutic level within the next seventy-two hours. Right now he's comatose, but all vegetative functions are within range."

"Great, thanks and would you leave a note in his chart to call me when he regains consciousness, please?" I was my most polite self.

"Not a problem." She assented and penned a note to that effect in his chart. "I'll also put you down as a contact person in case something untoward happens—it works both ways, I'm afraid."

"That's fine," I replied. "Thanks for your help, and let's keep our fingers crossed that he'll be out of the woods soon."

I left her station and walked down the row of beds each screened from the other by a thin cloth curtain until I came to Fred's bed. He was pathetic, and for the first time in five years, I actually felt sorry for him. As I looked at his shriveled body dwarfed by the size of the bed where he lay, I couldn't help but blame myself for his misery.

Talk about no good deed going unpunished; he had acted in the best interests of the students at the college in an unselfish fashion and now was paying a huge price. I stood there at the foot of his bed wracked with guilt. Walking up to the head of the bed, I put my hand gently on his shoulder and promised Fred that I would teach his classes and do all of the scut work that he did as chair of the department until he returned fully recovered. It was the least I could promise. Not wanting to tear up in maudlin self-recrimination, I turned quickly and left his bedside, the ward, and the hospital.

-37-

Back in my car, I debated whether to drive down to the college and check out the damage to my office or up to the clinics to see if any red flags had been hoisted. I decided, however, to head back to Chatham and have a late lunch with Chris. This was supposed to be a day of rest after all.

Swinging out onto the mid-Cape, I fiddled with the radio to see if the Sox were playing at Fenway when my cell phone chirped. I looked at the number; it was familiar, but I wasn't one hundred percent sure I recognized it.

"Dave Knight here," I said in a clipped salutation.

"Dave, this is Rachel Robbins calling. Where are you?" Her voice was up an octave in excitement.

Figuring she was calling about Lenny and the baseball bat, I said casually, "Hi Rachel, thought that might have been your number. I've heard all about your arrest yesterday from Manny this morning. Good work! If the bat tests out, and I know it will, then all three will face murder charges."

"Yeah that will be sweet and a good collar for my record, but I'm not calling about that at all." She went on, "I just heard over the scanner that there's a real dicey situation over in South Chatham where you live."

"Huh, what do you mean?"

"From what I'm getting there's an alert out for you from the Chatham police. Now that I've contacted you, I've got to call the locals so they can stop looking for you. I'll be back to you in a minute, got that?" She said and hung up.

What the fuck now, I thought as I waited for the longest minute in my life to tick down. Finally, the phone rang.

"Dave," she started in, "you know a guy named Pitts?"

"Well yeah, he's the director of the day treatment program," I answered cautiously. "What's he got to do with the cops looking for me and why are they looking for me?"

I heard Rachel take a deep breath and then say matter-of-factly, "Pitts went to your house sometime this morning and hosed it with an assault rifle. He must have poured gasoline all over before setting it on fire because it's a total loss."

"What the fuck!" I screamed this time out loud into the phone. "Rachel where is Pitts now?"

"Someone called when he heard the pops from the rifle. The cops showed up before the fire department. Pitts was standing outside the house with the rifle at port arms and refused to put it down. I guess he pointed it at them; it was 'suicide by cop.'"

"Oh my God, no!" I exclaimed. "I've got to get home."

"Easy big guy, you don't have a house anymore. It was a total conflagration. That's why the cops put out a BOLO for you."

"Huh?" was all I could muster.

"After all the shooting and then the fire, nobody knew whether you'd been killed in the house, and the fire had been set as a cover-up. I wouldn't go there if I were you; I'd head for the station house first." Her response was firm.

"I'm almost at Exit 10 now," I said. "Call the cops for me please and tell them I'm on my way to their new place across from the airport."

"Ok Dave, will do, and take care of yourself. Oh, I do owe you big time for your help with Lech. That's a topic for another day I guess," and with that she ended the call.

I spent a testy ninety minutes with the Chatham police as they grilled me about Mike Pitts and why he'd want to kill me. With apologies to Sergeant Shultz from

Hogan's Heroes, "I knew nothing." I did tell them that I had met with Pitts the day before and had an argument about the way he ran the program. I didn't tell them that the argument was over running drugs nor did I mention that Pitts' letter of resignation would be delivered Monday morning to the clinic. I feigned ignorance and suggested that Pitts had become enraged and unglued over my criticism. In the end, they let me go with a warning not to leave the Cape.

-38-

I drove slowly back to what had been my home. Not one wall was left standing, the whole place and everything in it was reduced to ashes. The firefighters were still there spraying hot spots, and the police had cordoned off access to the yard, as it was not only an arson and crime scene but also a murder scene. I pulled a three-point turn and headed for Chris' house.

Going over everything with her helped me frame what had happened and what I needed to do. Right now, I had nothing but the clothes on my back, an old Explorer, and an even older sailboat—the sum total of my life's possessions. I might have been poor in material things, but the support Chris offered me was a priceless commodity.

"Dave," she said softly after listening to my litany of the last few days' events, "I hope you'll stay here with me; we can get through this together. I'm serious, you need stability in your life, let me help."

"Thanks, and I mean it." I answered. "Right now I'm a cross between a basket case and a zombie, so a little guidance will be welcome. What do I do next?"

"Move in here first, then buy some new clothes tomorrow," she started to tick off the priorities. "You said you were going to go to the college and take over Fred's classes. You'd better talk to the Dean about his absence."

"For sure," I agreed knowing that I could figure out where Fred was in his syllabus and not embarrass myself in front of his students. I figured I'd volunteer to the Dean to fill in for Fred as long as he was out of action including giving finals and submitting grades if needed. I would even do the end of the year evaluations for the psych faculty if necessary. Yeah, I was feeling just a bit guilty about involving Fred and the college, so I would do penance.

"If you're going to take on extra work at the college for the next month or more, what are you going to do about your clinical work?" Chris prompted. "We talked this morning about how you were practically working for nothing after expenses at the clinics. Why continue especially with type of aggravation? It's not like you don't have enough experience with them to last you a lifetime's worth of case examples for the classroom."

"I know, I know, but what would I do with all my spare time? Take up golf?"

"Well we can expand upon the conversation from this morning," she began. "If you stay here, the insurance settlement for your house could go a long way toward a bigger boat. Cruising the coast of Maine in the summer in style wouldn't be a bad diversion."

"Let's work on this, sounds like a plan," I bit on Chris' pitch. "Tomorrow I'll be in the classroom where I really feel at home, wanted, and needed. Afterwards I'll try to work out a reduced schedule with both clinics. Let me leave the door open for staying on for a couple of months, then we'll see."

"Now you're talking! Let's seal the deal with dinner at the Land Ho tonight, and we'll get on with our lives tomorrow."

"Deal," I said and leaned over to give her kiss more intimate than affectionate. We didn't make it the restaurant at all.

＊

Six Days In May

ABOUT THE AUTHOR

Robertson Browne is the nom de plume of a retired university professor who has spent over three decades in clinical positions as a psychologist. Currently he lives on Cape Cod with his wife during the winters. Come summer, both of them enjoy sailing the coast of Maine. This is his first novel, a work of factual fiction.

1843607R00135

Made in the USA
San Bernardino, CA
08 February 2013